Elizabeth,
Enjoy!
Louise Crawford

HAT TRICK

LOUISE CRAWFORD

Hard Shell Word Factory

Special thanks to Sacramento Homicide Detective
John Cabrera for sharing his time and expertise,
and for inspiring the title of this book.
Thanks also to C.P.A. Don McKoughan for his input.
(Any errors in procedure are mine).
Last but not least,
thanks to my husband and daughter for their support,
and to my writing buddies, Jay MacLarty, Naida West,
Gene Munger, and Liz Crain for their tireless feedback.

©1999, Louise Crawford
Paperback ISBN: 0-7599-0280-1
Published March 2001

Ebook ISBN: 1-58200-119-7
Ebook Published July 1999

Hard Shell Word Factory
PO Box 161
Amherst Jct. WI 54407
books@hardshell.com
http://www.hardshell.com
Cover art © 1999, Dirk A. Wolf

Chapter 1

5:00 A.M. THE JAG slowed, gravel crunching beneath the tires while a blues riff blasted from the radio—loud music gave me energy. I eyed the pitch-black, vacant parking lot with a great deal of reluctance, then glanced at my boyfriend, Stephanos Zoloski—a much better view. The sight of his tousled dark hair, curling at the neck, and his muscled, six-foot-two frame gave me a rush of heat akin to a food binge. He looked more like a professional athlete than a homicide detective. I hoped I looked more like an aerobics instructor than a psychologist.

We'd met during a murder investigation, me as a counselor and potential victim, him as the detective in charge of the case. Lust and love followed. Hence, jogging at 5:00 a.m. with the Z-man. I hadn't smoked in months, but I craved a cigarette more than a run—and I would have *loved* a high fat, high cholesterol almond croissant even more. Zoloski—he stubbornly remained Zoloski in my mind, Stephanos in the throes of passion, the Z-man somewhere in between, turned off the ignition and opened his door, spilling light over the pavement.

"I need coffee," I grumbled, imagining a steaming cup of Java.

He hiked an eyebrow, said in Bogart-ese, "You had plenty of energy last night, Sweetheart." A delightfully wicked grin broke the planes of his face and got my blood pumping better than caffeine. He climbed from the car and stretched his achilles.

"Zat vas last night," I said, sounding more like a Gestapo agent than Marlene Dietrich. But in the back of my mind I wondered if our three-month honeymoon of living together could last. I was getting a bit winded keeping up with my professional life, my friends, and my lover's hectic work schedule, and this sort of 5:00 a.m. nonsense.

Zoloski's grin broadened to a mock leer. I felt a twinge of guilt for the pessimism creeping through my brain. Generations of negativity ran though my veins and although I'd done a lot of work to change, sometimes the past snuck into my attitude. This morning it seemed particularly heavy. *Happiness can't last,* my mind whispered. It's just a prelude to disaster. I felt suspended in time, waiting for the perverbial shoe to drop.

Jeez, get going. I struggled from the bucket seat, touched the reassuring canister of pepper spray in the pocket of my shorts, then reluctantly extended each leg until my hamstrings twinged.

Ten minutes later, our stretches finished, Zoloski cut across the old baseball diamond to the horse trail, me a step behind. After three months of jogging at Renfree Park, I knew the dirt path by foot braille. Still, I kept a penlight velcro'd to my wrist. Zoloski led the way through the towering canopy of twisted oaks and sycamores.

Maybe *Stephanos* was too damn scary. Made me think of a more permanent arrangement than our six-month trial live-together. Maybe *Zoloski* kept a distance in my psyche that made me feel safe. Psychoanalyzing myself was like a lawyer who has himself for a client, counterproductive. I could get lost in my own psycho-babble and forget I had a life. A life I'd almost lost three months ago and was determined to get the most out of now.

I took a deep breath, inhaled the smell of dirt, grass, oak, and sage as the trail dipped and climbed. I imagined the firm lines of Zoloski's gluteus maximus leading down to his long, well-muscled legs. He'd lost the hint of love handles from a few months earlier, and at thirty-eight, was in great shape. My face warmed as I thought of his broad shoulders and bulging biceps—no sleep for the wicked.

He pulled further ahead. Move it, Blaize, I told myself, my feet like dead weights. Last night had been heaven, *this* was hell. Visualizing my thirty-one year-old body with sleeker curves and definition, I picked up the pace. This was the only thing that kept me a size eight and one step ahead of the "fat free" munchie mountain I ate daily.

Zoloski stumbled, staggered, and righted himself. "Watch it—"

My toe hit something. It gave slightly as I tripped and nearly did the splits. Zoloski caught my arm.

I flashed the penlight across the dirt to a lump the size of a big log. A log wrapped in black satin? It looked like a sheet. I smelled something unpleasant, like a body unwashed for a thousand years, and my stomach roiled. One of the homeless?

Zoloski moved closer as I nudged the semi-soft thing with my toe. No response. With my pen light, I pulled the wrapping back and peeked inside. Pale, flaccid skin flecked with blood, mouth open in a giant yawn, something stirring in the toothless cavern—flies. I fell back, jerking on the sheet, exposing an arm.

Look ma, no hands.

My thoughts ricocheted like a pinball machine on electro-shock therapy while my gaze remained riveted on the arm. Definitely not looking for a hand-out.

I gulped air, and choked. Another image flashed: a magician sawing someone in half, lots of blood. I dropped the light.

Zoloski grabbed my shoulder and steered me down the trail as I heaved toast and orange juice. "Stay here." He left for a couple of seconds, returned with my penlight, wrapped an arm around my shoulders. "You okay?"

No! my stomach shrieked. I wiped my mouth on my T-shirt, the bitter taste of bile stinging my tongue. "Sure."

Zoloski faked a smile. "No jogging today, Sweetheart," he said in his worst Bogart voice.

"Jeez, no kidding!" Finding a mutilated corpse wasn't exactly on my how-to-start-the-day list either.

His mouth tightened. "I'm sorry you had to see that." He brushed my hair off my forehead, ran his finger gently along the scar on my jawline. We were both thinking about Mac the Knife, his attack too recent to have faded from my nightmares. I shivered, trying not to remember. Three months of bliss and now this. "Say it isn't the company I keep."

He didn't respond, his gaze followed the penlight beam as it moved over the surrounding area, his expression in detect mode. "I need to keep the scene intact. Can you call it in?"

"Sure." I stepped carefully over what had been my breakfast and called back to him, "I'll wait at the car."

I climbed into the Jag and locked the doors. It took two tries to hit the right sequence of numbers on Zoloski's cellular. The sun rose in a brilliant splash of hot pink, orange and yellow as I waited inside the car, the windows cracked for fresh air, trying not to think of the grotesque corpse. The more I tried to distract myself, the more my thoughts chugged their own course. The corpse hadn't been there yesterday at 5:15 a.m. A lot of American River College students used the path, so the body was probably dumped after dark. Someone from the college might have noticed something.

The breeze whispered through the oaks as my brain kicked in. Why was I assuming it was murder? Just because he had no teeth and hands? Ah, sarcasm! Damn. Watching the early morning glow, I rubbed the backs of my arms, cold in spite of the ripening heat. The corpse hadn't been there long or the smell would have stopped us before we got to it. Or would the night air stave off the reek? Sacramento, in August? Where the lows got to 70? Get real.

I had about as much reality as I could take. I tried to shut off the mental conversation, but questions pressed: If the guy was a bum, why had he been rolled in satin? Nearest thing at hand? Ha, ha. Was he young or was that my mental aberration? I tried to visualize the face and saw only the horrible toothless cavern.

Zoloski would be churning along the same brainstorming route. We'd made a good team—looking for Mac. Maybe I could help? No way, José. I didn't need to ask to know the Z-man's answer. I told myself I didn't mind—my college days of earning an extra buck as a PI were over—so why did I feel jump-started by adrenalin? Excited? I didn't, I argued, I was just shaken. Hell, it wasn't everyday one tripped over a corpse.

As a clinical psychologist, I sometimes got involved in murder peripherally, but normally I dealt with recovering addicts, usually struggling to live a life different from their parents. I enjoyed the challenge, and was successful enough to share office space with a lawyer in the Senator Hotel, a cushy location across from the Capitol. The lawyer and I didn't talk much: I waved as I sailed through to my cubbyhole in the back, he smiled. I wrote a check every month, he collected. Was he any good as a lawyer? I had no idea. He threw me an occasional client—and a donut.

The surrounding quiet overwhelmed my efforts at distraction. Traffic hummed in the distance, but the noise was too far off for comfort. I switched on the radio, flinched as heavy metal crashed and bounced off my eardrums, and turned it down. Uneasy, I forced my thoughts back to my work. Right now I had two compulsive/obsessives who needed a boot in the right direction, also a husband and wife who were in a 12-step group and trying to learn new ways to relate beside addiction and co-addiction. My goal was to have the two obsessive/compulsives firmly entrenched in Overeaters Anonymous and on their way by September. The other couple had twenty years of destruction to mend. What could I substitute for their negative intimacy—the baiting statements, and button-pushing fun? Boxing gloves?

Meanwhile my nomadic streak had me chomping at the bit. Now that Zoloski and I were cohabiting, I was having wild urges to fly. Alone, I knew who I was, with a man my identity wanted to slip into a coma. It took hard communication with the Z-man to maintain my own life and still be a part of his. "New behavior gets easier with practice," I told my clients.

A police car peeled into the lot, lights flashing, no siren. About time. Relieved, I opened the door, climbed from the bucket seat.

An unmarked car followed at a more leisurely pace.

I waved. I'd done my job. I didn't recognize the two officers, but the man who climbed from the second car was unfortunately familiar. "Zoloski's with the body," I said. The younger of the two cops smiled, then introduced me to the medical examiner who didn't acknowledge my words.

"We've met," I murmured, remembering the cocktail party Zoloski had drug me to as I eyed the small, thin man. A grey fringe of hair above his ears, he wore clothes Columbo would have been proud of. But hey, this was California—the land of casual—or "cazj" as we natives like to say. The guy offered me a cool look as he pulled on a pair of latex gloves.

Up yours, fella. Not exactly good psychoanalysis, but I try. He was one of the many who disapproved of Zoloski living with a shrink. At the party where we'd met, I offered him my services *gratis* since he appeared in such need of professional help. Didn't earn me points.

"Just follow the horse trail," I said, pointing them in the right direction, thinking the ME was an ass. "Can't miss it."

The sun, now a bright yellow ball had reached the top of the trees, making me squint as I watched the officers split up, one following the ME, the other going back to the patrol car. I closed the Jag's door. The car was a soothing mellow yellow. No mellow in my morning—only Mr. Toothless and handless. Every scar on my body twinged, from my jaw to the healed bullet wound in my shoulder to the knife slash on my calf. Time for more distraction. I rummaged under the seat for the mangled paperback romance I kept stashed there—another addiction I had yet to address.

Trying to lose myself in a hot, steamy paradise with a guy that rivaled Zoloski's charms, my mind kept painting a machete behind the guy's back. I kept rereading the same page, trying to make sense of the black and white scrawl. Every little noise brought my head up from the page, sent a chill of alarm down my spine. What was taking the Z-man so long?

I leaned back against the seat and closed my eyes. Even though I was sleep-deprived, it didn't come. I rolled the windows down all the way to catch the breeze and tried again. I finally flipped another page in the book.

Suddenly, the Z-man leaned through the window and whispered my name.

After I peeled myself off the ceiling, I punched his arm. "Damn sneak!"

His grin vanished. "Ow! Watch those snappy hands!"

"You deserved it!" But I smiled. If I was going to be saved from savage love and dismemberment in the tropics, who better than the Z-man! Not that I remembered anything I'd read. I closed the book and shoved it under the seat. Zoloski's green, green eyes glinted with humor. "I like the clinch cover. Sex Slave of Sacramento? Good book?"

Sex slave? Try Eddie Kruger. I had the urge to pull the book out and read him the real title, but stifled it with a shrug, my face growing warm with embarrassment.

He handed me the keys. "I'll have to read it sometime. Get some erudition, like you PhD's."

A smile tugged at my lips. "Fat chance." I'd stash it somewhere else ASAP—keep the cheap thrills to myself. I nodded toward the trail. "Any idea who it might be? Anything *else* missing?" I thought "Bobbit" but figured Zoloski wouldn't appreciate my humor.

"No, and I don't know." Zoloski shook his head. "Forget it."

At his parental tone, I gritted my teeth and counted to ten. Good therapy.

"Hey listen, you go on. I've gotta hang around. I'll catch a ride home at lunch to get my car." Zoloski leaned further through the window, kissed me, then whispered, "Maybe tonight we can—practice something from that book."

My cheeks were on fire. "You don't need any practice to melt my knee-caps."

"Oh yeah?" His grin slowly faded. "I might be late."

What else was new? I sensed the gears in his head switch from personal to business, felt like a distraction as he glanced around the parking lot, taking in the scene.

"In case you get off at a decent hour," I said in a surly tone, "I'll be eating dinner at six, and working out from seven-thirty to nine-thirty."

His gaze returned, eyebrows raised, lips curled into a half-smile. "Racquetball if I get to the club by eight?"

I knew how to get his blood racing. It didn't take a corpse, just a friendly competitive, cut-throat game—and a reward. "The winner gets a massage."

Zoloski delivered another of his devastating smiles. "Deal."

I revved the engine and waved. I intended to win. The man had magic hands.

BUT THE CORPSE DIDN'T. No hands, teeth, clothes, or ID of any kind. And that held Zoloski up. He missed our game, and I missed the massage. Bummer days, Blaize.

The next morning he was out the door before I cleared the bed. So much for maintaining a relationship, I thought, feeling prickly as a porcupine. His absence made me feel abandoned, so I picked up the phone and called Lon, my best buddy. A golden man of muscles and masculinity, he looked anything but gay. He was gorgeous, great company, my soul-confessor and no threat to the Z-man.

No answer at his office, I tried his condo, he sometimes worked at home.

"Ken?" His voice sounded strange, high-strung, panicked.

"No, it's Blaize." We hadn't seen each other since June. Usually we chatted on the phone once or twice a week, but over the last few weeks he hadn't called. I figured he'd be thrilled to connect. We always had a blast going out to dinner, or monopolizing the phone line for an hour or two to discuss our latest romantic escapades. But instead of thrilled, I heard deflated. "Sorry Blaize, can't talk now. I'll call you back." *Click.*

I stared at the phone. Jeez, Louise. I felt as though I'd missed half an argument—my half. I dialed again. No answer. I grabbed my purse, big as an overnight bag, heavy as a bowling ball, and headed downtown. I'd stop by my office, then buzz by his condo, make sure everything was okay.

ON MY DESK I found a stack of mail four inches thick. Shuffling like a card shark, I pitched obvious junk at the round file, and shoved the important stuff in my bottom desk drawer. Out of sight, out of mind. I checked my appointment calendar. No clients till this afternoon. The answering machine flashed like an airport beacon. I tried to ignore it, picked up my binoculars and glanced out the window, scanning the park from its wealth of roses to the edge of the hallowed Capitol steps. A bunch of high school kids with placards circled the area. I caught Colusa County on one, something about rapists on another. Shades of Mac the Knife, the rapist who'd barged back into my life a few months ago, and now he was dead. Had it only been three months? Sometimes when I was alone, I still heard his whisper, "Roses are red, violets are blue" ...saw the butchered bodies....

I hit the answering machine button. The couple in recovery had canceled. A pause. Another beep.

"Hey, Blaize! When are you and Zoloski coming to see the slides?

Europe was great...." Pat Dryden's voice ran at a fast clip like in our college days, not like the person who manned the city's Missing Person's desk.

I rummaged through my bottom desk drawer for a stick of gum, trying to ignore my craving for a cigarette, or worse yet, something chocolate and pure fat, preferably a truckload of it. To a recovering food addict like me, pure heaven, followed by pure hell.

Pat bubbled on about Arnold, her new hubby, the diametric opposite of Swartzenegger, and I smiled, imagining the sparkle in her blue eyes. Ah, what a little love, marriage, and sex can do. *For awhile*, my skeptical, die-hard inner voice added. I left a message on her machine, Saturday might work. Then I tried Lon. Busy.

I waved to the legal beagles in the conference room as I sailed out the door. Later, gator.

LON, A VERY successful engineer, lived off Garden Highway in a ritzy condo on the Sacramento River. Within shouting distance of restaurants and bars that edged the water, it had everything: trees, bushes, birds, water, sun....and only five or six minutes from the Capitol.

I headed down the aggregate walk, admiring the man-made lake in the complex's interior. A central fountain shot cooling spray straight up a hundred feet, the mist tingling my skin as I passed. A giant weeping willow stood off in the distance like something out of *Lord of the Rings*. Grey painted exteriors with turquoise trim spoke of peace and tranquility. Beemers and Mercedes speckled the parking lot. I didn't see Lon's red Supra, knew he normally parked in back, under cover.

My sandals sank into the manicured lawn as I cut from the walkway to the stairs, reminding me Zoloski's lawn needed mowing— my turn to sweat and sneeze. Ain't equality fun.

From across the road, hammers pounded, saws buzzed, and the smell of sawdust drifted on the warm breeze. Despite the relative comfort of my light linen jacket over a cotton gauze dress, sweat trickled down my back. Eighty-five degrees by ten meant one-hundred and fifteen by four in good old Sweat City.

My eyes lit on a small clump of flowers: red and white Sweet Williams, pink Carnations, and yellow Day Lilies at the bottom of the stairs. Similar splashes of color dotted all the staircases and I found myself wishing I could move in—just to have someone else do the yard.

I climbed to Lon's top floor, corner unit. As I knocked, I glanced around, disturbed by the quiet, then realized it was mid-morning on a work day.

I thought about Lon. On the phone, his voice had sounded strange. Frightened? Angry? Nervous? Were he and Ken having problems? *More than that*, my mind whispered, recalling the note of panic. Like avoiding a grocery store when I have a binge on the brain, something in the pit of my stomach reacted, urging me to turn around and run. I felt a prickly sensation as though I was being watched. I swept the area with my gaze, saw only a woman lying beside the pool, her back soaking sun, her head turned toward me. From what I could tell, she was asleep. Since I'd stumbled over Toothless, my hyper-alertness seemed to be working overtime.

I knocked on the door, waited, knocked again. Great—as in *not*. Where the hell was he? His line was busy ten minutes ago. Scrounging a piece of paper from my purse I scratched out a semi-legible note, asking him to call, and wedged it in the doorjamb.

Puzzlement and curiosity made me walk around the complex. I closed in on the woman on the chaise lounge by the pool. No fat. Zero. Muscle that made *me,* a workout workaholic, want to run to the gym. Her body was tanned to mahogany, dark hair in a pony tail, cold soda by her hand. I said, "Hello?"

She lifted her head slightly, her mirrored sunglasses reflecting two of me.

I resisted the prideful urge to flex my biceps. "I'm looking for Lon Wilson. Have you seen him?"

She sat up. "You a friend of his?" Her voice came out wispy as her bikini.

"Yes. I just talked to him on the phone ten minutes ago. You see where he went?"

She hesitated and I wondered what the big deal was about answering a simple question. But there was something going on behind those glasses. "Sorry...I've been asleep." Her head returned to its resting spot.

Now why the hell would Ms. Olympia lie? She hadn't been sleeping or she would have startled when I said hello. Puzzled and irritated, I murmured, "Thanks." Feeling as though I was spinning my wheels, I returned to my Saturn, my dark red pride and joy, and to my office and the pursuit of the almighty dollar. Consulting work—in this case analyzing data collected by two local businessmen who'd put together a new personnel questionnaire to target the values they wanted in their employees. So far the test validity was shot to hell by the data. I should have demanded payment up front. Life is joy.

Around 1:00 p.m. my phone rang, dragging me from a dream. I'd fallen asleep in the middle of a computer run. My forehead felt imprinted with ink. I knocked the print-out off my desk to grab the receiver, swore as it unraveled into a mess, and said in my professional voice, "Blaize McCue and Associates." My computer was my only associate, Andrea my given name. But Pat had dubbed me Blaize for all the potential romances I'd run from in a blaze of glory—the name stuck.

"It's Lon."

I recognized the voice, not the tone. Flat as a soda can run over by a semi. Either someone had nixed a building he'd designed, or Ken had burned him—bad.

"Sorry I missed you," he slurred.

Drugs? He'd been clean ten years. Couldn't be drunk. This guy had an alcoholic mother and wouldn't touch booze with a telephone pole. "What happened?"

"He's gone, Blaize."

My stomach tightened. "Ken?" I tried to conjure up the face I'd met briefly at Pat and Arnie's wedding, and failed.

"Yeah." Lon breathed. "I'm at home."

I heard the plea. He'd always been there for me. "Ten minutes, tops," I said.

It took seven.

Chapter 2

LON OPENED THE door. Only thirty, he looked like a dragged through the dirt, Robert Redford. His clothes were askew, blond hair as lop-sided as the attempted smile. My gaze fell to the blood-stained bandage on his right hand, returned to the fading shiner around his eye. What the hell?

I closed the door and followed him into the living room, a sunken area that looked and smelled like it had barely survived a bar-room brawl. Like an earthquake fault, a crack ran across the glass cloverleaf cocktail table. Broken glass and bottle chards littered the fireplace hearth. Crimson spots trailed down the hallway to the bathroom. My stomach knotted. "What happened?"

Lon dropped onto the couch, its cushions scattered on the floor. He shook his head. I measured his glazed blue eyes and detoured to the kitchen. The man needed a caffeine jump start. Whatever his troubles, I wanted to hear it from him sober.

As the water bubbled and hissed its way to the filter, I put the cushions back on the sofa and picked up the broken glass. Lon watched, silent.

Later, coffee in hand, I settled in beside him. "It's hot," I warned. The air conditioner whirred on in the background. If only I could fix people as easily as the room. Sometimes I took on responsibilities that weren't mine—"co'd out"—and sometimes I took R & R so I could find detachment, but I always kept friends and clients separate. I wasn't sure friendship would be enough to cope with this. Yet I felt closer to Lon than my brother, whom I seldom saw. Lon and I—in the words of *Anne of Green Gables*—were kindred spirits. We laughed at the same silly jokes, loved the same kinds of coffee, a good book, good movie, good game of chess.

I put my hand over his. His urbane veneer reminded me of Humpty Dumpty about to fall. I could feel the tightness of his knuckles beneath my palms. A tear slid down his tanned cheek, got lost in reddish stubble. His wide-set blue eyes glistened, but no more came. He wiped the one away, took a sip of coffee, set it on the table, stared at the crack and grimaced.

"You want to talk?"

He shook his head, glanced toward the hall, seeing or remembering something, then nodded. "We had a fight."

No kidding. "Last night?"

His brow furrowed. "Monday. He got home late."

"Is that how you hurt your hand?"

His lips curled in disgust. "Yeah." A long thoughtful pause. "He came home drunk. Plastered. Poured himself a bourbon while I watched. Damn him! Doing that to me!" Lon's anguished eyes locked on mine.

I took a deep breath, let it out slow.

"He knows how I feel about booze! He knows!" His gaze clouded. "I grabbed his drink, threw it at the fireplace. Threw the bottle too. We got into a screaming match, then a fist-fight." He shuddered. "It was awful...the worst part is... I don't know why!"

His voice said otherwise. I waited.

He glanced at me, glanced at the rug again. "For the last month or so he's been secretive... wouldn't talk... claimed it was work..."

"But you think it was something else?" Someone else?

He looked confused. "He *said* everything was fine. But shit—you don't start coming home late, drinking, clamming up for no reason."

My gaze shot around the room as though a reason might be found on the walls or in the jagged crack across the cocktail table. "Has he been back?"

Lon shook his head.

"Called?"

He ran his fingers through his short hair.

Anxiety? Fatigue? Both? Probably.

"No," he said. "And that's not like him either!" He stood and started to pace, all traces of drunkenness gone. He was as lean and tan as a tennis player, knock-out handsome even in wrinkled chinos, misbuttoned neon shirt and three-day beard. "I called his work, even drove by—that bastard Cain claims he hasn't been in. Drove by the Lavender Rose..."

I recognized the name of a gay bar, and jumped back to what he'd said before, "Who's Cain?"

"A security guy at the building where Ken works. Ken didn't like him."

"Any idea why?"

Lon shook his head, but I caught a flicker of evasion. I let it go. I was here as a friend.

Lon continued, "No one's seen him." He paused. "Would you help me look for him? You're good at that sort of thing."

Taken by surprise, I stared, suddenly wary.

Lon's mournful eyes reminded me of a Saint Bernard. Everything about him appealed for help. "I have to stick around here," he explained, "in case he comes back."

Five and a half months ago someone else had uttered a variation of that plea about her teenage daughter. "Help me find her, please. You can do it." Instead, the police found her butchered body, compliments of Mac the Knife. I rubbed my jaw, felt the scar Mac had given me.

This is different, I told myself. Why didn't I believe it? Thoughts of Mac made me uncomfortable. I'd managed to stop him, but memories lingered. Damn.

"Please—" Lon's puppy dog eyes glistened.

I sighed, the sound loud in my ears. "I'm a psychologist, Lon. Not a cop." How did I explain about Mac? That I was happy counseling people who were putting their lives back together. Happy in my safe little office. Happy falling asleep over data runs. My internal monologue of "happy's" bothered me. Irritated, I squelched the memory of adrenalin highs. There was nothing wrong with safe and dull. "Ken may not want to be found," I ventured. "Why don't you call Pat?" The three of us had become friends in college, although Pat and Lon kept more in touch with me than with each other.

His mouth settled into a determined line and he shook his head. "Ken would kill me if I made an official report. But I can't stand another day like today...." He blinked, inhaled, ran his fingers through his hair.

"Call Pat," I insisted. "Off the record. She'll help." I handed him the phone and dialed her number, hoping she was in and that she would.

Lon held the receiver to his ear, his words reluctant. "Pat, this is Lon. I'm at home. Please call me." He hung up. "Voice mail."

I sighed.

His St. Bernard expression begged for a bone. "If it gets out Ken's gay, he'll be ruined. The people at his firm are a bunch of stuffed shirts." He paused. "He'd never forgive me."

Feeling like I was sticking my head in a noose, I said, "Until Pat calls—I'll see what I can do."

An appreciative half-smile flared.

Just call me Marshmallow McCue. "I'll need to know *everything* you can tell me," I warned, giving him a hard look I hoped would give him second thoughts. "No holding back. And don't expect miracles."

He nodded, became effusive in his thanks, patting my hand, saying what a bud I was. I wanted to stall until Pat called, but that might be tomorrow. I knew the investigative drill and I had the afternoon free, and darned if I wasn't getting a bit excited at doing something different. "Do you have a picture of Ken?"

He smiled, a flicker of the Lon I loved in his expression, padded down the hall and returned with a polaroid: Ken by the river—bright orange and yellow awning, white patio furnishings, the yuppie crowd at Crawdad's restaurant in the background.

Now I remembered him. "He's a lawyer, right?" Lon had brought him to Pat's wedding.

"Yeah, corporate tax."

Ken was small, slender, with dark hair, olive skin, and nice regular features that would impress clients. Snappy pinstripe suit. But he wasn't smiling in the picture. If anything, he looked worried, eyes tight. I felt a vague sense of unease I didn't understand. "Did you take this?"

Lon peered over my shoulder. "No." He shifted feet.

"You weren't there?"

Lon sat down. "I found the picture in his suit jacket—" He held up his hands, "I was looking for car keys. Anyway, I asked him about the picture. He said it was nothing—just business and gave it to me."

I stared at the photo, noticed four suits similar to Ken's in the background; behind them several jocks, male and female, in swimsuits that enticed rather than covered; and near the deck tourists in loud T-shirts, shorts and boat shoes. "So who was he with?"

Lon shrugged. "Ken *said* no one." His expression tightened. "He was lying. His voice gets all squeaky when he lies." Lon frowned and jabbed a finger at the group of businessmen in the back. "That's Cain. Ken said he hates the guy." A pause.

"You think that was a ruse?"

A shrug.

"Did you ever confront him?"

"He looked upset. I let it go."

I gave the picture another once over, noticed nothing out of the ordinary. I pushed. "Why would he lie?"

"How the hell should I know!" Lon snapped, but the anger seemed manufactured. He glared when I didn't respond.

In a soft voice I asked, "Was he faithful?"

"Of course he was!" But his tone rang with defensiveness.

I wanted to get up, walk out the door and let him sort out his own love life. But he had that whipped look. I gave him a dubious frown. "You *know* that, or you *think* that?"

Lon stalked to the fireplace, looked out the side window, his arms crossed. I doubted he was taking in the view. "No one ever *knows*." Evasiveness.

Why did men always think in terms of sex? "Was he in trouble at work? Drugs? Booze? Gambling?"

He shook his head, his back to me.

I laid the picture on the coffee table and tapped my foot, wishing Pat would call, wishing Ken would walk through the door, and I could walk out. "What was he wearing the last time you saw him?"

"The suit in the picture."

Blue pinstripe. "It would be helpful if you'd make a list of every place he might have gone."

Lon turned. "What if something's happened to him?" His gaze fell to his injured hand.

It caught me off guard and my nose for trouble quivered. "Why do you say that?"

Lon sank to the couch, his tone a shade too bland to believe, "Just a feeling."

I raised my eyebrows and fixed him with a tough stare, wondering how hard I could push him and how much he could take.

He fidgeted. "As he left...he called me a bastard. And he said I'd be sorry." He grimaced.

A death threat? "Was he drunk?"

Lon nodded.

I patted his hand. "He's probably just holed up somewhere—too embarrassed to call." Was I trying to convince him or myself? "I'd like to go through his things."

Lon bobbed his blond head, and led me to the spare bedroom. "He kept his clothes in this closet and whatever work he brought home in the desk." He pointed to an antique desk I instantly fell in love with. Roll top, ornate carved designs along the top and sides, obviously refinished with great care.

Lon left as I started through the clothes. Everything was first class, high class, big bucks. Other than that, nothing exciting—until the last jacket. I found a business card that read: XXX Showgirls—24 hours a day. Interesting. A switch-hitter? I recognized the address, a section of commercial buildings in the north area of the city, gone to seed. The place had once been a dance hall for Tush Pushers. I set the card on top of the desk and started through its drawers. Lots of tax forms, both blank and used. Feeling nosey, I flipped through them. Ken pulled down a six figure income, had several business investments with innocuous names that told me nothing. I jotted a few notes and replaced everything.

I found Lon in the kitchen, handed him the triple X card.

He frowned. "Where'd you find this?"

"Jacket pocket. Was he—into women?" Just call me Blunt Blaize.

Lon's gaze skidded away. "No."

I didn't press.

He turned the card over, frowned. "A phone number."

I put my hand out, "Let me." I dialed, got an answering machine, heard a guy with a heavy middle-eastern accent say to leave a message. I left my name and business number.

Lon watched me like a hawk.

"Answering machine. No name."

"A client?" Lon offered.

I shrugged, "Could be. Where's Ken work?"

"The Ban building. Kensington and Chadwell."

In spite of Lon's problems, I smiled. The "Ban" building was a high-rise near the downtown Civic Center, covered with polished granite and glass that resembled a giant roll-on deodorant. Lon said it was like a woman with one breast—off-kilter.

I glanced at the kitchen counter, Lon's list consisted of four names. "What about family? Friends? Acquaintances?"

He thought a moment, then shrugged. "Parents are in the Bay area. Just Curly and Moe here in town."

Stooges? My brain clicked in. They ran a bar on K street, catering to upper-crust, and mostly gay, clientele.

"We've gone out to dinner with them a few times."

"Have you called his parents?"

Lon shook his head. "No way he'd go there. Believe me."

I didn't argue, but jotted Curly, Moe, Trent, the bartender across the street who was everyone's friend, and Cynthia Pronowske in my notebook. "Who's she?" I asked, tapping my pen against the last name.

"The receptionist at his office. He took her out to lunch once in a while. She was sweet on him and he figured it would help his image." He shrugged.

I retrieved my purse and paused at the door. "When Pat calls, have her contact me. I'll pass everything on."

Lon agreed, looking grateful and miserable at the same time.

I hugged him. "Hang in there. Call me if you hear anything."

"No, I'll let you spin your beautiful wheels," he teased, the Lon I knew resurfacing for a second. We hugged.

Inhaling the smell of water, fish, fruit, and sawdust, I bypassed my car, slipped on my sunglasses, and crossed the street to Crawdad's. The sawing, pounding, and building noises were deafening as I bounced down the steps to the pier. A motor boat roared past, sending out waves. Another buzzed close to the dock, abruptly cut its engine, and moored. So much for riverside peace.

Eleven o'clock. The lunch crowd was multiplying like rabbits. The temperature had risen another five degrees. I scurried into the cool interior, waved over Trent, the bartender, asked if he recognized anyone in the picture. He hesitated, then shook his head. "Sorry, no."

Waiting while he shifted from foot to foot, I read the sign behind the bar "Safe Sex on the beach" then gave him a hard stare. "You sure?"

He pushed a couple of bottles around. "Yeah, I'm sure."

"Okay." For now. I glanced at my watch, wondering how much more asking around I was up for. This wasn't my *forte* anymore. *I should be outta here*, I told myself. But seven years ago Lon had given me a shoulder to cry on when Ross, my ex-boyfriend, and I had a break-up fight. Lon hadn't tried to fix me or offer any unwelcome advice.

I questioned my way down the pier, talking with restaurant staff until my gauze top was wet with perspiration. No help.

On the gangplank to The Virgin Sturgeon's outside deck, I heard my name. Oh joy. Ross. I turned.

He towered over my five foot eight, "Hey, Blaize, what're ya doing in this neck of the woods? Join me for a drink?" He gestured toward the Sturgeon's inner bowels. A slow, lazy grin crawled over his tanned face, lechery reflected in his Clint Eastwood eyes. Most women loved it. I gave him a look that said cockroaches had something on him. "Need someone to pick up the bar tab?"

He frowned. "Still living with the cop?"

I thanked HP, my Higher Power, for sending Zoloski my way. "Get lost." I grumbled and started past, but he grabbed my arm, not too hard, not too gentle—kinda like old times. I shoved my elbow in his side and he let go with a grunt. I smiled. "Don't bother to call."

He snarled an obscenity. More old times.

Some days start out bad and stay that way. I had a hunch this was only the beginning.

Chapter 3

MY NEXT STOP was the Weatherspoon, a little hole-in-the-wall paradise for coffee and croissant lovers like me. With an old-time feel, the place was a haven for readers, thinkers, and would-be artists. Books grew like moss from the walls. Newspapers were heaped on rickety round tables, and pictures spackled here and there.

My stomach growled as I grabbed my lunch. On the way out I and bypassed a chess match beneath a massive oak. Queen to queen's bishop four; White lost a pawn as the croissant melted on my tongue. I inhaled the rest before I reached the car. The iced coffee held on until my seat belt snapped in place. I glanced back longingly, remembering when Lon and I met there to study for college finals, play chess, or just blab. We both laughed when women gave Lon the eye. Those days were simple. My goal then: graduation, a PhD program, a license as a psychologist—and no more PI work. Now I had the degree but kept veering back onto the PI path.

Enough ruminating. Stoked up, I sat for a moment, considering my options. I could go to the office, or try to reach Pat, then tell Lon I did my best. That didn't feel right. I decided to head for the Ban building, ask a few questions about Ken. That would satisfy my promise to Lon, and my own sense of honor. But would it satisfy my need for excitement, intensity? Maybe the dissatisfaction I was feeling had nothing to do with Zoloski and me, but with my profession. Uncomfortable, I left that thought in the dust as I pulled out. I had a good life, steady income, nice office—I was not chucking it for a few PI thrills. If I wanted thrills I could hit the State Fair and bungee jump.

I had my mind settled by the time I ended up on I Street, near 19th. Due to construction, I fought a crane for parking space. After walking two blocks in ninety-five degree heat, I dove into the air conditioned lobby of armpit heaven. Pneumonia weather. What happened to energy conservation? My feet sank into royal blue plush carpet as I shivered my way to the directory. Ken's office being part of a conglomerate on the 12th floor, I stepped into the mouth of a set of gleaming elevators that reminded me of Star Trek. Polished chrome reflections made me look like a short, stubby Ferengi. Swell. Nice professional image.   Thoughts of Ms. Olympia flashed through my mind. I could use a little exercise. Leaving my fatter ego behind, I stepped out and took the stairs.

Twelve floors left me winded. Whew! What a mistake. I needed a cigarette. I paused to catch my breath, and eyed the velvet awning over the law firm's entry. Elegant, white letters, all caps, stated: Kensington and Chadwell. Beyond it, stood a massive vase at least eight feet tall.

My heels clicked across marble tile. Moving past a small settee set into a recessed wall, I resisted the temptation to take a seat. The receptionist was eyeing me with curiosity from behind a massive redwood desk. Her nameplate read "Cynthia Pronowske." She was young, almost pretty, well-dressed, and obviously bored.

Ah, yes, the receptionist sweet on Ken. If anyone knew anything, she probably did. I smiled. "Are you the only receptionist for this big place?"

She straightened, pushing out her chest proudly, "Yes," her tone questioning.

Not a whole lot to flaunt, I thought, but who was I to tallk—at least we had a positive rapport. "Well I hope you don't have to handle all the calls too?" I said sympathetically, as though the phone rang off the hook from eight to five.

She nodded. "It's not too busy today." The hint of a frown appeared on her forehead. Her gaze asked what I wanted.

"Ken mentioned what a great receptionist you are and I hope everyone appreciates you."

"Ken? Mr. Woods?"

I thought about the Triple X card. Was her interest in Ken one-sided, or was Lon off base? I fluttered a hand like I had half a brain. "Yes, I'm a little early. I have an appointment at noon."

Worry shone in her eyes. She hesitated, then gestured me toward one of the chairs that flanked the settee. I detoured a couple of feet to examine the fake Egyptian urn. Hollywood wedded to Ancient Thebes. The place reeked of money.

The receptionist scampered down the hallway and I scurried past her desk to the glass-enclosed board room.

Sixteen leather roll-around chairs surrounded a cherry wood table, its inlaid top set with triangular patterns. Everything was dark brown and top of the line. Beyond the windows I could see the Hyatt, the gold Capitol dome, and practically next door, the Church of the Blessed Sacrament—Our Lady of K Street Mall. The tree-lined streets looked like a miniature train set.

"Excuse me?" A male voice, light Middle-East accent full of

authority, made me want to whirl around.

I forced myself to move slow, casual, found myself eye to eye with a darkly tanned, fifty-ish face that appeared as friendly as a Great White. This guy's suit had to be even more expensive than the ones in Ken's closet, something from Gieves and Hawkes, One Savile Row, where James Bond and the Royal Family spent their ill-gotten gains.

Behind gold wire-rimmed glasses, his dark eyes seemed to get darker. "The receptionist said you had an appointment with Ken Woods?" His gravelly voice questioned who I was—as though he knew something I didn't. Could Ken be here? But then he would have come himself. I smiled. If he wanted an explanation, he could ask. Was he one of the men in the photograph Lon had given me earlier? My hand tightened around my purse strap. We played "stare down."

Finally, he extended his hand. "I'm Victor Amerol. And you?"

Shaking his hand, I said with fake warmth, "I'm Ken's cousin. In town for a few days. We have a lunch date." Why the hell did I say that? Gut instinct?

We shook some more, and eyed each other some more. Was he one of those men who thought women should be covered from head to toe in public? "Your name?" he asked with a softness that said he was used to control.

I bristled, but offered a coy simper, "Andrea McCue."

He flashed a cutting smile, smoothed back his short black hair and gestured toward the reception area. I preceded him to the vase. "Lovely decor," I murmured, wondering if this guy could warm to anyone in clothes off the rack.

"Ken called in sick today," he said. "However, I did check his calendar. He had nothing listed for this afternoon. Nothing about a lunch date...."

Beyond Amerol's shoulder, I saw the receptionist staring in surprise.

I wrinkled my brow, Columbo style. "That's funny...."

"What?" His placid look said it'd take an earthquake to shake him up.

"I called him at home to say I might be early. He didn't answer." I forced a chatty cadence into my tone. "My plane leaves tonight. And I haven't seen Ken in ages! You're sure he called in sick?"

Amerol shrugged, but deceit flickered in his gaze. "I'm sure." He knew something. His shark eyes deadened again and his gaze dropped. "So, how do you like our fair city?"

Man, smooth as silk. I felt like a tap dancer caught in a boxing ring with no gloves. "Oh," I drawled with a flirtatious wink, "It's fun! I bought a ton of stuff. For the family back home."

He arched an eyebrow, a flash of interest reflected in his expression. "Back home?" His gaze flickered toward my left hand. No ring.

For a moment I felt like a mouse in a cat's paw. Well, hey, I was liberated. I smiled, ignored the question, and took a hopeful step toward the hallway. "I'll just leave a note on Ken's desk."

Amerol stopped me, his hand heavy on my arm. "That's not necessary. I'll tell him you were here."

I glanced past him to the receptionist who was listening. Sympathetic to my cause? Giving Amerol a disappointed smile, I uttered some blithering apology about being a nuisance and retreated to elevator heaven. I hit the button, plotting my next move, wondering how I could talk to the receptionist—alone. Amerol gave off bad vibes. She interested me.

AN INNER WAR raged as I rode the elevator down. I'd gone way beyond the call of duty. I should call Lon, tell him what I'd learned, which wasn't much, then dump the matter into Pat's lap. But Bad Vibes Amerol irritated me, and he scared the receptionist. I wanted to know why. I took the elevator back up, pulling off one earring as I stepped out. The receptionist gave me a confused stare. She looked a young, flustered twenty.

Amerol was no where in sight.

I kept my voice low. "I dropped one of my earrings. I held up a gold dangly bauble that had cost fifty bucks at Nordstrom's. "It wasn't in the elevator. I thought—well, I hoped it came off in here." I swept the floor with my gaze.

In a conspiratorial tone, I asked, "Did you talk to Ken when he called in?"

Her face colored and she stammered, "No." I wasn't sure if it was because I'd taken her off guard, or because she was lying. The office phone rang and she plucked it, mouthing to me, "Go ahead and look."

Oh yeah, the earring. I listened to her "Yes, Sir, No, Sir," for a moment and edged my way toward the hallway. Ken's office was the first one. Eureka. I stepped inside, my heart thudding in my chest, wondering why I was doing this. This was way beyond looking for a missing boyfriend. Yet if it had been Zoloski who disappeared, I knew Lon would help me any way he could.

So I'd lied to Victor Amerol. He'd lied to me. Ken had *not* called in sick, the receptionist's face told me that. So, where was Ken? And why had Amerol lied?

I closed the door, tip-toed to Ken's mahogany desk and checked his calendar for the last week. Monday's page was torn out. Monday night Ken had gotten drunk, picked a fight with Lon, threatened him, then left. I flipped forward a week. Nothing.

I tore a piece of paper from the back of his calendar and scrawled him a lovey-dovey note from his distant cousin. I searched every drawer. *Nada.*

The row of filing cabinets behind me beckoned, but my nerve was running out. In spite of the air conditioning, sweat ran down between my shoulder blades. Jitters? Creepy-crawlies? Like a fish gasping for water I needed out of there.

Swallowing my fears, I quietly slid open the first drawer. I felt like I was in a dream, searching for something, didn't know what, but felt compelled to look. Belatedly, I hoped I wouldn't get Ken in trouble with my snooping.

The first drawer contained information on clients with business or last names beginning with A, B, and C. Anytime, Inc. leaped out at me. The name had been in Ken's tax stuff at Lon's. I jotted the name and looked for a list of investors. Couldn't find them. Strange. Antsy, I stuck the paper in my purse and moved on. I had just closed the fourth and bottom drawer, stood up to get a kink out of my knee when the door opened abruptly. "Oh dear!" My hand fluttered to my chest, my heart threatening to break a few ribs and escape Victor Amerol's murderous look. Several men stood behind him, along with the secretary, her hands knitting an invisible sweater. Oh boy.

"Miss McCue!" Amerol snapped, his red face saying he wanted to kill me—but now was not the time nor place.

I refrained from correcting his "Miss" to Ms.

"What are you doing here?"

I gestured toward the desk. My hand didn't shake, thank God. "Well, Ken's my cousin," I blustered, "and you were so rude...I really felt I should leave him a note." I gave him my best "little woman" defiant look.

He checked the desk, read my scrawl, frowned and murmured something to one of the men behind him. A language I recognized as somewhere near the Sudan. His tone was master to slave.

Locking my arm in an unfriendly grip, the "slave" whose tongue flicked between his lips like a snake, escorted me to the elevators, punched the button, saw me inside. All the way down his eyes remained fixed on mine, taking my measure in some undefinable way. In the lobby, he escorted me straight to the guard's security desk. "Please see that she has an escort *if* she comes back." His tone said "You'd better not." Nodding, the guard glared.

The "slave's" narrowed gaze and another flick of his tongue across his bottom lip reminded me of a cobra, and also made me wonder if I made him nervous. Cobra Face disappeared into the elevator, but not before I caught a backwards glance at me that bespoke concern, not menace. Had he meant me to see? Puzzled, I sat down on one of the oak benches, kicked off my right shoe and rubbed my instep. The pink and grey granite reflected my flushed face back at me. I slid my gaze across it's gleaming surface toward the security desk. "Is that guy always like that?" I asked in a half-joking tone.

"Cain's okay. He works for the building's owner." The guard gave me a once over that I ignored.

Cain. Lon's words about Ken and Cain came rushing back. "The owner? Who's that?"

"Victor Amerol."

Jeez, talk about pissing off the man at the top! I replaced my shoe and retreated to the bar across the street. I needed a diet coke, straight up, no ice. It burned nicely all the way down and left me clear-headed.

I'd done more than enough gum-shoeing. Time to return to my real job. I would try to reach Pat from my office—like I should have done in the first place—and then see if I could entice Zoloski into a racquetball game. I had another diet coke, waiting for my heart to resume its normal rhythm. Victor Amerol and his henchman, Cobra Face Cain, scared me and the more I thought about Amerol, the more he reminded me of my step-father, a scary man—especially to a seven year-old. I psychoanalyzed myself for the next five minutes, until the panic attack passed, then dug out the photograph of Ken. Cain and Amerol stood in the background with two other men. Four of the five men were about the same height, five-nine or ten, the other probably six-one. Ken, Cain, and Amerol were slender, the two men behind Amerol were tanks, one six foot, the other my height, all muscle. Bodyguards? From the picture, I figured Ken and Amerol were doing a little business. So why Cain and the other two? I told myself it didn't matter, finished my soda, dropped a buck on the table and left.

It was only two blocks to my car, but I didn't quite make it. Footsteps came up fast. I started to turn.... WHACK. The lights went out.

Chapter 4

SIRENS FILLED my ears. Someone was moaning. Zoloski? I swam toward consciousness, realized it was me and tried to emerge from the black lake over my head. The inside of my mouth tasted like sour apples, throat dry as burnt toast. My nose burned as though I'd inhaled the wrong end of a cigarette. I had to get to the surface. Breathe.

As I closed in on light, my skull exploded. Somebody gimme some heavy duty drugs. Light pierced my eyes before I closed them again. Pain shot across my scalp, and I wanted to retreat back to the warm, dark womb.

Plastic covered my nose and mouth. Panicked, I opened my eyes for another dazzle of glaring light. Squinting, I saw something dangle near my face. It swung close, then away. A clear, hot water bottle? No, too small.

The swerving, shaking, roller coaster ride continued. I closed my eyes, my stomach roiling, a volcano of acid about to erupt. No puking in the bus please.

Bus?

"Can you tell me your name?" A soft genderless inquiry.

I blinked, saw a blue blur of uniform, a figure leaning over. My head throbbed and I sank back toward the muddled dark place.

Fingers prodded and pressed my chest. I yelped. My vision cleared for a moment, revealing a feminine face, dark eyes, dark hair, white letters embroidered on blue coveralls. Paramedic.

"What happened?" The words stuck in my throat. I closed my eyes as the vise around my head tightened and my stomach flip-flopped.

"UCD Med Center AMR 128 Paramedic Jackson. We're en route to your facility, code 3, critical trauma on board. Approximately 25 to 30 year old female. Unconscious."

Twenty-five to thirty? Me? Yeah. Unconscious? Sort of.

The disembodied voice continued, "Appears to have been hit on the head..."

Was that what happened? Scrambled brains on board? A groan began working its way up my throat.

"Patient has a large hematoma to the right parietal area with a one inch laceration. Bleeding is controlled at this time..."

That's a relief.

"...NPA..."

NBA? Did I get hit with a basketball?

"...Adequate respiration. Good tidal volume..."

Tidal? I drifted back to sea. More words floated by. Pressure on my sternum forced me awake. "Yow!" I half-gasped, half-yelled.

I tried to move, protest, do something.

Someone held my arm down. "Stay still."

Suddenly the sirens stopped. Two paramedics lifted the gurney out and down, and rolled me through sliding doors into a madhouse of green aliens all gibbering med-tech. We took a right, then a quick left. I was in a room with another gurney rider. Light glared overhead. Green garbed MDs flanked me, poking, prodding. "What's your name?"

I pulled at the mask on my face.

"It's oxygen. Leave it on. We can hear you."

I felt hemmed in.

"Do you know your name?"

My identity sizzled through my thoughts along with a hundred other facts. "Blaize McCue," I rasped to a pair of impatient eyes.

"Good. How about today's date?"

Shit, a test. Memories rushed at me. Noon. The Ban building. WHACK.

The doctor looked exhausted. "Do you know where you are?"

I cleared my throat. "Hospital?"

"Were you mugged?"

"Was I?"

The MD shot a questioning gaze at someone beyond my vision, then shrugged in answer.

"My purse?" I tried to lift my head, see who he'd glanced at, regretted it as red pain tried to take off the top of my skull.

"No purse," the doctor said.

Damn. Dark waters swirled.

WHEN I WOKE, the tube, an NPA, was out of my nose, the IV out of my arm, and I was sequestered in a nice quiet hospital room. I felt almost human.

The door swung open. Zoloski paused in the doorway, his mouth a worried line, his gorgeous green, green eyes concerned. He moved closer, took my hand, planted a gentle kiss on my brow, then my lips. "What you do to get attention," he murmured, but questions lay in the back of his eyes.

"Nothing like a concussion to expand my horizons." Not my wittiest comeback. "How long have I been here?"

"You were brought in a couple of hours ago. One of the nurses found my business card in your pocket."

I remembered stashing it there months ago when my friend Pat had given me the Z-man's card so I could talk to him about a murdered client. I hadn't worn the jacket since. I smiled up at Zoloski, feeling woozy and dry-mouthed. Funny how things worked out.

He hiked an eyebrow, tossed a duffle bag on the chair beside the bed and gave me an unreadable look. "I brought you some clothes, toothbrush, etcetera." His awkward tone made me wonder if a lecture about being more careful downtown was coming.

"Thanks."

He gently squeezed my hand. "They're keeping you overnight. Just in case. I'll take you home in the morning."

I struggled into a sitting position, my head agreeing with the doctor's orders, the rest of me determined to exit.

Zoloski leaned closer. "Did you see who hit you?"

I shook my head, setting off a zillion pin balls behind my eyes. "No."

He rubbed my hand, his touch comforting, his tone taking on a business edge. "Your purse was stolen. Someone called 911, reported you down. Didn't leave a name. Were you on your way to lunch?"

The Ban Building was only a few blocks from my office. "I'll explain later." I gulped back a wave of nausea. "I want to go home. Now."

"Oh yeah?" An unfamiliar voice interrupted.

Zoloski turned. I stared. Ms. Olympia in a blue jump suit, dark hair touching her shoulder above a white label: Paramedic. I rubbed my nose. "You the one who gave me a nasal enema?"

"Thought you might be fakin' it," she replied without remorse as she crossed to the bed, her gaze flashing from me to Zoloski, back to me. Something flickered in her dark eyes.

"Faking unconsciousness?"

Her reply surprised me. "Yeah. Lots of people do. You'd be amazed."

"Well, I wasn't."

She shrugged. "Just dropped off a DOA. Thought I'd see how you were doing."

"I'm alive. Thanks." My gaze fell to the name tag embroidered on her uniform's right shoulder. "Nick?"

She extended her hand, her gaze warmer after my thanks. "Nicole Jackson."

I gave her a firm shake. "Blaize McCue." I nodded slightly toward the Z-man. "Detective Stephanos Zoloski."

She shook hands, then backed to the door. "Gotta go. Glad you're okay."

I called out, "Hey Jackson..."

She paused, her hand on the doorknob.

"I meant it. Thanks."

A brief flash of white teeth and she was gone.

My next task was convincing the doctor I was ready to go home. He didn't buy it. "You've had a serious head trauma. Everything looks good, but you need to stay overnight. Make sure."

"I'm going home," I repeated. "I know my name, today's date, and where I am. You can't keep me here."

He sighed, the sound tired and frustrated. "You're absolutely right. Go!" He left the room.

Grumbling, Zoloski helped me dress. "You should stay here." Like he would know.

"If I'm going to feel like shit, I want to feel like shit in my own bed," I grumped as he helped me into the car.

"Our bed," Zoloski corrected. *His* actually.

I sighed, gingerly leaned back against the seat. "Right," I agreed, suddenly sleepy. "Ours." The word grew on me.

He threw me a sidelong glance that spelled COP. "You sure you didn't see anyone?"

I closed my eyes. "The lump I have is on the back of my head, Stephanos. I heard footsteps, started to turn, then *nada*."

I suddenly remembered Mr. Bad Vibes, Victor Amerol, his shark-like smile, and told Zoloski about looking for Ken Woods.

His expression closed down. Not a happy camper, but at least he didn't crack any "queer" jokes. Most cops would. I could almost hear his inner dialogue, the part where he asks when am I going to say "no" to my friends, and keep my nose out of trouble. "Like when hell freezes over," I murmured.

He threw me a questioning glance, his jaw tighter than my new bra. "What?"

"Nothing."

A sigh of pure frustration. "Look, I shouldn't tell you this. But knowing you—I'd better."

I started to protest. His glare shriveled the words in my throat.

"Victor Amerol is not someone you should mess with. He's big. He's powerful. He's got nasty connections. And if he had anything to do with that whack on the head, it was a warning. The next time you won't wake up."

"Jesus." Was I mugged or had I poked a wasp's nest? "You're kidding, right?"

"No." Zoloski snapped.

I remembered the flat, dark eyes; they'd looked ready to roll back any moment as he took a chunk out of my hide. No feeling in those babies.

Stress overload set in. I turned my thoughts to safer things, like canceling credit cards, renewing my license and replacing the mace, pepper spray, pocket knife, and make-up in my purse. And worst of all, trying to find another one big enough for the kitchen sink. On a scale of one to ten, my spirits sank into negative numbers.

Zoloski zipped onto the freeway, the Jag's engine purring with power. He patted my knee. "I canceled all your credit cards—from the list in the desk."

Did he read my mind? I'd forgotten the list we'd put there. "Thanks." I rolled my head gently to one side, studying his profile. His chiseled features, once-broken nose, reddish-tanned skin and dark hair curling up at the shirt collar made me want to whistle in appreciation. "Hey, Zoloski..."

"Yeah?"

I swallowed my cowardice. "I love you, Big Guy."

He grinned. "Maybe you should get hit on the head more often."

"Hey, I've said I love you before." Hadn't I?

His eyebrows did a little dance. "Once. After I asked you to stay with me."

I remembered. The romantic dinner, flowers, the endearing note. Three months ago. Three to go... "You ready to turn me in for a new model?" I wondered aloud.

He shot me a questioning look. "No. How about you?"

Was he kidding! I shrugged.

"Well?" he rasped.

"I'm thinking," I teased.

A satisfied, smug expression settled over his face as he pulled into the driveway. "And...?"

"Home Sweet Home," I quipped. My dreams of happiness had always painted me alone. Our relationship had pulled me in a new direction, sometimes painfully, sometimes joyfully.

Against my protests, Zoloski carried me into the house, his biceps bulging. As always, the feel and smell of him turned me on. How could I feel this good after being mugged? Aspirin acceleration? Frisky hormones? Naw.

He laid me on "our" bed and pulled the covers up to my chin. "Sleep," he ordered a twinkle in his eyes.

Amazingly, I did

I AWOKE TO darkness. Red numbers on the radio-clock showed eleven-thirty. Where was the Z-man?

I sat up, glad no pin balls erupted, and swung my feet over the edge of the bed. Still no pain. Yee Haw! I padded into the living room with a show-off gait. Takes a licking and keeps on ticking.

Zoloski sat barefoot at the dining room table, photographs and file papers covering the surface, shoes and socks sprawled across the tile. He wore an expression of intense concentration that I loved.

"What's up, doc?" I croaked. I cleared my throat.

He pushed back his chair, threw me a smile. "How ya feeling?"

"Pretty good." I touched the back of my head, the golf ball lump tender. Darn if my mood wasn't up around a ten. Zoloski's charms, or gratefulness to be alive?

"What's all this?" I gestured at the table, the nearest photograph. A dead man's chest, bruised and bloodied. Almost looked fake—almost.

"That guy we found on the horse trail."

Look Ma no hands. I sank into a chair. "Toothless?"

"Yeah."

"What's the skinny?"

Zoloski shrugged. "The guy's in his late twenties, early thirties. No ID. No wallet. Bloodied shirt. No jacket. Expensive slacks. Cause of death unconfirmed. But looks like a whack on the head."

WHACK. I recalled the split second eruption of painful fireworks, the lights going out, and the sky spinning above. My mouth felt dry as cotton balls. Coincidence? Had to be. Still, if I hadn't turned.... "Read the description again."

Zoloski did.

Why did I keep seeing Ken Woods? Dark hair. Dark eyes. Expensive clothes. The right age group. So were a million other men. But if it were Ken, it offered an explanation for Victor Amerol's reaction to Ken's "cousin"—if he knew Ken was dead. A giant leap based on absolutely nothing but dislike, which the Z-man would never buy.

Uneasy, I reached for a face shot of the dead guy, stared at it and concentrated on holding back the bile in my throat. I covered the bottom half, leaving just his eyes and nose and started shaking. I could be wrong.

"You okay?"

"Sure." Old Iron stomach Mcqueasy? Naw.

Zoloski shot me a look of disbelief. "What is it?"

I didn't want to say until I was sure. And I no longer had the picture of Ken. Still... "He reminds me of Ken Woods, Lon's missing boyfriend."

Zoloski and I had met Ken at Pat's wedding. Now, he shuffled through photos and papers, found another head shot, studied it, then stared off in space. "It could be him. Is Lon's number in your rollidex?"

"You really think it could be Ken?"

He picked up the phone. "One way to find out." He slipped the photos and papers inside a folder. "I'm going to ask him to take a look at the body. First thing in the morning."

Zoloski punched in Lon's number.

I touched Zoloski's arm. "Lon's a close friend," I said, wondering how a request for special treatment would go down. Probably as well as *his* advice about one of my clients. "Let me tell him."

He gave me the COP look. "This guy's got no teeth, no hands. Somebody wanted him buried as a John Doe. I want to know why." He shifted toward the wall, his tone all business. "Lon?" A pause. "This is Detective Zoloski. Blaize's friend."

Another pause.

"Sorry I woke you. No, Blaize is fine. No, she got a tap on the head, spent a few hours in the hospital. I'll tell her to call Pat tomorrow." A pause. "I'd like you to meet me at the morgue in the morning."

Nothing like breaking it to him gently, I thought. But then, maybe there wasn't a gentle way to say it.

Lon's anxiety-ridden voice erupted from the other end.

"It's probably nothing. But we have a guy with no ID and need to check all leads."

A long pause. Lon's voice rose to an furious pitch I knew covered worry.

Zoloski interrupted. "Okay, okay. We'll do it now. But it's probably just some drunk."

My hands tightened around the edge of my chair. It was no drunk and we both knew it. Someone had gone to a lot of trouble to obliterate this guy's identity. I should be with Lon, not listening to a one-way conversation. I hurried to the bedroom and threw on some clothes, came out as Zoloski was strapping on his gun. He grabbed his jacket and scowled. "No way José. You're going back to bed."

I didn't argue. Merely continued on to the car while he blustered.

Chapter 5

THE MORGUE AFTER midnight wore an eerie yellow glow from overhead light. I climbed from the Jag, my gaze flickering across the empty parking lot to Lon's red Supra. My head ached, my eyes hurt. I wanted to be anywhere but here.

Lon was pacing by the front door, tennis shoes silent on the pavement, cigarette in his right hand. The smoke spiraled across his leather jacket like stray fog. Two years of trying to quit down the tubes. So what? my sarcasm kicked in, he already looked like death. Ice settled in my stomach. What could I say?

Zoloski put his hand on my arm and shot me a hard look. A warning? His expression softened. "Trouble with a capital T, huh?"

So I'd said during our first few dates. Did he have to remind me? Usually it made me smile. Not now. Lon looked ready to take a step off a high bridge.

He dropped his cigarette and took me into his arms. "Blaize!" he croaked. "Jesus I can't believe this!"

I hugged him and made sounds of comfort.

He pulled back. "How's your head? Pat told me you were mugged." He glanced toward Zoloski, then back to me. "Shouldn't you be in bed?"

His concern under the circumstances touched me, bringing tears to my eyes. I swallowed them back.

Zoloski started inside.

Patting Lon's arm, I led him through the glass doors to the Netherworld. My memory of the place made me queasy. The odor—death and disinfectant—the melancholy coldness seeping into my bones.

Zoloski took care of formalities. Lon and I held hands while the Z-man led the way. He motioned to the coroner, who pulled open a big drawer and peeled back the sheet.

I squeezed Lon's hand. The blood rushed from his face like an elevator dropping 50 floors. He sank into a chair, fumbled in his jacket for a cigarette, then couldn't light it. I gently took the lighter and lit it for him as Zoloski watched. A glance at the Z-man told me nothing about his thoughts.

Zoloski spoke, his tone businesslike yet soft, "Is that a positive ID?"

A quick nod from Lon as he sucked on the cigarette like it was dope.

I felt angry at my own helplessness and had to stifle the urge to snap at Zoloski, tell him to talk to Lon later.

Zoloski frowned at me, hesitated, then said to Lon, "You're sure it's Ken Woods?"

Lon, his gaze cloudy, kept shaking his head as though to say, "This is all a bad dream."

I patted his hand, murmured his name. His gaze skidded from Zoloski to me. "What?"

"He's in shock," I said. "He needs to go home."

"Ken Woods?" Zoloski asked gently. "You're sure?"

Lon shuddered, looked around for an ash tray, then despairingly dropped the cigarette butt on the floor and stepped on it. "Yes. It's him." He looked at me like a drowning man eyes a lifeboat. "I need to get out of here."

I glanced at Zoloski.

He sighed, the sound telling me to stay out of this. "I need to ask some questions, Lon."

"In the morning," I interrupted, pulling Lon to his feet. "I'm taking him home."

Zoloski's gaze narrowed, his jaw tightened, and he said through clenched teeth, "I'll follow you over."

To pick me up or grill Lon? An unfair thought, but I was uncomfortable. Zoloski was in COP mode, and Lon was my friend. "Thanks," I said.

In the car, Lon choked out, "What happened? Where was he found?"

I shook my head, unable to answer, thinking of pliers in some man's hands. Teeth yanked out. I just hoped Ken was dead first. As my stomach danced an unwholesome jig, I pushed away visions of a meat cleaver chopping off hands.

As though his thoughts dragged the same nightmare river, Lon hastened to light a cigarette, then rolled down the window. I'd never let anyone smoke in my car—but I couldn't tell him to put it out. It was probably the only thing holding him together. After inhaling half the cancer stick, he looked at me. "What kind of creep would do something like that?"

I threw Lon an appraising glance as I took the Garden Highway exit. "I don't know." He and Ken had fought. There'd been blood in his apartment. I felt a twinge of disloyalty to the Z-man as I said, "Don't talk to Zoloski tonight. Answer his questions in the morning, but don't volunteer *any* information."

Alarm showed in his eyes as I parked. "You think I killed him?"

Zoloski's headlights flashed behind us.

"Of course not. But you don't want anybody jumping to conclusions." Victor Amerol's dull shark eyes swam through my consciousness. I rubbed the lump on the back of my head and winced. Tender—but not as the night. This night was anything but. Zoloski pulled open Lon's door, ending our conversation.

I got out, gave Zoloski a "stay back" look, walked Lon upstairs, gave him a hug and said goodnight.

In the Jag, I ignored the dark look in Zoloski's eyes and asked if the autopsy report was finished.

"Preliminary only. Should have it tomorrow." His voice was stiff. An awkward pause followed as he zipped down the left lane of the freeway. Finally he sighed, the sound heavy with frustration.

Loved those non-verbal cues. I picked up the gauntlet. "Lon's my friend. I can't just ignore what's happening."

"And I'm a cop," he shot back. "And you should be in bed, not interfering in my case."

"Oh yeah?" My jaw suddenly felt as tight as piano wire. "You're a homicide cop. That means Ken was murdered. *You're* looking for a suspect."

He threw me a sidelong look that was both speculative and wary. "And you're looking for a reason to get involved." His hands strangled the steering wheel. "It's not enough for you to skydive on vacation, or take on class-five rapids in a fourteen foot raft, is it?" He didn't wait for an answer. "Damn it, I've never seen anyone as driven as you. You want life to be a roller-coaster ride."

"So do you," I squeezed in, wishing I could deny what he said. But I was hooked on *his* work—the excitement. Had been since we'd tripped over Toothless—even if I hated to admit it.

He switched gears. "You know something I should know?"

I hesitated a moment too long. "About what?"

"You know damn well what! Something that would implicate Lon!"

I thought about the mess in Lon's apartment, the bandage on his hand. I hadn't mentioned either. Damn, damn, damn. I racked my brain for a comeback. "Ken worked in Victor Amerol's building."

Zoloski snorted as he pulled into the driveway. "Yeah, you told me." He waited, his eyes asking for the rest of it.

A staring contest ensued. Lon had asked for my help, was my friend, and I wouldn't abandon him—not even for Zoloski. The Z-man and I had shared barely six months of our lives. A great six months, but Lon and I went back a decade. I groped for some offering. "I got hit outside Amerol's building. You said he's dangerous."

"A lot of people work in Amerol's building. Muggings happen."

"Well..." I threw out my hands, wishing I had something better to offer than Lon's broken-up apartment. Must have been one hell of a fight. Would Lon have asked me for help if he'd killed Ken? No.

Unless he was covering up, a part of me whispered. But he'd insisted on going to the morgue, I argued back. Why would he do that?

Because he's smart.

Why did I feel so uncertain? I'd never seen Lon so distraught, never seen him drunk, never seen his apartment a mess. He maintained the image of a straight successful engineer, but his knuckles had been raw, the cut on his hand deep. Could it have been an accident he'd tried to cover up?

Toothless and handless? Could Lon have done that to his lover? No way, José. I felt better. "What about gay-bashing?" I said as Zoloski ushered me inside.

Zoloski grunted. "And as an afterthought the perpetrator whacks off Ken's hands and yanks his teeth?"

I stripped and climbed into bed in mute agreement.

As he slipped between the sheets, he whispered, "A penny for your thoughts."

"I'm a blank," I lied, feeling instantly guilty, then angry because he had me looking at Lon as a suspect.

He arched an eyebrow, gave me a wry smile that said he was letting me off, for now, but tomorrow I wouldn't be so lucky.

Pulling me close, he kissed my ear. "I love you, Blaize," he murmured, "but I'm still a cop."

I felt warmed by the love part, and threatened by the last. How important was the JOB? More important than us? Zoloski's identity was tied up with being a cop. Mine was floundering between wild urges. Shrink and PI were becoming items of critical mass—two opposing forces which threatened to explode in my face. I closed my eyes, and mentally repeated the twelve-step slogan "One day at a time." Thus far it had kept me from going bonkers.

Of course, I forgot to apply it in the morning when Zoloski asked me if I had anything to tell him. I kept seeing the future—Lon in jail on a murder charge. Although Zoloski didn't say it, a challenge of "him or me" lay in his eyes. His jaw looked tighter than a nut-cracker jammed shut.

Cold silence hung between us as we walked to our respective cars. Zoloski threw his case book into the Jag. "You're obviously not telling me something," he ground out. He slammed his door and rolled down the window. "You decide to talk, give me a call." He backed out of the driveway and I heard him mutter, "Damn woman's driving me nuts!"

I climbed into my car and slammed my own door. Sitting there, I realized that as much as I wanted to, I couldn't rescue Lon from the police. Ken had been murdered, Lon was an obvious suspect. I had to let it go. But if I did, would I resent Zoloski? Resentments could build up like granules of sand, not seem like much, then suddenly turn to a mountain of rage. Or they could pile up like garbage and molder, rot, and reek... Shades of my grandparents. Shades of Zoloski and me in the future? Not if I stayed current, I told myself.

Resolving to talk with him after work, I jammed my extra car key in the ignition and headed for the office. Along with a headache and argument, I still had to cope with replacing my purse, wallet, license and other essentials. As I walked through the spacious lobby of the Senator Hotel, I tried to distract myself by imagining the days when "lobbying" originated in places like this. Back when the rooms were living quarters for the Legislators, and railroad men hung out trying to snag votes.

The distraction lasted until I was at my desk staring at the blinking red light of the answering machine. Political chants drifted from the Capitol, filtering through the window with the already hot sun. I couldn't quite make out the message, but I could sure feel the heat. Eighty degrees by 8:00 spelled one hundred and ten by 3:00. Fried brains for lunch, Madam? I had the inane picture of someone flipping gray matter on the sizzling sidewalk and serving them up. Jeez Louise.

Missing hands. Missing teeth. Fried brains. A dull ache spread across the back of my neck. What next?

Chapter 6

I CENTERED MYSELF by reading a daily meditation book by Al-Anon members, for people in relationships with an addict, past or present.

Today's page reminded me that blaming my discomfort on outside events can be a way to avoid facing the real cause—my own attitudes. But in this case outside events *had* disturbed my life. Ken Woods was dead. Murdered. Lon was distraught. I was his best friend. And damned if I didn't like wearing a PI hat. Changing my attitude couldn't change that. I closed the book.

My gut said I'd done the right thing last night—warning Lon not to volunteer information—but would Zoloski see it that way? Showdown at the OK corral. I didn't want to dodge bullets or spew them, but if Lon needed me I would be there—Zoloski would just have to understand.

With that wonderful insight, I counseled my two morning clients. The first, in Overeaters Anonymous, didn't realize she reacted to everything as a victim. I gave her a nudge toward awareness. She resisted.

"Resistance is pain, acceptance is relief," I wanted to tell her as she talked about her latest binge, unable to get to the feelings buried beneath thirty extra pounds. No instant success today, I thought as I ushered her to the door.

The second client twitched and squirmed as he talked. Ants in his pants? Using again? His eyes were clear. No matter how I prodded for feelings he stayed in his head, using the words "I think" persistently.

With an inner sigh of frustration I sent him off to cope with the real world for another week, and turned to the answering machine. I hit the button, afraid I'd hear Lon's voice asking me to come over, asking me to give comfort and "feel" emotions I'd rather advise my clients to walk through than experience myself.

An unfamiliar, heavy middle-eastern accent spouted from the tape. "Blaize McCue I am returning your call. If you would like to meet I am available after ten p.m. Come by the club." A pause. Was he reading a cue card? The voice had little inflection. Victor Amerol's voice had reminded me of silk covered steel. This guy sounded younger, rougher. Less educated. What club? After 10:00? I didn't think he meant my health club.

"Ask for Mohammed," the message concluded.

Who the hell was he?

The machine beeped. Pat's voice.

Damn. I'd forgotten the European slide show. I called Zoloski and passed on the message. Did he want to go? I wanted to call her up and asked about Lon, but bit my tongue.

Curious about "Mohammed," I pulled out the tape, stuck a new one in the machine, and looked around for my purse. Damn again. I had a lump on the head and no purse. I stuck the tape in my desk.

11:30. My next client wasn't due until 1:00. I headed for the bank, seven blocks away, withdrew some cash, then hit Macy's. Exercise, and a new purse. Not a bad lunch break.

But who in blazes was Mohammed?

THE ANSWER came to me as I handed the clerk crisp green bills and watched him ring up $175 worth of leather—soft, buttercream leather, with lots of pockets inside and out. I loved it.

The pockets reminded me of Ken Woods suit jacket, and the business card I'd found in the pocket—I'd called the number on the card and left my name. At least my memory had kicked in. Now I knew he was returning my call—but I no longer had the card.

Numbers stick in my brain. Sometimes. I closed my eyes, visualized the card, phone number on one corner, the address on the other. Quickly, I jotted down both on the back of my receipt. Maybe Zoloski would come with me to talk to the guy. Or would he think I was interfering?

Pushing the thought aside, I hurried down K Street. My stomach growled and I fed it some gum.

Three more messages were on the machine by the time I reached my office. Zoloski: "Saturday's fine with me. Why don't we go sailing in the morning, picnic, soak up a little sun, then pick up Chinese food to share with Pat and Arnie."

No mention of Lon. But he came next. "Blaize, Zoloski left a while ago. I think everything went okay." Doubt in his voice? "He's going to call Ken's parents in San Francisco. Tell them what happened... They don't know about me." Pause. His voice dropped to a strangled whisper. "I still can't believe it. Who would do *that* to such a beautiful person? It doesn't make sense."

It made sense to somebody. I sighed. Five minutes to my next patient.

Last message. Pat: "Zoloski called and confirmed Saturday at seven. I heard about Lon's, uh, friend. How's he doing?" Pause. "Dumb question, forget I asked. I'll call him."

Good. Maybe she'd get over some of her homophobia and I could retire at playing middle-person.

I ushered in my next client.

Afterwards, I flipped up my lap-top and finished the final test analysis. God, how I hated numbers, but got massive satisfaction from mastering them. My fingers burned up the keys. Satisfaction swelled as I slipped the report and my invoice inside a manila envelope and shoved the packet into the mail slot. At least my professional life was rolling along.

New purse over my shoulder, I double-timed to the DMV, renewed my license, got a temporary, and sped off to La Bou for a bowl of minestrone, whole wheat roll and cafe mocha. A heavenly break for my tastebuds and my brain.

Stoked up, I drove to the gym. In deference to my head wound I took it easy—let my thoughts ramble. They consistently returned to Mohammed and what he might know about Ken. I went home. No one there. Ate dinner with Dan Rather, thinking I'd RATHER be with Zoloski.

Tired, but restless, I switched channels, couldn't stomach the commercials, zapped the TV off. I tried to read, couldn't remember the preceding chapter, and gave it up. Nine-fifteen. Where was Zoloski? I dialed his office. Surprisingly, he answered on the first ring.

"It's me, Lover, just wondering where my bed warmer is. It's after nine." I doodled Mohammed's name on the note pad beside the phone, wondering how best to bring him up.

"Sorry Blaize. I'm hung-up." His tone said he was waiting for a call, wanted me off the line.

"If it's a she, I'll kill her," I joked.

"It's work, don't worry. Well... worry a little. I like it."

I pictured a small smile tugging at his firm lips. It warmed me. "Jay Leno's looking good, Stephanos," I warned, referring to my past life as an unattached woman when I'd stayed up late with TV personalities.

He laughed. "As soon as this call comes in I'll be on my way." On cue, the line gave a call-waiting double-click. "Ah," he said.

"Talk to you later," I said.

"Be home soon."

But at nine-fifty he still wasn't home. I jotted him a note about Mohammed and left.

THE XXX CLUB sparkled like a cheap dress with a rhinestone pin. The male population glutted the inside like maggots on a rotting corpse. My curiosity had brought me here and now I had second thoughts. But hell, I was here. Might as well meet the guy.

Music blared from an unknown source, the sexually suggestive notes dripping like saliva, encouraging impatient hoots and hollers. The bouncer looked like your average college kid on a football scholarship; big, beefy, short blond hair, nice smile and a grip that could tear the arms off a Grizzly. But I was grateful for his presence.

Like a good coach, he pointed me toward a doorway in the far corner, and I zigzagged through the roomful of rowdy, yelling, sweating males. "Start the show!" someone howled.

Swell, I hadn't missed the fun. Some guy whistled as I passed. Dream on. If looks could freeze *cojones* mine did.

The door said PRIVATE. I rapped on it and it opened, giving me a second's respite before a big six-foot frame waltzed into view. It belonged to a baritone that rivaled Zoloski's. "Ms. McCue?"

I nodded. "Mohammed?"

His liquid brown eyes reminded me of Omar Sharif as he moved back a step. He was every bit as handsome, and probably not much older than me. He nodded and guided me down a dingy, dimly lit hall, the narrow tight space making me uncomfortable. We passed a dressing room and stopped at a door marked "office." He unlocked it and preceded me in. The place surprised me. It was nicely furnished, two upholstered chairs, large desk, filing cabinets, expensive brocade curtain across a small window.

Gesturing toward a chair, he held out a pack of cigarettes. Did he think this was a date? I gave him a smile of goodwill. "I quit. But go ahead."

"You're not one of those non-smokers who hate the self-indulgent?" His accent had sounded menacing over the phone but now radiated charm. Charming as a scorpion?

"No." Why did Ken Woods have this guy's business card? I remembered the photograph from Crawdad's: Ken, Amerol, Cobra Face Cain, and two big guys. One very good looking, the other more of a bulldog. Damn if I wasn't ninety-percent sure this was Handsome himself.

He lit a cigarette, inhaled, and waited, eying me as I observed him.

The impressive claw-legged desk put a wall between us. "So..." he blew out a puff of smoke, "what do you wish to talk of?" Knowledge gleamed in his eyes even though I'd only given him my name and office number.

"You already know."

His face remained studiously blank as he inhaled again. Smoke swirled like a belly dancer's veil before my eyes. I blinked. "You appear to be an intelligent, professional lady. I think one who is out of your..." He reflected a moment, "league."

"You knew Ken Woods." He had to, my instincts told me, and the picture in my old purse—people didn't have their picture taken with total strangers. Ken, Amerol, Cain, and this guy were connected. It wouldn't be the last time I wished I had that photograph.

A flicker of curiosity. A shrug. "I meet many people..."

"He told me you were a business partner."

He took another drag and smiled. I could hear his foot tap beneath the desk. "I'm an enterprising man, I have many interests. What business would that be?"

I glanced around the office. "Anytime, Inc."

Coldness settled over his face like a death mask. Like he could stick a blade between my ribs and not bat an eye. It gave me shivers. Lawrence of Arabia come back. But it was the confirmation I needed. I was on the right track with Anytime, Inc. and the men in the photograph at Crawdad's.

His voice softened which only made it sound menacing. "*You* called me, Ms. McCue." His gaze met mine—the mark of a good liar. "I don't recall the name, Ken Woods. I've never heard of this—" he paused again, "Anytime, Inc."

Damn, did I wish I had that list of the investors and photograph!

He stubbed out his cigarette. "But I am curious. Who is this Ken Woods?" He gave me the once over with his Omar eyes.

"He was a patient."

Surprise registered in his eyes, then vanished so quickly I wondered if I'd imagined it. Mohammed tapped his forehead. "A man with problems? Crazy? Why would you care what he said?"

"Why do you say he was crazy?" I asked with my counselor's voice.

He shrugged. "You said this Ken Woods was a patient. I assume you are some kind of doctor. A head-doctor?" His smirk told me he knew a whole lot more about me than that.

I found myself wondering if he'd stolen my purse. Had my

questions about Ken worried Amerol? Had he sicced this guy on me? I got back to his guess about my profession. "Are you psychic or what?"

"A lucky guess." He gave me an innocent look I wasn't buying. "You said this Ken Woods told you I was a business partner... I've never heard of him... he must be crazy." He gaze drifted down my front. "Why would you care what a crazy man says?" he repeated.

"He was murdered."

His foot stopped tapping and he stood. "Ms. McCue. If this Ken Woods did have my name, he was probably a patron here, nothing more."

Damn. "A gay man? Come on."

Another flicker. He hadn't known or was a superb actor. He leaned against the edge of his desk, disgust now etched in the line of his mouth. "A woman as attractive as you should be at home with her man, not out worrying about such filth."

I narrowed my gaze, hardened my tone. "How do you know I'm not one of the flock?"

He came around the desk, stopped beside my chair. "Perhaps the right man could change your mind."

My skin crawled. Fighting the shakes, I stood up. "Maybe I'll give you a call." In my next life.

His hand fell to my shoulder, the sexual invitation blatantly written in his eyes. "I could be a good friend," he murmured.

Nice euphemism for sex partner. Running around without a man in the Middle East was tantamount to asking for rape—suddenly I wondered how long this guy had been in the USA and if he knew we had a different moral code.

His white teeth flashed a threatening smile.

Stifling the urge to bolt, I got slowly to my feet, my gaze locked with his. His palm slid down my arm, fell back to his side. "Think about it, Ms. McCue. You may need a friend."

I took a step back, and offered the kind of tight-lipped smile I used in photographs I didn't want to be in. "Oh, I will."

Traces of his malevolent sneer lingered.

I hurried down the claustrophobic hallway, sure in my own mind that Ken and Mohammed were connected to Anytime, Inc. But he hadn't known Ken was gay. So what? Where did that get me? There had to be more.

As I threaded my way toward the door, the crowd was riveted on three women in G-strings gyrating on the small stage. "Lean over!" someone yelled. Several wolf whistles followed.

"Over here, baby!"

"Spread 'em!"

Adrenalin surged. I wanted to clobber the guy. Then I caught the dull as gunmetal eyes of the closest "dancer," and realized she could care less. My anger wouldn't change her or put this place out of business. I slowly unclenched my hands.

The woman's red painted lips remained fixed in place as she swiveled her hips, slithering her arms up and down her body like stroking snakes. Every part of her got caught up in the gyrating rhythm—except her two giant grapefruit breasts which looked frozen in place. God, that was one botched boob job. I'd never complain about my bust again.

A guy near the edge of the stage jabbed his companion, "...could hang your hat on those babies."

Laughter spilled like beer from a broken keg as a guy slipped a ten-spot into the dancer's G-string. Smack. Her heel caught him in the face. Must have had slippery hands. I hoped he'd have a black eye to explain to his wife.

Pausing near the door, I glanced back and my nape hairs prickled. Mohammed stood in the hallway, his narrowed gaze fastened on me. He inclined his head. I painted on a smile and jetted past the collegiate bouncer.

Oh, peaceful quiet—oh, gentle hum of passing traffic. I exhaled in relief, loving the reassuring normality of the sounds. Then whack—like being hit on the head again—an out-of-place whir of machinery pricked my ears.

Twenty feet away, two dark figures stood over my car, one leaning inside. My heart rocketed into my throat. "Hey!" I ran toward them.

They took off like olympic sprinters. My door lock was drilled out, the stereo ripped from the dash. Wires dangled like severed veins.

I SWORE ALL the way home. You'd think living with a cop would have some fringe benefits when it came to crime. I should be so lucky.

The house was empty. Where was the Z-man when I needed him? I washed off the smell of booze and smoke and crawled into bed. Sometime during the night Zoloski's warm body curled next to mine, his arm wrapped around me. But when I woke, no Z-man. Only a stiff neck and the back of my head throbbing. Morning light filtered through the windows. I checked the message board on the fridge as I downed two aspirin.

"Blaize, see you tonight. Dinner at seven. Here. My treat. P.S. Who's Mohammed?" I wondered what he'd make of the interview when I described it.

A mild warning went off in my head. Zoloski usually volunteered for kitchen duty after an argument, or when he was feeling guilty about something. We had a sailboat date for Saturday. He hadn't canceled—yet.

It was his week for the laundry. I checked the basket. Empty. I left the ruminations behind and went to work. At lunch, I swung by Lon's place with two Taqueria burrito monsters that could be split in half and still add pounds to one's backside. His favorite, and mine.

He opened the door a crack, just enough for me to see his red eyes and the purplish shadows beneath. "Blaize!" He let me in. We hugged, nearly crushing the chicken and cheese stomach-stuffers.

"Thought you might be hungry," I said, holding up the bag. He ushered me to the bar that ran between dining room and kitchen. I tried again to elicit conversation. "You hanging in there?"

He shrugged.

I bustled into the kitchen, put two plates on the bar, then took the stool next to his. His lower lip trembled. "Thanks for the thought." He smoothed the front of his wrinkled t-shirt. "I haven't been very hungry. Everything tastes like sawdust."

I reached over and squeezed his hand, wishing I could be more helpful, wondering if I should tell him about my meeting with Mohammed, ask him about Anytime, Inc. I decided to wait until I'd learned more about both. Oh boy, Zoloski was going to love me poking into his investigation. That thought almost made me lose my appetite.

"I talked to Ken's parents this morning. They called me."

"They knew who you were?"

He opened the Taqueria bag and plopped a burrito on my plate, then his. "Yes." Surprise lifted his voice. "Ken told them about me last month." It deflated. "Also told them he'd made out a will naming me as beneficiary."

Uh-oh. Motive for murder. Zoloski might think so. "But Ken never told you?" I snapped open the two sodas, put one in front of Lon.

Lon's gaze met mine, honest, open, hurting. "No." He gulped soda. "His Dad said the funeral is on Saturday." His jaw tightened. "He hinted it might be inconvenient for me to drive to the Bay area... *You know*, his expression said.

Anger sparked in his cloudy blue eyes, then died. He took a bite of burrito, swallowed mechanically, no recognition of the tangy, spicy sauce, the cool crisp lettuce and melted cheddar. He flopped it back on the plate, wiped his hands and stared into space. "I'm going to the funeral." He looked at me. "I'd like you to come."

My stomach tightened. I'd miss the sailing. A friend in need, or a date with the Z? Zoloski would be pissed.

ZOLOSKI AND I dined under the back porch awning. He barbecued chicken, filling the air with smokey, woodsy smells I loved almost as much as the meat and the man. New potatoes brushed with olive oil, a little garlic, and lots of BAD salt, cooked over hot coals. My favorite. My mouth watered in appreciation as he heaped everything on my plate, poured white wine, brought out steamed veggies, and lowered the music. We munched and crunched in silence.

Sated, I sat back, and thanked him for the best dinner in eons.

He grinned. "There's still dessert."

I groaned.

"A nice Irish coffee for my coffee addict."

I laughed. "I can find room for that."

He returned with a tray. I watched him put two cubes of sugar in a mug, pour in brandy and hot water, drip heavy cream over the spoon.

"You trying to keep me awake?"

He gave me a slow grin, warming me in all the right places.

I dreaded telling him about Omar Sharif Mohammed, and going to the funeral with Lon. The mood was too good. Still...I cleared my throat, took a sip, set the cup down and plunged in. "Stephanos..."

"Blaize, about..."

We both stopped, covered curiosity with polite smiles. We knew each other too well.

"Ladies first."

Damn, the one time having a gentlemanly male was a disadvantage. I spoke in a neutral tone. "I'm going to Ken's funeral with Lon. Saturday morning. It's at ten. I'll be back around one." Cutting it tight, my inner voice chided.

He digested the news. Too calmly. What was chugging through his brain? "Why don't you meet me at Folsom at two. We'll have a snack, sail a couple hours, then head over to Arnie's and Pat's."

I smiled, relieved. "Sounds good." Then I readied for the next hurdle.

Zoloski stretched his arms over his head, flexing his muscles. "Anything else?"

The lines of fatigue around his eyes tightened as I told him about the XXX club, Mohammed, the photograph I no longer had, the belief that Mohammed knew Ken, and was an investor in Anytime, Inc. "He denied it, but I could tell he was lying."

Zoloski's fingers choked his coffee mug. Oh boy, warm fuzzies had turned to Antarctic vibrations. He gave me the one-eye. "Anytime, Inc. is under investigation, and I don't want you involved." A hard edge of anger lay beneath the civil warning. "Stay away from Mohammed, okay?"

"Why?" I asked, before adding half-teasingly, "Other than the feeling he could stick a knife in my heart with little regret, and might enjoy fucking me beforehand, he seemed like a nice guy."

He snorted. "Two damn good reasons." He leaned forward. "You heard what I said, right?"

"Yes, Sir."

His jaw tightened. Irritation flashed in his eyes. "I'm serious."

"Okay, I get the message," I said in my best mediator's tone. I should tell him I could help, I thought. Try to convince him we could work together. But the look on his face said, "Don't even try."

"Look, I appreciate the information." He patted my hand.

Trying to salvage the evening, I wondered.

"I don't want you to get hurt," he said. "You already got a concussion."

"That was a mugging."

"Probably," he conceded. He gave me a sharp look. "Anything else you want to share?"

I shook my head. "Your turn."

His mouth compressed. "I was just going to say I didn't want this Ken Woods case to come between us. No matter how I feel about you, I can't let it influence my job."

The JOB. The job and the man were inseparable, like the fizz in soda—and I knew how he got on a case—the high energy, long hours, obsessive need to find the perp—and at this moment I envied it, wanted to be a part of it. "I know that," I acknowledged. *There's more*, my mind whispered.

Passion crept into his voice. "Blaize, this thing is big—" The phone rang. He gave me an unreadable look. "I'll get it." He went inside.

Was he expecting the call? Work? My fingers curled. His job made me feel like an outsider and I resented it.

Did the call have to do with Ken? Lon? Some other case? I was champing at the bit, dying to ask, determined not to.

I watched Zoloski through the glass as he paced the kitchen, nodding, gesturing with his hands as he talked, pausing at the counter to jot a note, every so often glancing my way.

Uh-oh. I put the lid on the barbecue, went inside and snapped on the TV. Low volume.

Zoloski was rinsing the dishes, phone stuck under his chin. "...searched the place. The lab'll...when they've analyzed all the samples..."

Lon's place? What samples? Darn the sound of running water.

Zoloski's voice lowered to a disguised hum I couldn't decipher without being too obvious. I reined in my curiosity and turned up the sound.

He hung up and joined me on the couch. Nuzzling my neck, he whispered sweet nothings, his breath warm, his male smell a full throttle turn on. I forgot my questions until Friday morning, but by then he'd left for work.

Never one to be distracted by frisky hormones, I took stock of the fact Zoloski had distracted me to distraction. On purpose? He'd avoided my questions for two days.

Tonight I planned an ambush.

Chapter 7

11:00 P.M. NO ZOLOSKI. Just a hastily scrawled note that said he'd zoomed by in the afternoon, grabbed some notes, and wouldn't be home until late. No ambush. I went to bed with Leno and a bowl of Rocky Road. My mouth had an orgasm while the rest of me felt lonely and abandoned, dreading the funeral on the horizon. On the good side, my brother Ian had repaired my car and put in a new stereo so my baby was ready to roll.

Zoloski must have crawled in around three. At least that's what one bleary eyed glance at the clock said before I rolled over and dropped back into oblivion. He was still asleep when I left.

At 6:45 a.m., I was on the freeway, right on time to pick up Lon. On weekends Bay Area traffic can rip along or crawl, and there's absolutely nothing to do except allow plenty of lag time. Long habit directed the car to Lon's place, while I sipped hot coffee, enjoyed the aroma, and hoped I wouldn't slop any Java down my somber blue dress. High-necked, the knit dress covered my "Mac" scar and flattered my waistline. The long sleeves would keep me warm if the weather was cold and damp. Sixty-eight degrees on the coast made us Sacramentans shiver; we were used to frying in August.

Edgy, I tapped the horn, put the coffee in the cup-holder and clicked open the passenger door as Lon came down the stairs.

He also wore navy blue. Pinstripe. White shirt with a gold collar pin, and navy silk tie. He slid into the passenger seat and gave me an unconvincing "I'm okay," smile. His pearly whites glistened, so did his black shoes. All proclaimed, "I'm all right." Yet he fumbled with the seat belt and looked in desperate need of high octane caffeine. My guess was he'd been up most the night.

I touched him on the shoulder. "You want to talk. Feel free."

He shook his head.

Stoic to the end, I thought. It took a whole lot of energy to hold back a tidal wave. "How are you holding up?"

He shrugged.

I wanted to shake him, say, *Lon, Lon, talk to me, buddy. I'm here.* I held out my coffee. "Hazelnut, black, no sugar, still hot. You can finish it off."

He smiled, took a swig, then another, sighed, put the mug down on the floor.

I stifled the urge to "fix" him with some helpful words and remained silent, the rich odor of coffee wafting between us.

"I just feel so guilty," he rasped as though he'd smoked an entire pack of cigarettes before climbing into the car. "If we hadn't fought and he'd stayed home, he'd be alive...."

"You don't know that," I chided gently, touching his hand lightly, my own throat tightening.

He swiped his eyes, looked ready to eat his knuckles rather than shed a tear.

I did a quick internal feelings check-in to clear my head.

I was nervous.

Anxious.

Hated driving in the City.

I moved down my inner checklist and paused at ANGRY. I was angry at Zoloski for not waking up this morning to say "I love you." It would've been nice.

I turned the ignition and got back on the freeway, ignoring Lon's gaze. My checklist continued. Was I scared? Of being needed by a friend? No. I liked feeling needed.

Scared of what might happen at the funeral? Yes. Definitely. Funerals were not my scene and I didn't want to create one. Grieving people did crazy things. Like lash out. Lon wasn't wanted. He was inviting trouble. But he had every right to say goodbye.

"Music?" Lon didn't wait for an answer but reached over and switched on the radio. A commercial.

I slid a tape in the player. George Winston's *Autumn* came on. Piano at its best. Melancholy. Lon leaned back against the headrest. His soft voice mixed with the music so at first I thought he was humming. "They got a search warrant yesterday. Searched my place." Dead calm. Hands clasped in his lap like a Sunday school choirboy. The cut on his right hand was a dark line, almost healed.

"Zoloski?" I remembered the phone conversation I'd overheard. The SOB should have told me. I snapped into my man-hating role as though I'd never left it. Damn. My grandmother's feelings about men had reared up in me. I took a deep breath, coaxed the old lady back down, and got back on track. Zoloski and I had some talking to do, but I'd learned *not* to pile the sins of all men on his shoulders.

Lon's eyes stayed shut, his eyelids moving. "He was doing his job, Blaize. He was polite. Helped me put everything in order after the others swabbed the place."

A knot formed in my stomach, an image in my head. I saw plastic bags with hair, skin, blood, taken from Lon's carpet.

"Did they find anything?"

Lon exploded. "Of course they did! We had a fight! Jesus Christ! You saw the place..." A pause. "But I wouldn't have— couldn't have—"

Ripped out his teeth and chopped off his hands?

"You saw his face. It was awful." He choked and fumbled in his pocket for a cigarette. "If I roll down the window?" he pleaded. Now he was asking?

Hell, I'd broken the rule the night of the morgue. I couldn't say no this time either. "Roll down the window."

As he happily inhaled, I drove in silence, thinking about anything but corpses, murder, and blood. My ambush last night had flopped because Zoloski got hung up—and now I damn well wanted to know where. If he was putting together a case against Lon, I wanted to see it. His message, "I'll be in late. Don't wake me before you leave in the morning," was evasive.

Conflict avoidance? Yeah. Thoughts of murder and murderers intruded again. Just what I needed, a John Carpenter frame of mind for a funeral. I turned up the music to drown them out, tired already. The Golden Gate bridge was swathed in forbidding fog that cut through my dress. Lon rolled up the window. Neither of us said anything until we reached the grey stone gothic cathedral on Nob Hill.

"We're here," I announced, following Lon's gaze to the towering church spires. He clenched my hand as we walked in and sat in the back. I felt conspicuous. Only twenty or so people were up front. Mostly family members I guessed, ranging in age from five to ninety. Behind them, occupying a couple of pews, sat colleagues and friends; I recognized the receptionist from Ken's office. Did a double take and saw a flash of profile, white teeth and tanned skin. The hair on the back of my neck bristled. Victor Amerol flashed his shark-like smile at the man beside him: Cobra Face Cain. Several dark-haired men with wives or girlfriends sat between them and the receptionist. Mohammed sat at the end of the pew. My stomach clenched. All the men in the missing photograph. Except Ken, and one other man whom I remembered as short and powerful looking, but I hadn't paid much attention to his face.

Without pointing Amerol out, I asked Lon if he knew the name.

He shrugged. "Ken dropped the name a few times. The guy's

some wheeler-dealer, into a lot of things. Ken did some tax work for him." He threw me a curious glance.

I sidestepped. "You ever hear him mention a guy named Mohammed?"

A blank look. "No. Why?"

The music started, which was good because I wasn't sure how to answer. I mouthed "later," focused on the first speaker, and told myself I wasn't a cop. This was Zoloski's province. So why did I feel like a dog worrying a bone that didn't want to let go? Damn, I could almost hear Zoloski later, "You need another whack on the head to set you straight?"

But questions continued their uphill march through the eulogy. If Lon were arrested for Ken's murder would the police quit looking for another suspect? Would guilt or innocence be affected by Lon's sexual preference? Could I sit on the sidelines and watch him go under without assuring myself of his guilt? And damnitall, why were Amerol and his henchman, Cobra Face, here? And Mohammed? Were they all investors in Anytime, Inc.? How could I find out? Zoloski. But he'd told me in no uncertain terms to drop it.

By the end of the service I'd convinced myself to do just that. After all, Lon hadn't been arrested, and Zoloski was a good cop.

Without a problem, we made it outside, and I took a deep breath of relief. No family scene. Thank you, HP.

Too soon.

Victor Amerol tapped me on the shoulder. "Miss McCue. Good to see you again." His dark eyes flicked away. "I don't believe we've met," he said to Lon. I could see Lon trying to place him. I should have pointed Amerol out, warned Lon the guy was a shark. "I'm Victor Amerol."

Something jumped in Lon's eyes, but he squelched it. He shook Amerol's hand. "Lon Wilson." His tone gave nothing away.

I pulled gently on Lon's arm, not wanting him to volunteer any information, needing to bolt before the guy pinned me with his eyes. Cain stepped behind me, close, so I couldn't move.

Amerol said, "Ken was a fine young man."

Lon's neck tightened, his voice grew thick. "Yes. He was."

Amerol's voice softened like Brando's Don Corleone, but his eyes remained hard as bone. "You a school friend? A colleague?"

My hackles rose. What was this sleaze-bag after?

Lon shook his head. "A—friend."

I interrupted. "We really have to go, *dear*."

Amerol touched my arm, sending shivers down my spine. "Leaving so soon, Miss McCue?" Animosity flickered in the black obsidian eyes, in direct contrast to his concerned tone.

The "Miss" instead of "Ms." really bugged me, but Zoloski's warning kept me silent.

"I heard you were robbed. I hope you weren't hurt."

I gave him a cold stare. *Con somebody else, buster.* Behind him, Mohammed moved into view. Sharks circling prey?

Amerol's gaze caught mine, cold as Antarctica. "Any idea who did it?"

Yeah, you, shark-breath. But I shook my head. "Didn't see a thing," I drawled, doing my blithering cousin act. "Some nasty person snuck up on me and the next thing I knew I was on the ground. It's just not safe on the streets." I smiled and fluttered my eyelids. Gag me with a spoon.

"That's too bad," he said, knowledge in his eyes.

Too bad *what*? That I got mugged or it wasn't safe on the streets? Damn, the guy acted like he wanted me to think it was him! And if so, he knew who I was—certainly not Ken's out-of-town cousin. "Isn't it though," I simpered, fear settling like rocks in my stomach. Was he warning me off? Was that why I could feel Cobra Face breathing down my neck?

On the periphery, I saw Mohammed move closer. I grabbed Lon's arm and nearly jerked him out of his shoes as I pushed past Cain. "We have to go now, darling."

Victor Amerol's eyes burned holes in my back.

Just as we reached the car, Mohammed called my name. Now what? A lesson from the "right man?" I handed Lon my keys. "Get in the car, I'll be right there."

I turned, took two steps and stopped on the edge of the grass. His Omar eyes and smile were all charm. Curiosity flickered as he glanced toward Lon, then back to me. "Here for the funeral of someone you never met?" I asked, a touch of sarcasm dripping from each word.

He shook his head. "My cousin knew him, worked with him. He was very upset by his death."

Does he think all women are this gullible or just me? I crossed my arms. "And who might that be?"

"Vic." He said it with an arrogant smile.

"All in the family, huh?" I quipped, thinking he and his cousin gave me the creeps.

His black bushy eyebrows rose. "Family can be trusted."

"Is Anytime Inc. a family-owned business?" I stabbed, hoping to get a reaction.

The charming grin vanished and his eyes went cold. "My cousin asked me to give you a message. Forget Anytime, Inc. Forget Ken Woods."

"Thanks for setting me straight." Wrong final word. A glimmer of sexual invitation flared. He didn't have a wedding ring on, but that meant nothing. The old double-standard applied, mistresses for the husband, no misters for the wife.

"Mohammed!" Cain's voice carried on the ocean breeze as he strode quickly across the grass. I shivered, and turned on my heel without a goodbye. I felt both pairs of eyes on my back, like four lumps of hot coal.

I SPENT THE drive home explaining my dislike of Amerol, his henchman, Cain, and his cousin, Mohammed. They were all at the funeral, but that was hardly enough to swerve Zoloski from his current path—he had plenty of evidence, against Lon. "What did Ken tell you about Amerol?"

Lon shrugged. "Not much," his tone reluctant. "He admired the guy. Said he was smart. He called them all 'smart guys.' Do we have to go into this?"

My ears pricked up. "All?"

Lon sighed. "A group of investors Ken consulted for. Amerol was one of them." He sounded weary.

I felt a flutter of excitement. "Anytime, Inc.?"

"I don't know."

Deflation. "Did Ken keep any other records? Besides the ones I saw in the desk?"

"Just at work."

Well, that didn't help.

He closed his eyes, shutting me out. At his condo he said, "I'm tired. I'll call you later." His gaze was thoughtful. I'd triggered something. "Thanks for coming with me," he murmured as he leaned over and gave me a hug.

"Anytime," I said automatically.

I watched him climb the stairs. A glance at the dashboard clock showed one-thirty. I was going to make Folsom after all. Would Zoloski and I blast each other out of the water? Life is joy.

A familiar female voice interrupted the worry. "Hey, you're alive!"

Ms. Olympia grinned, and leaned through the window, while I searched my memory for a name. "Nicole..."

"Jackson," she supplied, then nodded toward the stairs. "That the friend you were looking for the other day?"

So she did remember. "Yes." I liked her snappy dark eyes, her confidence and down-to-earth manner. I sensed friendship if I wanted it.

Her eyebrows rose. "Your other 'friend' know about this one?"

"Who?"

She smiled. "The detective."

I chuckled. "They know each other. One's a friend, the detective's a bit more." I wondered how Zoloski would feel about being referred to as a "bit more."

A pause. I asked, "Ever eat lunch downtown?" eyeing the clock.

"Sometimes."

"How about Monday? My treat. It's not everyday I get such excellent care for head trauma."

"Sounds good."

I got her pager number, gave her my number and left.

BY THE TIME I reached Folsom Lake 2:30 had come and gone. Gravel crunched under my tires as I searched the dock area for Zoloski's six-foot-two, lean-mean-muscle-machine. *Nada.*

Gym bag under my arm, I followed my nose to the women's restroom. I waited in a long line for the right to shoo a ton of flies away and hold my breath while I changed into a blue bikini, overgrown t-shirt and boat shoes. Zoloski would appreciate the bikini. I'd caught him eyeing it when I pulled out my comfy one-piece.

I trotted down to the dock. A few people were scattered to either side on the rocky beach, but most of the crowd was further down the strip, frying their brains and bodies.

The rainbow sail of the Z-man's catamaran was halfway across the lake. My stomach growled. By now Zoloski had probably eaten my lunch and his. We were both working on curbing our passive-aggressive tendencies, but it would be just like him to eat my sandwich as retribution for tardiness. Sweat trickled between my shoulder blades and breasts. I cooled my heels in the water.

Zoloski sailed in twenty minutes later, face slightly sun-burned around his mirrored sunglasses. His hair was wind-blown, his clothes wet. He jumped from the cat and tied off, his ragged tank shirt and low-slung cut-offs exposing a flat, hard stomach and lots of tan muscle. A feast for feminine eyes.

His greeting was as cool as my feet. "So, you made it." The sunglasses made him seem remote.

No kiss, no hug. No food? Bummer days, Blaize. I tried on a smile. "Only an hour late. Traffic was bad. Any lunch left?"

"In the Jag." He pulled the keys from his pocket and led me up to the parking lot. He'd gotten a nice shady spot under an oak. Lucky. My car would be 190 degrees when I opened the door.

Sans T-shirt, sitting on the blanket, I ate half a turkey sandwich and slugged down a diet soda. He munched a few peanuts and swigged root beer.

Punch line time. "You want to talk first, or me?"

He shrugged. "How was the funeral?"

My turn to shrug. "Okay. You should have come." His sunglasses annoyed me. I reached over and tapped them. "I feel like I'm talking to myself."

He took them off.

"Thanks."

"You're welcome, Sweetheart." His Bogie cut some of the tension.

I put down my soda. "Victor Amerol was there." I shivered. "The guy really gives me a creepy feeling, Stephanos. He's a cold fish."

No comment.

"I'm a psychologist, I know what I'm talking about."

Bogie disappeared. "He's from the middle-east. They don't approve of women out of the harem—or running around uncovered." His gaze said he'd noticed my bikini. "Didn't we just have a conversation about you staying away from him?"

"He approached *me* after the funeral," I snapped defensively. "Asked how my head was, like he knew all about it. And the entire time, his flunky, or whatever he is, Cain was standing behind me, breathing down my neck. Then Mohammed joins the crowd. He's Amerol's cousin!" In spite of the broiling heat, I shivered. "Talk about a scary family."

That really caught Zoloski's attention, and he eyed me. "How do you know Ken wasn't a buddy?"

"Mohammed definitely didn't know Ken was gay so I hardly think they were mourning fun-and-games."

Zoloski's gaze narrowed. Pissed off or interested, I couldn't tell. "Go on."

"Ken did tax work for Amerol. So I can understand why Amerol might show up at his funeral. But Cain? And Mohammed? And Mohammed warned me to forget Ken and Anytime, Inc."

"So, take his advice—since you won't take mine."

I bit back a reply, not wanting the conversation to derail into a fight.

Zoloski seemed to collect himself, his tone more conversational. "How did you find out Ken did tax work for Amerol?"

"From Lon. He said Ken talked about Amerol. Invested in some business with him."

"We haven't found anything to prove Ken invested in anything besides stocks and bonds."

"What about Anytime, Inc.?" I was imagining a front company for smuggling of some sort.

Zoloski's expression was somewhere between annoyed and smokin'. I was "Trouble with a capital T" and he looked like he was fighting the concept. "What about it?"

"Who are the investors? What kind of company is it?"

Zoloski leaned back against the beach blanket and closed his eyes against the sun. "As I recall we had a discussion regarding Mr. Amerol and Anytime, Inc." A sharp edge to his voice. "We went through Ken's work records. Amerol's name shows as a client. That's it. No group of investors, no company records for Anytime, Inc."

I'd seen the file in Ken's office before Cain gave me the boot. But I had no proof. If I told Zoloski, I'd just start an argument. Like a big German Shepherd, he looked ready to defend his territory.

His voice took on a "superior" know-it-all tone I disliked. "However, we turned up some interesting stuff in Lon's apartment."

Like blood? Hair? I knew he was waiting for me to ask, but I was not about to give him the satisfaction—it made me furious that he would do that without telling me first. Unwilling to give an inch more, I ran my fingers up his sides to his armpits.

He convulsed, laughing and growling. "Shit!" At least that's what it sounded like as he pinned me to the ground and began his own tickling campaign.

I squealed, using my knees and elbows, trying to push away. Without success. Out of breath, I yelled, "Truce!"

His fingers did one last slide down my abs.

Laughing, I untangled my legs from his and sat up. He leaned over and kissed me lightly. "You feel great. I missed you," he confessed.

"Me too." Lovey-dovey thoughts turned me to mush. I took a

deep breath and realized that I wanted to trust him. Needed to, in fact. He was a good cop. He wasn't out to hang an innocent person. "Look, there's something I haven't told you." I thought of the state of Lon's condo, his drunkenness and wondered where to start.

He crossed his arms.

I glared. "Don't smirk."

Who me? his green, green eyes asked, his expression all innocent.

I gave him my best superior, confident, PhD look. "I tell you my stuff, you show me the autopsy report and update me on the case." I felt we had to be on an equal basis, and needed to know what he knew.

He seemed to consider. A slow smile pulled at his lips.

I felt a flush crawl up my face.

He had a wicked gleam in his eyes. "Okay—but not until tomorrow. And—"

Here it comes.

"You go for a spin out on the lake with me—no top."

"I'd get burnt to a crisp!" I glanced around, gratified to see people packing up to leave. It was nearly 4:00.

Zoloski rummaged through the picnic basket and waved SPF45 sunscreen under my nose.

"Out on the lake then," I agreed. "In a cove. Someplace private."

He grinned, lust in his raspy Bogie answer. "It's a deal, Sweetheart."

Teenage insecurities flashed through my brain about big boobs and tiny waists. For all my working out, I was not Wonder Woman—and if I was close, I couldn't see it.

Zoloski smeared sunscreen across my shoulders and back, and then down my front. We almost didn't make it onto the lake.

PICTIONARY WITH Pat and Arnie had Zoloski and me screaming with laughter, and left me with a sore throat. Their slides of Europe entertained us when we were yelled out. But their pictures of Muslim women in the middle-east made me think of Amerol. Thoughts of him led to worry about Lon. I banished both with two helpings of cheese cake, and went home happy.

Until Sunday morning. Ken Woods' autopsy report—with pictures—brought back the grim realities.

Chapter 8

ACROSS THE KITCHEN table from Zoloski, I skimmed the coroner's report and glanced through the photographs. For a toothless corpse of twenty-nine, Ken looked good. The expensive jacket I'd seen in his closet matched the slacks he was wearing. The blood stains on his $150 shirt were of two groups. One was A-negative, Ken's. The other, O-positive. Not Lon's, I hoped.

Watching me read, Zoloski drank an orange, cranberry, and grape juice concoction that resembled mud.

The air temperature where Zoloski and I found Ken's body was 68, the low for the night 65. His body was 92.5. Rigor had started in the small muscles, which meant that Ken had been dead four to six hours. Someone had killed him between 11:30 p.m. Monday and 1:30 Tuesday morning. Lon had said it was late when they fought. How late?

I tried various scenarios, my mind playing the murder like a virtual reality flick behind my eyes. Not Lon. Damn it.

I pictured the murderer. A dark silhouette resembling Cobra Face Cain or Omar Sharif Mohammed. He meets Ken in some lonely place and bops him on the head with a metal pipe. Perhaps Ken had stumbled on something he shouldn't have. My mind jumped to tax dodges and Al Capone. The IRS sent Capone to prison. Ken was a tax attorney. Maybe Amerol wasn't willing to risk a run-in with the IRS. Another part of my brain said I'd watched "The Untouchables" too many times.

Back to *my scenario*. Ken is not killed outright by the blow, but is on his way through the "golden hour," when victims follow the white light or recover. Would he have lived if his hands hadn't been chopped off? From what I'd read, there was that possibility—with brain damage. Yuck.

So—Cain drags Ken to a car—not his own—and carts him off someplace lonely and dark. He chops off Ken's hands, Ken goes into shock and dies. Then Cain yanks out Ken's teeth with some rusty instrument—rust was found in his mouth—and dumps the body. The police had yet to find the actual death site. It wasn't at Lon's, not enough blood. Not on the horse trail either, no blood, except on the sheet.

I glanced up from the table and caught Zoloski studying me, a half-smile curling his lips. He liked watching me concentrate. Told me once it was like a movie, my thoughts rolling across the screen in facial contortions. What did he see today?

I smiled back, feeling momentary warmth before gesturing at the material. "So how do you interpret all this?"

"Sure you want to know?"

No. "Yes."

"Lon inherits all Ken's assets—unless he's convicted of murder."

So, he knew about the will.

"They have a fight. It gets out of hand. Lon hits Ken over the head, then panics. Figures Renfree Park is a good place to dump the body. He took several classes at American River College, he'd know the area."

Over ten years ago. I felt my lips compress, a protest trying to escape. I held it back, but couldn't help shaking my head.

"At the park he gets scared. Has a brilliant idea. If the body remains unidentified, it won't get traced to him." Zoloski shrugged. "So he cuts off Ken's hands. Yanks out his teeth."

"He'd have to have a very sharp knife handy. Pliers too. Not to mention a strong stomach. That's not Lon."

"So maybe he recruited someone. Someone who brought the knife and pliers with him, did the dirty work, then dumped hands and teeth in the river."

"Like who?" I was incredulous. "He'd have to pay some thug a heap of money!   And if Ken remained unidentified Lon wouldn't inherit anything!"

"Just a theory."

Well it stunk. "If Lon did it, and I'm not saying he did, I could see him panicking and dumping Ken's body—*maybe*. But there's no way he'd do the rest. And I can't think of anyone who would help him mutilate a body like that." We were missing something. "Someone must have seen Ken leave Lon's apartment that night...."

"No one saw or heard anything." He gave me the COP look. "Or wants to get involved."

Feeling desperate, I picked up a picture of the body wrapped in black satin. "What about the sheet?"

Zoloski shrugged. "Lon didn't have the mate if that's what you're asking."

I wasn't sure what I was asking or what I wanted to know. "Well, that's something."

"Okay, that's my end. Quid pro quo."

When I hesitated, he said, "Come on, brain dump. We had a deal."

Reluctantly, I dumped about the mess at Lon's place and what he'd told me about the fight with Ken. "Why would Lon ask me to find Ken if he'd killed him?"

"Guilty conscience. Trying to avert suspicion. Take your pick."

I hiked a challenging eyebrow. "What now?"

Zoloski got up, poured coffee, brought me a cup. He rested his hand briefly on my shoulder. "Tomorrow morning we question Lon."

Arrest him lay beneath the sugar-coated cop jargon. The coffee burned my throat. Had what I said just sealed Lon's fate? "That business card I found in Ken's jacket has to mean something. It and the photograph were stolen with my purse. The picture was of Ken, Amerol, Cain, Mohammed, and one other suit." I suppressed a shudder. "They were all at the funeral."

Zoloski sat down. "They were Ken's clients. Ken was a CPA and a tax attorney." The words came slow and measured as though I only had half a brain. "He had many clients."

Resentment flared. My hair was honey colored, but he was treating me like a dumb blond. "I know that!" I remembered Trent, the bartender, the too quick shake of the head when I asked if he recognized anyone in the photograph. Had he held something back? Was it worth mentioning?

So far, Zoloski wasn't buying my sales pitch, or he already had his mind made up. Would he care about my intuition regarding Trent?

"I think the bartender knows something," I ventured.

Zoloski jotted a note in his notebook, and gave me the "Back off" glare. Anyone else, I figured he'd have said "thank you." Was he afraid I'd get too involved, end up in the hospital like the last time a client had asked for help? Worry made him grumpy.

I continued, hoping to fish something from his expression. "I think Ken found out something about Anytime, Inc. that he shouldn't have, and Amerol sicced Cain on him."

Zoloski leaned forward. "When are you going to stop?"

His tone rang all my warning bells and a knot formed in my stomach. Now was the time to tell him how much I liked brainstorming with him—figuring angles—investigating.... From the set of his face he wasn't about to listen. I cleared my throat. "When you tell me Lon's not a suspect."

His lips disappeared. "I can't say Lon's not a suspect, but I will say he's not the only one. Is that enough?"

"Maybe."

He gave me the one-eye. "You going to keep courting Amerol, Cain, and Mohammed?"

I hesitated. "No." I grumbled. "They're your department."

"You better mean it."

"I'd like to help."

Zoloski glared then flipped a page in his notebook. "Okay. Then give me the whole rundown. From the time Lon called you about Ken—everything. I want to make sure I got it all."

That wasn't the kind of help I meant and he knew it—but I obliged. I felt lousy every time he asked for clarification or noted something, like I'd just hung a noose around Lon's neck.

"You'll need to come in, sign a statement. Tomorrow." It was a command.

"Yes, sir!"

Irritation flickered in his eyes. "Is it me, the women I pick, what? I'm trying to give you some good advice, and you're pissed off." His tone had risen.

"So are you!" Mine matched his.

"That's because you're not appreciative—"

"Appreciative!" I cut in. "Why should I be appreciative when you're trying to hang a murder rap on my friend? If it were Pat in trouble, you'd be looking under every rock for another suspect!"

"I've known Pat since she was ten! I trust her!"

And I trust Lon! I held up my hands and lowered my voice. "Okay, okay. I'm just going to trust in the process...." In twelve step, trusting the process meant letting go.

In a mollified tone, Zoloski repeated, "You'll come in to sign a statement?"

"Eight o'clock?" I volunteered. My tone was a bit stiff, but at least I'd headed off a fight.

"Fine," he muttered before moving into the den.

I took another pass over the autopsy report and pictures, wondering why I thought I'd see something Zoloski's trained eye would miss. Ego? Frustration? Both. Hard to believe we'd tripped over the body less than a week ago.

We spent the rest of Sunday being cool and polite. I hated it, but couldn't seem to get past it. Tomorrow, I promised myself, I'd do something great for the Z-man.

But dawn came too quick. Zoloski was headed out the door when I dripped out of the shower. "See you later," he called, leaving me in an irritable mood.

I hurried to my office, found out I had a client scheduled and called Zoloski, left a message: "Be in to sign a statement later," and ushered her in. She was in a good place. I wasn't. Halfway through the session, feeling like a split personality, part of me listening, part of me wondering if Zoloski was putting the squeeze on Lon, I stopped the session and promised not to bill her for the time. We rescheduled for Thursday.

I needed to get to the homicide division, needed to know what was happening, get my signature on a statement, and check on Lon.

I was feeling like one of my own clients: taking on too much responsibility, or in program lingo, co-ing out to the max.

THE OLD JAIL WAS dark and gloomy. I climbed the stairs to the landing and announced myself to the person behind the frosted window. She announced me to Zoloski, behind a door marked "Felony Assaults and Homicide Division." I sat and waited.

Cops were everywhere, crisscrossing the landing—some giving me the eye, some a curious once over, everybody but Zoloski.

Finally he came out, ushered me inside. We passed a closed door to a room with a small table and two chairs. Interrogation Room? I pictured Zoloski questioning Lon. Had I interrupted? Or was I too late?

I strained my ears as I followed the Z-man to his cubicle. Sitting beside him in the small space between his desk and credenza, I did a double take seeing a framed picture of me resting alongside the penal code.

Zoloski was all business—until I'd signed my life away, which was what it felt like—then he smiled. Uh-oh, a chink in the armor. I held up the photograph, a snapshot of me on the catamaran, my hair blowing every which way above a dazzling smile—if I do say so myself. If he liked it so well, I'd give him another. I turned on the burners.

He leaned over, took the picture, then kissed me, the kind of melting kiss that made my knees weak. His phone interrupted.

"Damn." He whirled around, snatched up the receiver. "Zoloski."

The warmth of his kiss lingered like a shot of fine brandy. It wore off as I skimmed the framed newspaper and magazine clippings of cases he'd worked. He loved his job. I heard it in the high energy way he asked if "the perp wanted to cut a deal." The air around him charged with electricity. It was one of the things I understood and admired. The problem was I *liked* my job, but I didn't love it—I loved his—and was only now beginning to realize how much.

He hung up. "Where were we?"

Did he really need a clue? "I believe you were about to fill me in on your morning."

He cocked an eyebrow. "I thought we had something else on our minds." His gaze could have toasted marshmallows. "How about a long lunch at home starting right now?"

I considered cancelling my lunch date with Nicole Jackson. "First, tell me what's happening with Lon."

Disappointment lodged in his eyes. The wind went out of his sails. He scooted the chair back. "Nothing. He came in, answered some questions, signed a statement, went home."

My heart thudded happily. "That's great."

Zoloski's mouth turned down a fraction. His look dampened my thrill. "Doesn't mean we won't talk to him again," he said, his words implying it was more than probable.

My uneasiness returned. "What'd he say?"

Zoloski picked up the phone. "You want to talk to him? Make sure he's okay?"

The edge to Zoloski's voice made me stop mid-reach. "What's eating you?"

"The guy's up to his eyeballs. You just can't see it!"

"The guy's someone you don't approve of," I shot back, "and that's all you see!" I stood up.

"Well don't let me keep you from running into his arms!"

Whoa doggies, I missed a turn signal. I stared at him. "What?"

"Ask him." His gaze fixed on me.

"Ask him what?" Frustration.

"About his sexual preference."

The game of hints infuriated me—but Zoloski's come-on, the offer of a long-lunch, and now his watchful eyes needled me. "Are you saying he's not gay?"

"Good guess, Sweetheart."

"But—" I felt shaky. "You're saying he's bi?" I felt like a parrot struggling to learn words. "I don't believe it! How do you know?"

He suddenly clammed up.

"Tell me!" I sputtered, furious.

Two detectives came through the office door and moved down the corridor. Zoloski waited until they were out of sight, then said in a low, hard voice, "I asked him a question regarding his sexual preference, he answered it." Zoloski paused, his gaze narrowed, measuring. "The guy's jealous of me. I felt it the first time we met. Now he's hiding his come-on for you under that teary-eyed innocent act."

Shee-it! Lon had never mentioned "bi" to me. I gaped, shocked. Lon had always had a male partner. The shock brought on anger, with a bit of dysfunctional pleasure at Zoloski's jealousy thrown in. I whispered harshly, "I'm not your ex-wife, Stephanos," aware of the two cops farther down the corridor. "If I'm unhappy I'll let you know firsthand—*before* I exit our relationship."

The words brought a flicker of apology to his green, green eyes. Jealous eyes? I'd never thought that before and it unsettled me. It challenged my notion of two independent professionals in love, without worries about infidelity. Yet his ex-wife and my ex-boyfriend had been unfaithful. Maybe the worries were there and I'd just refused to see them. Great. Just when I thought I'd snared the only fully adult male in Sacramento.

I slung my new purse over my shoulder; I'd had enough surprises and insights. "I've got a lunch date. I'm going to be late."

Zoloski pushed his chair back and stood, his tone conciliatory. "Racquetball at seven?"

I mustered an unhappy "Yes," and left, my thoughts shifting from Zoloski to Lon. Bisexual! Up to his eyeballs...Was he? Had he really said that? Was he playing games with the Z-man? The Lon I knew wouldn't do that...Shit. Shit. Shit.

I headed for Vasilio's, the Greek place where I'd arranged to meet Nicole Jackson. Protestors swamped the Capitol steps, the sidewalks, and half the K Street Mall as I race-walked past, grateful for the diversion. Placards held dire warnings about gun control. "Take the guns from the criminals, not the victims!"

I felt torn. A gun had saved my life. But only last week a two year old shot his friend with an "unloaded" gun. Maybe we should scrap all weapons and go back to sticks and stones. More civilized.

Across the busy lunchroom I saw Nicole already at a table. A short, heavy-set, dark-haired, man sat beside her. I did a double take. Dark-haired, dark-eyed men were coming out the woodwork. This guy looked like a well-groomed pit bull and rang an almost familiar bell.

Their gazes were locked, mouths moving. She noticed me as I threaded my way to the table. I sat down across from her and threw a curious glance at her companion. "Sorry I'm late," I said over the din of surrounding conversation. "Did you order?"

She shook her head, introduced the guy as her partner, Al Martinez, and nudged him playfully in the ribs. "He was going to eat with me if you didn't show."

The guy grinned as he shook hands. He had sharp eyes that seemed to measure me, and a strong grip that tested. An intense man. With a nod to me, a "See ya, Nick," at Nicole, he left.

Nicole smiled. "You saved me from boring talk about slasher movies. He's an avid fan."

Oh yeah? "Must have been some movie," I remarked, wondering why she'd lie or if I'd misread the intensity in their faces. The conversation had looked anything but boring. But maybe seeing blood and guts on the job everyday made them immune.

She shrugged.

I felt uncomfortable.

A waitress took our orders and Nicole chatted about the protestors, the weather. I forgot my uneasiness.

Then she leaned forward. "Your friend, the gorgeous guy at my complex, is he in trouble?"

Surprised, I hesitated. Gorgeous? All the girls and boys say that. "A friend of his died. He's having a rough time. Why?"

Another shrug. "I ran into him at the mail box. He looks like he could use some TLC."

"He needs *friends* right now."

An eyebrow rose. Noticing the edge in my voice? If Lon was bisexual why hadn't he made a pass at me? I wasn't exactly chopped liver. He'd always talked about male partners, never women. How well did I know him? A frown pulled at my lips. I hated myself when I doubted my friends.

"We all need friends," Nicole said lightly. She turned the conversation to weight-lifting, and within minutes I'd surprised myself by committing to a workout at her club Saturday morning. I felt like I'd just missed an unmarked turn, that I was manipulated in some obscure way.

She started in about her job. "You should have seen my last partner. What a jerk! There I am, straddling the patient, a druggie, trying to get him over one shoulder and into the ambulance. My partner won't help. Won't touch the guy because he's got AIDS. Then the wife starts demanding to know what's going on—is her husband going to be okay?" Her mouth tightened. "Shit. Sometimes the job sucks."

"So Al's an improvement?"

Her teeth flashed. "He's way cool."

The conversation turned to lighter subjects with a few ambulance jokes thrown in. An hour flew by.

"See you Saturday," she said as we stood up. I smiled, glad for the friendship and something to think about besides Lon. She hurried out. I paid the bill, checked my client calendar, and went out the door and up Eleventh Street. I saw Nicole and Martinez in the ambulance parked a half-block over, their gazes tracking me, faces serious. When she realized that I'd noticed, she waved. I waved back, but felt a quiver of uncertainty. Like a post-counseling review, I replayed our conversation.

She'd directed it in a very subtle manner, touching on subjects, then moving on as though she had a prescribed set of questions.

Jeez, Louise, you're getting paranoid. I shook it off. Get a grip.

Chapter 9

I RETURNED TO my office, called Lon, got a busy signal, saw my next client, then tried Lon again. Busy. I hoped he was talking to a good lawyer.

My 5:00 p.m., and last, client canceled due to bad cramps—for the second time in a month. Gimme a break. Our next session would deal with her obvious avoidance and hopefully get beyond the excuses to the real issue.

With two hours until racquetball with the Z-man, I swung by Lon's. Unsettled by Zoloski's surprise, I needed to talk to Lon. Lord knew what I would say.

Blue and red lights were flashing in the parking lot. An ambulance, its rear doors gaping, was parked next to the stairs leading to Lon's condo. The scene looked like something out of a movie: rubberneckers surrounding the steps, uniformed cops, paramedics coming down the stairs, a stretcher between them. I glimpsed blond hair, felt a wisp of disbelief, then cold fear. I bolted from the car, running and shoving my way through the onlookers. It was Lon. Unconscious, pasty-faced, I.V. dangling overhead.

The paramedic moved past. Nicole.

She gave me a short nod.

I followed along. "What happened?"

"911 call. Looks like heroin. We've got Nar-Can to boost his respiration. He should be okay." She climbed inside the ambulance.

My mind reeled. Lon had once confided he'd been a user in high school, that he'd been clean for over ten years. "Where are you taking him?"

Martinez looked at me through his sunglasses as he closed the back door. "UCD Med Center."

I dogged Martinez' steps to the front, hoping he'd let me ride along. He shook his head.

"He's my friend!"

Martinez gave me a hard stare that said I'd owe him one. The look in his eyes implied more than lunch.

Fat chance. I climbed in beside him, my nerves tingling as we hurtled onto the freeway. A couple of times he shot me a look I couldn't interpret, but didn't say anything until we'd slammed to a halt. "End of the line, babe. You'll have to find your own way back."

Babe? Nice Guy. I gave him a "Thanks," as though I meant it and followed as they wheeled the gurney inside.

Lon was placed in the same crowded room of med-tech, green-garbed aliens I'd encountered four days earlier. I wasn't allowed in. A female sumo wrestler disguised as a nurse with a mouth like an incision pointed me toward the waiting area.

Nicole joined me a moment later, diet cola in her hand. She'd unzipped her one-piece jump suit, exposing a sweaty exercise top. "Wanna soda? There's a machine down the hall."

I shook my head as she sat down, watched her press the cold can to her face.

"Did Lon call 911?"

She shrugged. "Must have. Al got the call." She glanced sideways, "You know your friend used?"

"No." His former addiction was none of her damn business. He'd once said nothing would make him go back to that hell. Had Ken's death pushed him into the abyss? Lon was a stoic introvert who had a smile that covered a multitude of emotions. I should have read suicide risk before now. I swallowed, worry churning in my gut like fermented coffee.

Nicole took a swig of soda. "You said a close friend of his died?"

Was this an interrogation, or was I being sensitive? "I'd better see how he's doing."

She dogged my steps. "He'll be okay. They'll keep him here until the heroin's out of his system. Then he'll be free to go."

That was reassuring, but her presence bothered me. I wondered how she could afford to live in an expensive condo. A paramedic didn't exactly rake in the big bucks. How coincidental that she and Martinez had responded to the 911. First lunch with Nicole, now this? What area did they work? "It's amazing you got the call."

She gave me a blank look, but I could see the wheels turning behind her intelligent eyes. "We were close by. You'd be surprised how often I get a call to people I know."

Both me and Lon? That sounded a little too convenient, but she sounded sincere. Why didn't I believe her?

She followed as I retraced my tracks to Lon's cubicle. The curtains were closed, the grim-faced nurse gone. "Warn me if the guard dog comes back." I slipped between the curtains, leaving Nicole outside.

Al Martinez was leaning over Lon, talking softly. I froze. Martinez talking to Lon while Ms. Olympia quizzed me? My neck hairs prickled, my suspicions on full alert.

Martinez glanced up, his expression friendly. Lon looked greenish white, like a bad batch of play dough.

"You okay?" I asked.

"I guess," he rasped.

Martinez gave me a grin as he moved past. Testosterone glimmered in his eyes before he threw Lon a parting glance. "See ya, pal."

Pal? A ton of questions trampled through my mind, but Lon looked done in and I didn't dare ask. "Have you seen a doctor yet?"

"Yeah."

"And?"

"I stay until the shit's out of my system," he muttered.

I'd never seen him so down, something eating at him from the inside. Had he tried to "off" himself, or had Ken's death pushed him into using, his overdose an accident. "No fifty-on-fifty?" I asked, referring to the 72-hour police hold for suicide attempts. Lon had once served as a volunteer for Suicide Prevention and knew the lingo.

He shook his head, the movement half-hearted, and turned to the wall. "Everyone thinks I killed Ken." I strained to hear him. "They're going to arrest me. I figured I'd save the state a little time and money..."

I didn't want to believe it. "But you didn't kill Ken!" *Did you?* hung in the air. Suicides by guilty parties were notoriously common.

He closed his eyes.

Damn. "You won't try it again?"

His eyelids opened, exposing bloodshot eyes. "I don't know...No. Not if you find out what happened to Ken."

Zoloski's green eyes flashed in my head like two warning beacons. How much strain could our relationship survive? Parental modeling had shown me friends were more important than spouses or kids. I'd survived neglect, and three step-fathers. I didn't want the same life as my mother. I looked at Lon. Did I believe in his innocence? I didn't know what to believe and I didn't want to make promises. "Do you have a lawyer?"

The tiniest shake of the head. The hopelessness in his eyes wrenched my heart. I squeezed his hand, thought of the time he'd rescued me; Ross made Zoloski sound like a prince when it came to making "gay" comments, especially when I was throwing my suitcase in Lon's trunk and leaving Ross behind. Now, knowing I was doing what felt right and so was probably dysfunctional as hell, I said, "I'll find who murdered Ken."

A brief flicker of hope flared in his eyes.

The therapist in me said now was the time to get a contract. "Only if you promise no more stunts like this."

He faked a smile. "Deal."

Feeling good, I left, wondering where to begin on my part of the bargain. Legal help, I decided. The trouble was, I only knew good lawyer jokes, not good lawyers.

Nicole Jackson and Al Martinez were gone when I emerged. What were the odds of them getting the emergency call? Ten to one? It didn't smell right. But then, I wasn't a bloodhound.

Homing in on the reception desk, I spied a bank of phones. I was supposed to meet Zoloski at 7:00 and it was already past 6:00. No way I was going to make it. He wasn't going to like my promise to Lon. I half-regretted it already. Could I keep it a secret? Hell, secrets are what fueled addictions. Damn. It could ruin the best relationship I'd ever had. I dialed, hoping for his voice mail so I wouldn't have to explain.

Naturally, he answered on the first ring. "Hey, honey, I'm on my way out." He sounded distracted. "Got to cancel our game. Sorry."

"Lon's in the hospital."

A pause. "I heard. You there?"

"Yes." I imagined a frown—knew he thought I was too involved with Lon and this case. It seemed incredible that we could be so close one day, and the next have the Gulf of Mexico between us. Yet that was how it felt.

"You okay?" he asked.

No. "Yes."

A distracted, "Great."

"Lon overdosed on heroin. But he's going to be—."

Zoloski interrupted. "Look, I've got company, Sweetheart. Can't talk now. We'll talk later." He hung up.

Jeeze, talk about the cold shoulder, should have saved my breath. I felt like I'd dropped into a virtual reality game where nothing made sense because I didn't know the rules. First Ken had disappeared, wound up murdered, mutilated, then Lon OD'd. Why? What did Zoloski know that I didn't? I'd grown up not knowing from day-to-day what awaited me at home, a fist fight, a screaming match, emptiness, quiet. The fear of not knowing had always driven me to want to find out more. As if unearthing the truth would keep me safe. My childish illusion was about to be busted again.

I gave my name to the nurse and asked to speak to Lon's doctor. Then I found a vending machine, drank bad coffee and paced around the reception area like a hound in search of a scent. After fifteen minutes, the doctor arrived, young, energetic, and reluctant to give information to a non-family member.

I flashed my card. "I'm Lon's therapist," I lied. "When can he go home?"

His expression softened. "Another hour. His respirations are back to normal, but I'd like to check him over one more time. There's some paperwork he'll need to sign before he leaves. Shouldn't be long."

I asked to see the paperwork, skimmed over processing forms and handed them back. Strange how an overdose on heroin didn't have to be reported. Buying and selling the drug was a crime, so was suicide, but not an accidental overdose.

"Anything else?" he asked, his tone slightly impatient. We were standing near the main doors. They opened with a sigh and Zoloski strode in, his unhappy gaze riveting me to the spot. Had he hoped I'd be gone? Or just forgotten to mention he was on his way over? Beside him was a woman, a Playboy centerfold dressed for success. They looked like Barbie and Ken. New partner? Since when?

He flashed a strained smile in my direction, followed it up with the briefest hug in our three-plus month history. He showed his badge to the doctor, then introduced "Federal Agent Brown" to both of us.

She appeared to be about thirty-five, with short dark hair that matched her eyes. Her handshake was firm and dry along with her smile and tone. "Ms. McCue."

I met her measuring gaze, thought about correcting her to "Doctor McCue," then decided not to be so petty.

Zoloski's lips curved the tiniest bit—as though he knew what I was thinking—and I felt better. Until Brown moved closer to Zoloski and he didn't seem to mind. Damn.

Zoloski plied the doctor with questions, while Brown looked down her patrician nose. I crossed my arms, wondering why the Z-man hadn't mentioned "Ms. Federal agent."

The doctor left us outside Lon's cubicle, said we could talk as long as Lon was willing.

Lon sat up, nodded, but his eyes angled away. Against the white sheets, he looked solitary as a man on death row.

Zoloski glanced toward me, his expression tense. "We'd like to speak with him alone."

The lack of warmth in his tone was like an upper cut to my ego—he was all business around his new partner. He'd practically accused me of having an affair with Lon, but maybe thoughts about Brown had sparked his outburst.

I looked at Lon, ready to stand my ground. "Want me to stay?"

He shrugged.

I wanted to throttle him. *I'm on your side.* "I think you need a lawyer before you say anything." I cautioned instead.

Zoloski's hand closed on my arm and he hissed, "We need to talk."

Fear flickered behind Lon's eyes, then slipped behind a wall of apathy. I wanted to wake him up. I yanked free of Zoloski, jerked back the curtain and started to leave. Lon's soft voice followed, "Blaize."

I turned, wishing I could douse him with cold water, jolt him back to the Lon I knew.

"Get me a lawyer."

Thank you, Bob-a-lou. I smiled.

Brown frowned. "We're not arresting you, Mr. Wilson. We just want to ask a few questions."

Zoloski shot me a look that said anything but *Thanks for all the help.*

"I think he should have a lawyer," I repeated firmly, hoping I wasn't pushing my relationship with Zoloski into a downward spiral we couldn't pull out of.

Who asked you? Brown's dark eyes shot back.

Zoloski took my arm again, his tone insistent. "I'll talk to you outside."

It felt like being arrested by my domestic associate. I glanced back at Lon, hoping he'd gotten the message to shut up.

The best defense being an offense, I beat Zoloski to the draw: "What are you trying to do, fry him?" I stared at the Z-man, daring him to bring up the curvaceous Agent Brown. I suddenly remembered him hanging up on me—he'd had someone with him. Well, I was no doormat.

He sighed, the sound pure frustration. "Look Blaize, they don't want you involved in this. Neither do I. Go home, go to work, go to the gym, but do me a favor and stay away from Lon."

"Why's the FBI involved?"

His fingers tightened gently on my arm, worry in his eyes. "Go home."

Damn. Was every cop uncommunicative and controlling? I'd

thought he was the exception. "Know any good lawyers?" I held his gaze. "Or should I ask Brown?" Quadruple damn, I'd mentioned her first.

"She's on the case."

"What's her interest?" *Besides you.*

He scowled. "When I find out, I'll let you know."

He didn't know? Or a lie? As to my promise to Lon, I kept my mouth shut.

The Z-man dropped his hand. "You going to stay clear?"

I shook my head. "Can't."

"Won't. Damn it, Blaize. You're out of control!"

I was hot and tired and ready to fight. "Meaning not under your thumb?"

"Meaning you never listen, or take advice," he ground out.

"And you do?" How many times had I felt like I was talking to a brick wall? I jumped at Brown's voice. "Doctor McCue, Mr. Wilson wants you." Her cool gaze dismissed me and moved on to Zoloski, warming appreciably.

"Talk to you later," I said in parting. Thoughts of getting my own apartment boiled through my brain. Out of control? Fuck him!

Lon was up and dressed. "Take me home."

I did. I stifled questions until I was sitting at his bedside with tea. A huge leopard watched balefully from overhead as I asked about Al Martinez.

"I think he moved into the complex a month ago." A shrug said he wasn't sure. "I've seen him around with his partner. I forget her name."

Ms. Olympia. "Nicole Jackson?" Were they more than work partners?

He nodded, took a sip of tea. "They helped Ken change a flat in the parking lot." His eyes clouded and his voice grew wistful. "Last month." He put down his cup, gave me a tired smile. "Feels like years."

"Do they share a condo?" That could help explain how Nick, as Martinez called her, paid the rent.

Lon shook his head. "Maybe."

A moment of silence passed. "What did Brown want?"

"I'm really tired..."

"Please..."

His gaze fixed on the zebra bedspread. "She asked if Ken had a rig, used smack, did he buy and sell..."

"Did he?"

"No." His eyes squeezed shut. Denial or an attempt to remember his conversation with Brown? I wasn't sure. He continued, "She asked if he had a place of his own. If he had any aliases." He opened his eyes as if to say, "That's it."

"Did he?"

"Not that I know of." Lon's gaze drifted.

I waited.

"He did spend time in San Francisco. Weekends sometimes and during the week if he had an appointment in the City."

"You tell this to Brown?"

He shook his head. "They'd only use it against me."

I wondered if Brown's questions had given me any answers. Drug money? That would explain the FBI. Did Ken have an alias? How would I find a missing apartment or alter ego? My brain felt sluggish, but my competitive drive had kicked in. Whatever Brown was looking for, I wanted to find it first.

A couple of ideas tickled my brain. "Guess we'll call it a night."

His eyebrows rose as I collected the tea cups. "No hug goodbye?"

Feeling slightly uncomfortable, I leaned over and hugged.

He gave me a hurt look. "You kept your distance in the hospital, too. Zoloski told you, didn't he?"

"I guessed from something he said, yes." I'd just forgotten the hug, hadn't I? I'd always thought that a therapist who had herself for a client was a fool, but here I was analyzing my actions and motivations. I sank against the edge of the bed.

He swallowed. "I didn't want to ruin our friendship."

Self-righteous words rolled off my tongue. "I'm a counselor, Lon. I've heard it all." I stopped and sorted through feelings of anger and hurt. "The fact you never told me makes me wonder what else you've never said. I feel betrayed."

He sighed. "Not long after we met, I introduced you to my lover—Vince. Do you remember?"

Eight or nine years ago. "Yes."

"You should have seen the way you relaxed once I'd made it clear we were more than friends. You were warmer. Even hugged me goodbye. I liked that—you." He touched my hand. "When Vince and I broke up you were living with Ross."

"You should have told me." Would we still be friends if he had?

His gaze met mine. "There's always been an attraction. You must have felt it back then or you wouldn't have been so uptight. You had a habit of "bolting in a blaze of glory" from every guy you dated. I figured if you ever asked, I'd tell you, otherwise, I wouldn't."

My mind spun. I stood up abruptly, unsure what I was feeling, except that I'd always liked Lon, felt safe around him... Now? "I said I'd call a lawyer."

I took the cups into the kitchen, remembering all the times we shared across the table, eating burritos, drinking coffee, talking about his job or mine. And he was right, my belief he wasn't interested in women had made a difference. Sex scared me back then, because of the rape years before, because I hadn't yet met Ross the Boss, who—if nothing else—showed me how good sex could be.

I picked up my jacket and purse, went to the bedroom door, eyed the huge leopard print over the black and white striped bed, and lowered my gaze to Lon. "I need to think." Lon was an attractive man. I used to kid him about "the women who were missing out on his handsome mug." I'd said a lot of silly things. My cheeks burned. "I'll call you later."

He watched me go, his blue eyes narrowing into worried lines.

I WENT TO THE gym, worked out hard, felt better, went home, ate in front of the boob tube feeling like one, and went to bed—with Jay Leno.

The phone rang at four a.m., waking me out of a sound sleep. I glanced at the empty side of the bed, thought of Centerfold Brown and felt instantly sick. "Hello?"

"Blaize?" Lon's voice, low, whispery, scared.

My first thought was he'd shot up again—in spite of his promise. I sat up, switched on the light. "Are you okay?"

"There's some guys outside my apartment. They're watching me."

Paranoia? "How do you know they're watching you?"

His tone sparked with frustration. "I don't *know*, I *think* they are. I tried to call the police, they put me on hold. Can you ask Zoloski what's going on?"

"He's not here." I squelched another worry about Brown.

"Oh."

Perhaps it was the Z-man? With Agent Centerfold? I sighed. I wasn't going back to sleep. I could either wait for Zoloski or... "I'll be right over."

He hung up. Only then did I wonder why he was up, eyeballing the parking lot at this hour.

Chapter 10

I PULLED ON jeans and a T-shirt, loaded my .32, rummaged through
Zoloski's things until I found his night goggles and stuffed them both
in my new purse. I scrawled Zoloski a note, but hoped it was him
camped outside Lon's.

I pulled into the well-lit parking lot, my lights off, conflicting
feelings churning through my gut. It was *late*. Nice people should be in
bed. I damn well should be. But the image of Zoloski and Brown
together hung behind my eyes. Was that why I came?

I sat in my car, studying the other vehicles. I spied Lon's Supra,
but none of the others looked familiar. A cat strolled down the walk as
though it owned the place. A woman near the pool retrieved her mail
and disappeared in the other direction. My hand rested on the door. Did
I really want to get out of the car?

Lon's kitchen light was on. Other than that and the parking lot
lights, the complex was dark. And quiet. Oh, what the hell. Hand inside
my purse, gripping the .32, I started down the sidewalk, pausing to peer
in cars and check out shadows, my heart thumping: be-ware, be-ware,
be-ware. Nervous as a cat on life number nine, I swallowed my fear and
forged ahead. Lon was probably just jumpy, had imagined the
watchers.

The breeze rustled through the trees, a country sound that seemed
left over from the previous century. I passed Lon's stairs, continued
down the walk, and stepped beneath the protective shadow of a
weeping willow before turning back to eye the lot through the night
vision goggles. I started with the furthest point and visually worked my
way through a green-tinged world. A pair of slightly off-kilter headrests
came into focus. Two people asleep?

I waited. Neither moved.

I stuck the goggles back in my purse and started forward when
one of the headrests turned. Mouth dry as old news, my heart
threatening attack, I ducked behind the bushes. If it was Zoloski—in
Brown's car—he'd kill me. Then I'd kill him...

The car door squeaked open and shut. Footsteps approached. I
wanted to burrow into the ground, all five feet, eight inches of me. My
palms turned sweaty, my breathing way too loud. What the hell was I

doing?

Heart thumping, I tossed my keys behind me, pulled out my penlight and began flashing it under the bush, then up, catching a man's face in the narrow beam. He brought up his hand to block the light.

"Oops, sorry," I said, recognizing instantly the angular chin and wide-set dark eyes of Cobra Face Cain.

He was not much bigger than me, but his stance intimidated. "Strange place to be at this time of night," he said.

I ignored him, flashing my light around. "Here they are!" I retrieved my key ring and tried to step past him. "Excuse me."

He didn't move, an unpleasant smile stretching his lips. The gun in my purse seemed miles away.

An apartment door opened and closed. Cobra Face turned and I shoved past him, moving toward Lon at the top of the stairs. "Blaize, is that you?"

Heart hammering, I managed a husky, "Yes," and started up the stairs. My legs felt like rubber cement.

A car door slammed, an engine revved, and a small sporty Mazda zipped from the lot. The living headrests had flown the coop. "If they're cops I'm Madonna."

Lon didn't laugh.

"Did you get a look at that guy?" I asked, holding the rail for support, my eyes trained on the Mazda's last known position as though the license plate would reappear.

"No... not really." His tone was doubtful, hesitant.

I shot him a sharp glance. "Are you tap dancing here or what?"

"No, of course not." His gaze skimmed the parking lot.

"It was Cain, Amerol's henchman," I said. "Why would he be watching you?"

He pulled a pack of cigarettes from his jacket. "I don't know."

I followed him into the kitchen, noticing for the first time the apartment needed mild cleaning—for him, slobsville.

"Why were you up? How did you notice those guys?" He seemed to consider my questions as he lit a cigarette, poured two cups of coffee and joined me at the table. Dressed in a crisp blue shirt, red tie, dark slacks, only his face showed the strain he'd been under.

Going to work at four-thirty in the morning? "So?"

Lon shrugged, inhaled like a vacuum, exhaled slowly. His hand trembled. "I had insomnia. I looked out the window. Those two guys were there, one smoking near his car, the other flashing a light into my front seat. I couldn't tell who they were."

I wondered what was going on in Lon's head. He wasn't wearing pajamas or something I'd expect an insomniac to wear. I inhaled the second-hand smoke like an addict. I couldn't imagine him dressing for me, but after what Zoloski said, and his own admission, what the hell did I know? "You were in a panic on the phone," I pointed out.

His blue eyes shifted from me to the floor.

When had getting the truth out of Lon turned into pulling teeth?

He took another drag, his tone reluctant. "An attorney in the City called. Some guy named Connor O'Malley. Ken gave him my name and number, and an envelope, told him if he failed to pick it up by August 30, he should give it to me."

Yesterday. Damn, I could feel another trip to the Bay Area coming on. "Did he say what was in the envelope?"

Lon shook his head. "I didn't ask. Said I'd pick it up this morning between six and eight. Then I noticed those guys. I thought I might be able to talk you into going with me..."

"To the City? Now?" I could just see Zoloski's reaction to a note saying I'd gone to San Francisco with Lon. If he was looking for an excuse to screw Brown, that would certainly open the door.

Jeez, Louise. Zoloski wasn't Ross. I needed to remind myself of that. Especially tonight—when he wasn't home.

Lon's blue eyes met mine. He stubbed out his cigarette and paced the kitchen. "I'm afraid if I go out I'll be followed by the cops, or those two goons..." Zoloski had accused Lon of seducing me with his baby blues and his innocent act. But those two guys in the parking lot were not figments of my imagination.

Cobra Face. Agent Centerfold. Zoloski. Ms. Olympia and Al Martinez. Hell, they all seemed like candidates for watch duty. But why? I understood Zoloski's motives, but the Fed's? And what about the others? Could the envelope provide the answers? Would it keep Lon out of jail or send him there forever?

I had to know. "Come to my office at nine. We'll go to the Capitol, mix with the Ecology marchers and lose any watchers. Then we'll head to San Francisco." It sounded good for about ten seconds. Until I remembered I wasn't Magnum P.I., or a cat with nine lives. "No. Let's call Zoloski, tell him what you have, and let the police pick it up."

Lon's jaw tightened. "What if it makes the case against me worse? I'm not going to jail for something I didn't do."

I touched his hand, a gesture of comfort and acquiescence. "Okay." I couldn't help it, I felt excited. Part of me wanted to leave

Centerfold Brown in the dust, part of me just wanted another hit of adrenalin. "See you at nine."

"Sure you're up for it?"

I heard two questions. "I'm sure you didn't kill Ken. And I'm still your friend." I took a sip of coffee, noting the relief that flooded his face.

He walked me to the bottom of the stairs. It was still dark, but I could make out the trampled Forget-me-nots. A sign of trouble to come?

Lon's tan face crinkled in all the right places when he thanked me and said goodbye. I felt good for all of two minutes.

A long white crease had been gouged into my driver-side door. Shit! I fumed all the way home, resentful that I was care-taking Lon and doing a lousy job of taking care of myself.

I pulled into the driveway right behind Zoloski. Hallelujah! Did I have the same bags under my eyes? We walked to the door together. I smelled smoke on his clothes—at least it wasn't perfume—and wondered if Ms. Centerfold indulged in cancer sticks.

"Where've you been?" he said.

"Out," I responded, dropping my purse by the door with a thud. "Where've you been?"

"Working." He tossed his jacket on the couch and loosened his tie. He looked big, tired, and angry. Bad night? He gave me the old eye-to-eye. "We need to talk."

Damn, how did he manage to sound reasonable and calm when he looked ready to strangle me? Was he still pissed about the hospital? "I'm listening," I said, matching his tone.

He dropped onto the couch, his gaze examining me for evidence. Double damn. Sometimes I wanted to kill his ex-wife for running off with another man. He asked, "What on earth do you think you're doing running around in the middle of the night?"

"Lon called," I rubbed my gritty eyes and sank onto the couch beside him. "Thought someone was watching him. I went over and took a look."

"The guy tries to off himself this afternoon and now he's worried about being watched?" His tone was skeptical, his expression less than thrilled.

"Lon's jumpy." I crossed my arms. "What can I say?"

Zoloski ran his hand through his hair, a gesture of frustration. "He's yanking your chain."

I resisted the urge to defend myself, asked with therapeutic calm,

"You think Lon's using me?"

Zoloski kicked off his shoes. "Only you can answer that."

Psycho-babble for "yes." My mouth felt tighter than a mousetrap, yet I was grateful he wasn't spouting lines about Lon's sexuality or warning me about AIDS. Those were the cracks Ross had spouted and I could never reconcile them to Lon. His sensitivity, humor, artistic architectural flair was what I saw in his drop-dead golden-boy looks. Not the intimacies of his private life or loves—those places I didn't go.

Zoloski was watching me, waiting for some response.

I could protest Lon wasn't using me, he was a friend asking for help. But Zoloski would not agree. "Ever since we found Ken's body you've been distant and wary, hard to talk to. Why?"

He sighed, but scooted over until our legs touched. Did he feel the current? "This wasn't supposed to be personal. But—" His gaze searched mine. "Lon's a great-looking guy, makes five times what I do. I've known you all of five, six months; he's known you ten years, and I can't believe he hasn't come on to you."

I gaped. *"I'm* not Ms. Centerfold." I couldn't resist the dig. "Every guy I meet doesn't fall head over heels, Stephanos."

"Then they're idiots!" We exchanged glances, his green eyes warm. He shook his head as though to shake off the sudden rush of heat between us. "Ten years—"

"Nine and a half," I corrected. "He was involved with a guy when we met. I met Ross a year later. Bad timing, bad history, lack of chemistry. Take your pick."

Zoloski considered my words—and my frustration? "Okay. Forget I said anything. I just needed to hear it." His killer smile flashed. Vulnerability softened the chiseled lines. The guy was jealous!

Sexy thoughts tickled my brain. "When are you going to work?"

His smile melted into a smirk. Lusty thoughts?

One way to find out.

ON MY WAY to work, I wondered where I would—or should—draw the line with Lon. Had my mother's obsessive need to meddle rubbed off on me? Family Theory said YES, YES, YES.

The idea that I alone could save the world, or in this case Lon, was crazy. I needed a reality check. Attending a recovery meeting for codependence might be sobering; like a wake-up call that says I've been down this road before. But a meeting wouldn't change the fact I liked the PI road, found it challenging in a way I'd missed since hanging up my psychologist shingle.

Instead of recovery, I found a muffled unfamiliar voice on my answering machine. "Tell your friend to forget Ken Woods. You too." *Click.* I stared, thinking I'd misheard. I replayed the message. I'd gotten it the first time. A chill ran down my spine.

I replayed it again, wanting it to make sense, to give me answers. "Which friend?" I asked, listening a fourth time, both Zoloski and Lon qualified. No answer. Repeating the same behavior, expecting different results, is dysfunctional. I turned off the tape and called Zoloski, got his voice mail.

I left a message. "I'm not sure what time I'll be home." The envelope in San Francisco might lead elsewhere.

As I shuffled five days' mail between the round file and desk drawer, I considered Lon's evasiveness. He was holding back and that made me edgy. It implied guilt. Doubt crept in. I remembered my promise to recommend a lawyer and jumped on it.

Harry, the attorney who rented me space, was in his office, door open, no clients. "Know any good criminal shysters?" I asked without preamble.

He grinned, but gave me an inquisitive look that crinkled his eyes, showing his fifty-plus years. "You in trouble with the meter maid?"

"Haw, haw." I sat down, liking the feel of his office: masculine, with warm colors and lots of texture. "You hear about that bus load of lawyers who went over the cliff?"

His eyes lit up and he shook his head, playing along.

"A real tragedy—two empty seats." I squelched a smile, glad I knew him well enough to get away with that kind of thing.

His look said he'd heard 'em all. He pressed his fingertips together like a priest at confessional, a professional expression settling over his doughy features.

"I think a friend of mine is about to be arrested for murder. He has money." That should cover what most lawyers want to know.

He took an address book from his desk and leafed through, jotting three names on the back of a business card. "If I were your friend, I'd hire one of these. They're good." His teeth flashed and his eyes crinkled again. "And expensive."

An old ditty my grandfather used to say about lawyers ran through my mind: Too poor, they slam the door.

Then I visualized Lon behind bars. Money be damned.

Chapter 11

LON KNOCKED ON my office door at exactly 9:00. Punctual as my electric bill. I turned off the radio, abruptly cutting off Chris Rea's "Road to Hell", grabbed my purse and hurried out the door. Hopefully we weren't hurrying off to a similar road.

"You look spiffy," I said my hand resting on his light grey silk tweed jacket. His royal blue shirt and red tie set off his blond good looks. Despite the dark circles of fatigue, he attracted female attention as we crossed the crowded crosswalk to the Capitol.

"Thanks." He grinned. "You too."

My chest swelled inside my red power suit. I extended a nylon-sheathed leg in mock curtsy. For a moment it felt like one of our fun outings until I remembered Cobra Face, and our destination. "You weren't followed?"

His jaw tightened. "Not that I could see."

From the huge Capitol doors in the distance, the rows of steps and long cement walkway looked rolled out across the manicured lawn like a carpet. Camped out were several hundred placard-holding protestors. We lost ourselves in the crowd.

"Save an endangered species. Eat a spotted owl."

"Recyclers do it again, and again, and again!"

I yanked Lon through the marchers. "Take off your jacket and tuck it under your arm." I did the same. We followed a small party of businessmen into the parking garage and climbed in my Saturn.

As I sped toward I-5, Lon tracked the cars behind. "No one seems to be following," he said as I took the off ramp to 580.

Good, if we were trained spies. I kept my eyes skimming the mirror. For the next hour and a half Lon rambled, talking about work, about packing Ken's things, and going East to visit his dad whom he hadn't seen in sixteen years.

I kept my eyes on the rearview mirror. "Bad blood still?" He'd talked about patching things up a year ago.

He shrugged. "Yeah. The guy's an asshole. Screws everything in a skirt."

I knew he had dumped Lon and his Mom when he was twelve.

Lon looked out the window, his expression tired. He looked closer to forty than thirty. I pushed back thoughts of my own father, deceased for over two decades but not dead in my mind. Amazing how long a reign of terror can last. Maybe that's why I bucked authority—a way to thumb my nose at him, and the shit-hole step-father's that followed. "I need directions."

Lon pulled a piece of paper from his pocket. "Take Market toward the Castro."

The Castro! A vision of seedy gay bars came to mind. Was I getting in too deep? I concentrated on pedestrians playing chicken with the traffic. Market Street was a nightmare of congestion and we couldn't turn left. Ever. I took right after right until I expected to land in Oregon. Ah, finally a left turn. It took us to the tarnished district of ill-repute.

Lon read off address numbers from the valley of buildings. Neon lights, shabby signs, trees, people, everything looked choked by cement. We finally found the place, a pale, dingy pink Victorian in need of gentrification.

On-street parking was next to impossible. I copped out for a $20 parking-garage fee, then led the way down Castro on foot. After two and a half hours on my butt it felt great to walk. An electric-blue-haired man with a siren-red-haired companion gave Lon the eye as we crossed the street. But he was a hunk. Naturally, he drew attention from at least half the males on every block—and they weren't noting his red tie.

I hesitated outside the Victorian—eyeing the paint as though it were skin on a leper—not sure I wanted to go in. My stomach gurgled. The sooner we got this mystery over with, the sooner we could eat. Optimism or pessimism?

A couple of women holding hands brushed past, a stray hand sliding over my shoulder. Jeez, Louise. I studiously avoided eye contact. Stifling a tremor of anxiety, I pushed open the glass door, found myself in a narrow corridor next to an elevator and a list of offices. Repo's, divorces, real estate, bail....

We rode the smokey closet of an elevator to the fourth and top floor and wound our way down the dark hall—several lights had burned out—until *voila*, Suite 404. Connor O'Malley.

"High class," Lon joked.

"Yeah." I pushed open the door, expecting Depressionville, but getting a surprise. The walls were painted off-white, sporting framed prints of the Sierras. Several old but fashionably eclectic chairs sat beneath them.

Beyond the waiting area a door stood ajar, exposing a thirtyish man who looked as polished as the walls, and as out of place as I felt. He gestured toward his inner sanctum. "You must be Lon." He had pale skin and a shock of dark hair, big dimples, and warm brown eyes. A man who'd be labeled "cute" till he reached sixty.

The nickname Dimples O'Malley flared in my brain. It suited him. His gaze moved to me. I stuck out my hand and we shook, his palm dry, firm grip matching mine. We were the same height. "Blaize McCue."

He smiled. "Have a seat."

I took the hardwood chair. It was cold and uncomfortable.

Lon spoke up. "Ken gave you an envelope for me?"

Dimples nodded, pulled open a desk drawer and withdrew a letter-sized envelope. I'd pictured something larger. Unless it was a microchip, I was going to be disappointed. He handed it to Lon.

Both of us watched Lon extract a business card. "The Pink Flamingo?" He turned it over. "Give this to Max."

Dimples' eyebrows rose.

I asked the apparent, "You know him?"

"He's the bartender." Dimples exchanged an inscrutable look with Lon.

"What kind of club?" My imagination painted a black dungeon, whips and chains.

"A drag-queen joint. Singing, dancing, opens at nine. Rowdy crowd."

"Males only?" I asked.

Lon searched his pockets, and pulled out a smoke, obviously uncomfortable with me hearing this. I watched him light up, waiting for an answer.

Dimples did the honors. "There's no requirement that you be a man—but the assumption will be that you are—no matter how you dress." He lit a cigarette too.

Great! Just what I needed. A lighting ceremony, and a visit to a drag-queen palace ahead. Ken must have left something for Lon at the bar. Why else the card? I also assumed Ken knew he might wind up dead. Why else the run-around?

I put out my hand. "May I see the card?"

Lon handed it over.

"Is this Ken's writing?"

Lon took another look. "Looks like it to me."

I addressed Dimples. "Why did Ken leave this with you?"

He shifted in his seat. "I met him at a bar a few months

back...May, sometime. We...talked..." his eyes angled toward the doorway.

And screwed around.

Lon squeezed the arm of his chair.

Dimples continued, his tone reluctant. "We arranged to meet the last Friday in June, then July. The last time he said he was in trouble." Dimples looked at Lon. "He gave me the envelope and your name."

What a thing for Lon to hear, that Ken was unfaithful. How do you unload on someone who's dead? Murdered. The wheels in my head shifted gears: uh-oh, motive. Jealousy and money. I could feel Zoloski and Agent Centerfold breathing down my neck. They'd love this. Then I wondered why Ken didn't just give Dimples whatever he wanted Lon to have. "Anything else you can tell us?"

Dimples stubbed out his cigarette. "No."

Something in his expression told me there was more. Maybe with Lon out of the picture he'd talk? Later, gator. I stood, slung my bowling bag purse over my shoulder and nodded toward the door. "Let's go."

Dimples walked us to the hall, said to Lon, "I'm sorry."

Me too.

Lon's face tightened, made me think of thick ice sealed over a smoking volcano. I took his arm and herded him into the elevator.

When we reached the street, he erupted. "Damn him! The fucking bastard!" He pulled ahead and I let him go, listening to him swear. A block later, he paused mid-stride and glanced around. In search of a wall to put his fist through?

He sucked the nicotine from his cigarette down to his toes, then exhaled and ground the butt under his heel as I caught up. He looked at me, his tone angry, "You never know do you?"

I squelched a thought. I trusted Zoloski. It was Ms. Centerfold I didn't trust. "No." I paused. "You know where this club is?"

"No."

We checked the map. I drove. Lon directed. Sandwiched between a giant purple wine glass, not yet lit, and a neon green parrot, the club was locked up tighter than a chastity belt.

I exchanged my red pumps for tennies I kept in the trunk, and we passed the afternoon walking around Golden Gate Park. Surrounded by thick carpets of grass and bushes, towering redwoods, and eucalyptus that smelled like Hall's cough drops, I relaxed. Cars droned by. Joggers and roller-bladers were out in force, moving along with the cool ocean breeze. Wisps of clouds drifted overhead as though drawn through the blue sky by the strains of a street musician, playing a saxophone in the distance. Arm in arm, Lon and I strolled. Seagulls soared and danced above the trees. The tension slowly drained from Lon's face. The emptiness in my stomach expanded.

In between the Japanese Tea Garden and the Steinhart Aquarium, I called my recorder, found that Mohammed had left a message: "I may have some information for you. Come by tomorrow—after ten." Information on how to make me, or something more concrete?

Zoloski was next. "Blaize, I've got to work late. Be home around eleven." A pause. "Love you."

Working late with Brown? Impulsively, I dialed his work and got his voice mail. "Can't wait to talk to you. Be home late too. Love you." I meant it. Did he? Or was Brown distracting him from the words. I trusted the Z-man, but not Brown. Still, I hung up feeling like I'd done a good deed.

Lon was wandering by the raptor exhibit, face blank, eyes cloudy. Miles away or years? About to be eaten by a velociraptor or snagged by the cops?

I gave him a light hug and offered to spring for dinner at Lil' Joe's, my favorite place. The best Italian cuisine in the City.

We sat at the bar, watching the cooks perform their magic over hot gas burners. One cook slid a huge plate of fettuccine my way. Topped by fresh chopped tomatoes and garlic, and jumbo prawns, it smelled heavenly. I inhaled a sweet, tangy mouthful, then another, tastebuds singing, stomach happily digesting every morsel.

Lon picked at his veal scallopini, ate a mushroom, picked some more.

"Not hungry?"

He stirred the veal and mushrooms around the plate. "Ken and I met last February." His tone was wistful. "Both of us were very cautious. We talked over coffee, just casual stuff, said goodbye, see ya around. After a couple of months, we met for dinner.

"We both knew it was a turning point. Either of us could have canceled, no risks, no worries, no bad feelings...it would have been okay." He squeezed out the last five words, his hand forming a fist. "He should have told me... the SOB should have told me..."

Suddenly, I had a glimpse of where his thoughts might be going. "Are you at risk? I mean—?" Jeez, I felt like a seventh grader trying to say SEX.

He gave me a look, like what kind of a fool do you take me for? He pushed away from the bar. "Don't worry, I'll live to be a hundred.

A nice long life—behind bars."

"Don't worry. You aren't going to jail. We'll find something."

Lon gave me a look that said he hadn't bought it.

I checked my watch. 8:30. "You ready?"

He nodded.

I glanced ahead for signs of trouble. Broadway was a haven of nude bars, XXX movie houses and adult book stores. Pure sleaze, except the restaurants. "Didn't you play football in high school?"

He gave me a blank look.

"The game isn't over until its over," I said, giving him a metaphoric shot in the arm.

Lon grimaced. "This isn't a game. Ken's dead. And I look guilty as hell."

His dark expression challenged me to deny it. I wished I could.

We rode the cable car to the Castro, reaching the Pink Flamingo at 9:30. Music blared from the jukebox, smoke lingering along the bar like a fog bank. A small stage, dance floor and a few tables and chairs populated the rest of the space. I caught a glimpse of Dimples as he disappeared behind the stage. I needed to find out what else Dimples knew about Ken, and where Ken stayed when he was in town. Talk about luck! I left Lon at the bar, identifying himself to the bartender.

I hurried up the stage steps, let the curtain fall behind me and moved into the darkness. A door cracked open ahead, emitting bright light, briefly silhouetting Dimples' profile. I got stopped in the hallway by a marine crew-cut carrying a Marilyn Monroe wig and sporting an evening gown. "What's your number?" His frilly voice didn't match the hair-cut.

"Magnum PI," I said before ducking into the brightly lit dressing room. The glare blinded me for a second. I stepped past a long row of dazzling costumes, saw Dimples' face reflected in the mirrored wall. He sat against the edge of the counter, talking to a woman, his tone low, urgent. Looking unimpressed, she applied eyeliner, studied herself in the mirror, applied some more. In this case, more was not better.

"Excuse me," I said. Their heads jerked around. "I have a couple more questions."

The woman glared at me in the mirror. "Who the hell are you?" Her male voice crunched like wheels over gravel.

Dimples laid a hand on her arm, said something unintelligible and moved toward me.

"Did Ken ever use another name?" I asked. "Tell you where he stayed in the City?"

"Yes and no." He glanced back at the woman. "Sometimes Ken used the name Karla."

"Karla Woods?"

"Look, I didn't want to say anything in front of your friend, but Ken was, well, two different people. To me, he was Karla, until the last time we met. He showed up dressed in a business suit, all sweaty and upset. Said things were out of control. They were pressuring him and he didn't know what to do."

"They who?"

Dimples shook his head. "Wouldn't say. Just *they*." He sighed. "Next thing I knew he was giving me that envelope with Lon's name and number, begging me to do what he asked." He paused. "I really thought he was just being dramatic, you know? Then when he turned up dead..."

"Thanks." I wasn't sure where this would lead but I could visualize Ms. Centerfold choking on my dust as I heroically discovered something to clear Lon. I turned, only to meet four young men, costumes draped over their arms, coming in. One was the Marine.

"Show time, girls," the Marine squealed.

Someone grabbed my arm. "Wait a minute! You're perfect! *She* can do the Rhonda number!"

They all gathered around. "Good face, nice bones."

These guys were good for my ego.

"Yeah, but it's raw material. 'needs more eye shadow and pencil."

"The hair's all wrong."

I looked at his buzz and shuddered at what he thought "right."

"The red suit looks good though."

Thanks a heap.

"Is there a red dress back here?" They moved toward the long rack of costumes. Dimples was laughing his head off.

I glared. "Sorry *boys,* but I don't think I'm your type." I left them staring, Dimples clutching his sides, his laughter rolling after me.

I found the bartender, but no Lon.

I leaned across the bar, "Max?"

"Yeah?" Total disinterest.

"A friend of mine was supposed to meet me here. Did he talk to you?" I gave him a brief description.

The bartender squinted through heavy glasses that made his eyes look too ten sizes too big for his face. "He's waiting for you outside."

As the stage lights came up and the curtain opened, I checked outside the door. No Lon. Went back to the bar. "Did you give him anything?"

Max glanced up, his face annoyed. "I do a lousy favor and all I get is hassles! Shit!" He slammed down a drink in front of the guy/gal seated to my left. The look in his/her eyes clearly asked what I was doing there? Good question.

I set my purse casually on the bar, leaned across and smiled my most endearing smile. "What did you give him?"

His face softened. "An envelope."

Another damn envelope?

I opened my purse, made sure the butt of my gun showed, and extracted a fake PI business card left over from my days with Ross. I handed him the card. "My friend could be in serious trouble. I'd hate to come back here with a subpoena. Hate to think what might happen to you." I smiled again, mimicking a patient I'd once counseled, one whose smile had chilled my blood. "Did he open the envelope? You see what's inside?"

"Looked like some ID, money, and a key." Max croaked hastily.

"Thanks." I went back outside, letting the cold smile linger. Dressed in my red power suit and sensible red heels on a street where men, some dressed as women, were coming out of the cracks and crannies was not my idea of fun. Damn, damn, damn. When I got my hands on Lon I'd use his head for a bowling ball.

Chapter 12

MY SATURN WAS where I'd left it. No Lon. I winced at the
scratched door. Cobra Face's fault? As I unlocked it, my skull tingled. I
whirled around only to confront empty air. The nearest pedestrian fired
a "weirdo" glance in my direction and leaped into his truck.

Fifty feet away, beyond him, a man ducked into a stairwell. Was
my imagination working overtime?

Damn, where was Lon? Unnerved by thoughts of Cobra Face
Cain, hazardous scenarios skidded through my brain: Lon running for
his life; Lon whacked on the head; Lon stripped of possessions. Were
his hands about to get chopped off? I nearly dropped my keys. Jerking
open the door, I sank into the seat, hit the locking mechanism, and tried
to calm down. My eyes felt like they were going to pop out of my head
as I watched the darkness around the stairwell. I could almost hear
Alfred Hitchcock music making the eeriness complete. In seconds, a
list of *should-haves* littered my thoughts like dirty laundry. I should
have called Zoloski and told him about Dimples. I should have told him
everything! I should have trusted him.

People came and went from the elevator, but not the stairway. Was
somebody scaring them off? My gaze latched onto a shoe protruding
from the darkness.

My fingers thought faster than my brain, pulling the mini-
binoculars from my purse. I zoomed in on the sole of an oxford. Lon's?
Someone was either sitting or lying in the stairwell at an awkward
angle.

I wished Zoloski would appear like a genie out of a lamp. Never a
cop around when you needed one. Gun in hand, mouth drier than paper
towels, heart hammering double-time, I left the security of my car.
Moving between parked vehicles in a half-crouch, telling myself I
would feel really stupid if it was a wino, I zeroed in on the shoe.

A group of teenagers suddenly erupted from the stairwell. One
said, "Yuck!"

I stuck my gun in my pocket as they zoomed past. Creeping to the
edge of the stairwell I risked a quick glance inside. The shoe was
attached to a familiar body sprawled on the stairs. "Lon!"

He sat up slowly, a trickle of blood running down his forehead.
Relief coursed through my veins like a shot of cafe mocha.

"Ow, watch the arm," he groaned as I helped him up. His jacket
and shirt sleeve were cut, blood seeping through.

"What happened?"

"Two guys were waiting outside the Flamingo."

"Cain?"

"Maybe. I didn't get a good look, just ran like hell when one of them tried to grab the envelope."

I glanced around. "Did they get it?"

He shook his head.

"Are they here?"

"I lost one up above. For all I know, he's still there. You scared the other one off."

"Well, let's not wait around for him to come down." I looped his arm over my shoulder and like three-legged racers we wobbled to my car.

I jammed my key in the door and swore as it stuck for a moment, sure I heard footsteps closing in. Every sound amplified into "hurry" inside my head. I jerked open the passenger door and shoved Lon inside.

A voice rang out. "Wait a minute!"

I didn't look, but dashed to the driver's side and jumped in. The voice could have been Cain's. Revving the engine, I burned rubber backwards, heard a thump and a vibrant curse as I slammed on the brakes. A hand jerked on my door handle. I screamed and stepped on the gas, roaring out of the lot like the devil was after me. The man fell away.

My hands were glued to the wheel. Perspiration sticking me to the seat, I wondered, how they'd tracked us and why.

I shot Lon a relieved glance as he removed his jacket and gingerly pulled up his sleeve. He had a nasty cut, still oozing blood. He folded his jacket and pressed it against the wound. Looking in the mirror, he dabbed at his forehead with a tissue. His hand shook and he dropped it back to his lap, folding it into the other hand as though praying for comfort.

I eyed the rearview mirror. "You have a doctor in Sac we can go to?"

"Yeah." He closed his eyes.

"Can you give me a blow-by-blow?" I wanted to keep him alert. The bump on his forehead was golf-ball size and turning bluish-purple. I swerved around a taxi, wondering if I should stop for ice or just head for Sacramento.

Lon's eyebrows drew together in a frown. "Ken left me a manilla clasp envelope." Emotional pain lay in the admission.

"Karla Woods ID?"

He shot me a surprised look.

"I ran into Dimples, uh, O'Malley in the bar. He told me Ken used the name Karla."

"Sounds like O'Malley knew Ken better than I did," Lon snapped.

"You didn't know?"

"That he masqueraded as Karla Woods? No!" Lon swallowed, his face clouded. "After I opened the envelope I stepped outside for a smoke. I was upset. Someone tried to grab the envelope and I ran. Two guys chased me."

My stomach tightened. "Did they get it?"

"No." The ghost of a smile lit his face. "I dodged in and out of several clubs, lost them for awhile. I wrote my address on the envelope and stuck it in a mailbox. Figured I'd get a postage due notice and go pick it up." He sighed. "I decided to wait for you at the car." He winced. "They found me. I made it into the elevator. Went to the top."

I thought of my scratched door—like a fingerprint—it would make tailing me easier, if Cain had followed us here.

"I lost one guy on the third floor. The one with the knife caught me on the stairs. I never saw his face. You arrived in the nick of time."

"What else?"

Lon hesitated. "The ID had an address."

Would we be coming back? Not a pleasant thought as I looked at Lon's bloody arm.

Lon continued, "A key ring with two keys and some cash. Don't know how much."

I finally found Harrison Street and the Bay Bridge. No place like home. I leaned on the gas.

LON'S ARM TOOK ten stitches. The doctor's eyebrows rose at his explanation—cutting himself while trying to open a package—but he sewed up the arm with a shrug and hygienic instructions.

It was after eleven and my eyelids were drooping as I revved the engine and flicked on the heat. It was a warm 70 degrees, but my blood felt like it needed anti-freeze.

"Now we're a matching pair," Lon said as I drove through midtown. He held his bandaged forearm next to the thin scar running up mine.

"Like bookends." I squelched a shiver, pushed down thoughts of Mac the Knife. "I called your friends, uh, Curly and Moe. They're putting you up for the night."

Lon shook his head. "I want to go home."

"So did Dorothy," I snapped. "And look where it got her—on a yellow brick road leading to trouble. For all we know those two goons will be waiting to pick us up." I pinned him with a glare. "I'll pick you up in the morning and drive you home." I smiled. "Besides, I handle trouble better in daylight."

Either he knew it was pointless to argue or he was too tired. I held out my hand. "Give me your mail key."

"No."

I gaped at the way he said it.

"I don't want your help anymore. I'll hire someone."

He was giving me the perfect out, but I couldn't take it. I had the end of a thread by the name of Karla Woods and a score to settle with Cobra Face—not to mention I liked being on the job. I wasn't about to hand this over to anyone. My obsessive, compulsive genes had kicked in. On the Global Assessment of Functioning Scale (GAF) of mental health-illness, I was zeroing in on 50; serious impairment in social functioning. I itched to shoot Cobra Face through the heart.

Curly and Moe lived in South Land Park; a neighborhood which thieves loved to hit. Although Labor Day was only a few days away, their prestigious colonial-style home was lit up like Christmas. They bustled Lon inside, swore to watch him like mother bears, and promised to keep him until I called.

I hustled home. Zoloski was waiting, wide awake, munching popcorn. He flicked off a late night movie as I dropped my purse by the door. He wolf-whistled and patted the empty space alongside. I sank into the couch, kicked off my heels, and leaned against his shoulder. Ahhh.

"Long day?" he asked, rubbing my calf, questions in his emerald eyes.

I yawned. "Talk in the morning? I'm fried." I wasn't sure how much I wanted to tell him, and my brain felt grittier than my eyes. "Bed?"

"How about a ride?" he said, scooping me into his arms.

"You up to it?"

He laughed.

I slipped my arms around his neck and nibbled on his ear as he carried me down the hall.

"Red is definitely your color," he whispered as he laid me on the bed.

THE NEXT MORNING promised to be another scorcher. Over breakfast I tried to pry information from the Z-man, my finesse on a par with a plumber using a jackhammer to dig pipe out of concrete. He and Brown had interviewed Mohammed at the XXX club. "So, Mohammed claimed Ken was just a customer?"

"Uh-huh."

"Did you ask him why a gay guy would frequent a bar that featured nude women?"

"Give me some credit, Blaize." A flicker of annoyance showed in his expression. "He said the guy was strange—a lot of their customers are—but as long as they don't cause trouble he doesn't care. He's just the manager."

I pinned Zoloski with a look. "Who owns the place?"

He knew, but his face was all hard planes. "Drop it." He got up and put on his gun, bent and kissed me on the cheek. "Last night was fun. Gotta go."

I padded after him to the door. "Does Anytime, Inc. own the bar?"

Pure exasperation. He yanked on his suit jacket, pulled open the front door and pinned me with his eyes. "Tonight its your turn to talk."

Uh-oh. I wanted to return Mohammed's call and follow up the Karla Woods lead first. Hand the Z-man some convincing evidence. "Can't. I've got a late evening planned—work. How about tomorrow? It's Friday—I'll treat. Dinner at Piatti's." Guilty conscience.

He gave me an unreadable look. "Ms. Brown wanted to discuss the case over dinner. Guess I will. I should be home by eleven."

I scowled as he closed the door. Damn. The thought of him with Agent Centerfold while I played ignorant PI burst my romantic bubbles. Green gushed out.

Stomping to the bedroom to get my shoes, I mentally ticked off the day: Two clients in the morning; a call to my brother to see when Ian could fix car door; lunch on the way to Lon's mailbox—if a postage-due notice was there, I'd pick up the envelope and see what secrets it held; a client in the afternoon; grab dinner; and zip by the XXX club. After that I'd mosey on back to the old homestead and see if the Z-man showed up with lipstick on his collar.

Feeling frazzled at the thought of what could be a crazy, intense day, I finger-combed my hair. It worked better than a light socket, but just. I pulled a rumpled block-print pastel jacket off the hanger, slipped it on over a silky cream shell, and smoothed the long, blue skirt with my palm. The look was "professional in a hurry." Oh, how I wanted a cigarette! Needed one! I hated that whiny, sniveling part of myself that said, "Just one!" My brain was tempting me with visions of sitting outside, smoking with my feet up, a cup of coffee at hand and putting off the day. One minute at a time, I told myself. At that rate it would be a hell of a long twenty-four hours.

On the way out, I called Lon.

Moe answered. "He's asleep."

"You're sure?"

He clucked like a mother hen. "Like a baby. Don't worry. He's in good hands."

For some reason, I thought about Ken's and muttered, "Just make sure he keeps his."

Chapter 13

MORNING ZIPPED BY. I picked up a chicken burrito and diet soda on my way to Lon's, and polished off both before I parked the car. Nervous jitters sent twinges up my legs as I walked to the bank of mailboxes, my gaze searching the lot for anyone who looked remotely capable of whacking me over the head or chopping off my hands. *Nada.*

I felt around inside the cool metal of Lon's mailbox. The blessed yellow piece of paper lay snug in the back: postage due—parcel at the post office. I jammed the paper in my purse as someone entered my peripheral vision.

"Hey, Blaize."

Ms. Olympia.

Nicole Jackson's voice carried, her stride confident as she approached. She was wearing her paramedic coveralls unzipped to the waist, black exercise top, a sheen of sweat over buffed muscles no one could miss. She arched an eyebrow, as though waiting for me to explain what I was doing in Lon's mailbox. I ignored the look.

"Still on for Saturday?" I asked, recalling our workout date.

She smiled and it warmed her face, made her light brown eyes shine. "Yes. Bring your boyfriend if you'd like. Al said he might come."

I didn't like the sound of that; it brought back the memory of Al alone with Lon, Nicole with me. Tag-team interrogation. I could see a friendship with Nicole derailing. Everything about her said, "hardworking, dedicated"—attributes I admired—but now I didn't trust her. "I'll invite him," I said over my shoulder. "See ya at ten."

I hurried to my car, the postage due notice burning a hole in my purse, my worries about Nicole shifted to the back burner. Was I closing in on something? I broke the speed limit getting to the post office, sweated in line, sweated some more and retrieved a manilla envelope.

I opened it in the car, the engine running, a cool air-conditioned breeze flowing across my face. Karla Woods ID slid out first: Karla Woods Johnson. A surname? Strange. The ID looked genuine. If I didn't know better I'd think Ken Woods had a twin sister. I fingered the two keys. Acura car key. Where was the car now? And a mailbox, postal box, or safe deposit box key. Lastly, a bundle of cash. I flashed through it, counting two grand in hundred dollar bills. Enough for a quick getaway? Why hadn't he left a note?

With that gnawing at my brain, I raced out to Rancho Cordova and Ian's shop. Second time in a week he had the pleasure of fixing my car. With a wry grin that made his lean face boyish, he gave into my plea for a "loaner." Hot damn! A Porsche 924, white with a blue interior and racing tires that rivaled Zoloski's Jag. Ian raced on weekends.

He shut the door after me, leaned through the window and kissed me on the cheek. "Bring it back tomorrow after five, my place. I'm racing Saturday." He smiled. "Watch the speed."

He knew me too well.

I drove off, foot weighing heavy on the gas. Hot wind blew my hair back. My mind shifted gears faster than my hand. One more client, then I was free until ten and Mohammed. My nerves did a little unpleasant jig at the thought of going to a XXX club again. Meat markets, nude or otherwise, did not appeal.

As I zoomed up the on ramp to Highway 50, a dark sedan that had been parked across from Ian's shop, pulled behind me. A shot of fear fired down my back. Coincidence? I stepped on the gas, sped between lanes and up through traffic like an Indy 500 driver. Looked in the rear view mirror again. *Nada.* Imagination working overtime. I breathed easier.

I called Lon as soon as I reached the office.

He sounded tired. "Hey Blaize."

"I got the envelope. The address on the ID is in the City, Noe Street."

His tone sharpened. "Noe Valley...I know it..."

He didn't volunteer why he knew the vicinity, and I let it go. For the time being.

He cleared his throat. "I thought you were taking me home today—daylight and all that."

"Stay another night, Lon. Sleep well. I'll pick you up in the morning."

"Then what?"

"Back to the City-by-the-Bay, what else?"

Did a smile cross his face? I pictured a brief one. I hung up and called Pat in Missing Persons. "How's life with Arnold?" I asked by way of introduction.

"Great!" she sounded jovial. "Hey, Blaize, what's up?"

Maybe marriage isn't so bad, a voice whispered treacherously. And tomorrow there'll be world peace, I shot back. Maybe I'd squelched that whisper for another decade. "If I wanted to get a fake Driver's License, where would I go and who would I talk to?"

"How many guesses do I get?" A pause. "One of your clients in trouble?"

"A friend."

A sigh. From the sound, she knew I meant Lon. "Are you barging into Zoloski's territory?" Pat's tone took on an edge. "I don't want to step on toes. Big toes especially."

"Don't worry," I reassured her.

I envisioned her shaking her head like she used to when I came home early from a date. "Hell, you can read about these places in the newspaper at least once a month...Come by in an hour. I'll have the latest. But not a word where you got it."

"Girl-scout's honor." I checked my watch. 3:55. My last client would be walking in the door any moment. "Five-thirty okay?"

Hesitation. "Okay. But no later. I got a hot date with my hubby."

"Hubby? Are we domesticated or what."

Pat chuckled as she clicked off.

My next and newest client stepped through the door. "Eleanor?" I held out my hand to the twenty-one year old college student. Her handshake was limp, her body language timid, her woebegone eyes wide with apology, as though facing a volcano about to erupt. First visit jitters? Environmental learning from raging parents?

In a gentle voice I explained, "My goal is to get you out of my office as soon as possible; give you tools to work with on your own," I smiled, "in other words, homework." I continued with the spiel, "All cases of sexual abuse must be reported to the authorities—unless the perpetrator is deceased or no longer a threat—so keep that in mind." I paused.

She nodded like an obedient puppy.

"Everything else is confidential." I leaned forward in my chair. "What are your expectations?"

She shrugged, melting farther into the chair. The lost child I saw tugged at my heart. I told myself I wasn't God, I couldn't save her or anyone else, I could only do my professional best. "You said over the phone you're in a twelve-step group?"

"Co-sa," she whispered. "My boyfriend's in SLAA."

SLAA, Sex and Love Addiction Anonymous. Not a group I was

very familiar with, but then being in AA or OA was no big deal—
people might not agree about SLAA—it touched on taboo subjects,
one's that I shied away from because of my past.

We followed a pattern of Q and As, her body giving more clues
than her words. As an eclectic therapist I used Gestalt to amplify on
such clues. I started with the crossed arms. Protection? Defense?

By the time she left she was breathing deeper and a little color had
crept into her cheeks. We made an appointment for the next week.

I raced over to I Street and Missing Persons. Striding up the old
jail steps, I searched the street for Zoloski's car, didn't see it and felt
disappointed, disgruntled, and hot.

The only thing the same about Pat was her short, stocky build.
From the glow in her face and the sparkle in her eyes to light brown
hair bouncing with a new cut that softened the line of her jaw, she'd
done a complete overhaul. She slipped on a light jacket and ushered me
back the way I'd come. "You're ten minutes late and so am I." On the
inner landing, she gave me a hug. Gardenias wafted from her skin.
Perfume, haircut, what next? She looked great. Maybe men weren't so
bad. Give it time. She handed me a piece of paper. "Pried that from the
files. Gotta run."

She left me standing outside Homicide. Oh joy. Feeling
conspicuous I stuffed the paper in my purse and wandered over to the
glass partition. "Detective Zoloski in?" I gave my name.

The woman's puffy, bloodshot eyes suggested chronic insomnia.
Too much "reality" here in jailsville? Her tone dragged. "I'll check."

A few minutes of twiddling my thumbs and I left. No message.

I headed straight to the car, climbed in and read Pat's notes about
the world of fake ID's. There were a number of options. A bar in the
South area, bad neighborhood; a hole-in-the-wall downtown, and an
adult movie place, also downtown, and—my heart leaped—a XXX
club on Auburn. Mohammed. Bingo. But was the fake ID the only
connection? Centerfold Brown had asked Lon about heroin. I thought
of the hundred dollar bills Ken had left in the envelope.

Speculations running rampant through my brain, I headed for the
gym. A good workout, some Lean Cuisine and I'd be ready for round
two with Macho Mohammed.

THE XXX CLUB still sparkled like a cheap rhinestone pin, and still
titillated the male population. The party was in full swing, a haze of
smoke swirling amidst the tables, nude dancers strutting up and down
the long ramp. Shrill whistles and howls promised the women a "good

time." As dollar bills slid into their G-stings, their dead eyes brightened. Gag me with a shovel.

The collegiate bouncer nodded toward the office. I zigzagged to the back and shoved open the hallway door, squinting in the dingy light. I paused by the dressing room. The door was ajar, that room quiet. Everyone on stage?

I stepped past and rapped on the office door. The sexual invitations and cat calls suddenly seemed remote. I had the distinctly uncomfortable feeling of being watched. I rapped on the door again and it opened an inch. "Mohammed?" I pushed the door and took a step inside.

The Omar Sharif eyes stared up at me from the floor, unblinking and lifeless. My gaze jumped from his eyes to the bloody slash across his neck. My stomach heaved but nothing came up. I backed out. Whatever he had to tell me was gone now. The crowd was riveted on three women in G-strings gyrating on stage as I edged toward the door.

"Yeah, baby. Take it all off!" someone yelled.

This time, I found the noise reassuring.

Mohammed's dead stare and gaping neck, the pool of blood, filled my mind as I smiled at the bouncer and walked out.

I inhaled the night air gratefully, reeling in the urge to bolt. The rhythmic hum of passing traffic calmed me. I unlocked the car. Inside, the Porsche, doors locked, I pulled my cellular from my purse. I heard a sound, turned, saw a short, husky figure dart out the back door of the building. My heart rocketed into my throat. I punched 911, waited a second, then realized that the phone needed a recharge.

"Bloody hell!" I threw it on the seat, turned the ignition and burned rubber as I craned my neck to see where the man had gone. Taillights flashed ahead, sped through a busy intersection. The light turned yellow. I punched the pedal and shot through a red, holding my breath. Where'd he go?

Gaze skidding across traffic, I wove in and out. No sign. At the next red, I slammed on the brakes and hit the wheel. Like a magician's trick, he'd disappeared, and I was left holding the empty hat.

FOR THE SECOND time in two weeks, I sat in a parking lot and gave police directions to a body. A rookie officer took down my statement, then questioned me some more. Zoloski and Brown showed up a few minutes later, together, some kind of chummy discussion going on. Did they have a nice dinner?

When Zoloski saw me, he left her behind, strode over, bypassed the rookie, and pulled me into his arms. "You okay?"

With his arms around me, what could I say? I murmured "I'm fine."

"I'm beginning to think I'd better put you on a leash," he whispered, his tone affectionate, brow furrowed.

A dead laugh escaped my lips. "How about giving me a bullet proof vest?"

"Would it slow you down?" A rhetorical question, I didn't bother to answer. He immediately had me review what happened. Brown kept her distance, as though I might bite.

Several more police cars pulled into the lot. The patrons inside weren't going anywhere fast. But I knew one man had gotten away. Just another porno junkie or a murderer? I wished I had the answer.

"Tell me what the guy looked like?" Zoloski waved Brown over. They both wore inquisitive masks as I described the squat silhouette that got away. Not much to go on, Zoloski's gaze said.

"He may have seen the body and panicked too," I mitigated. Hell, I'd done a slow run out the front door.

Silent communication passed from Brown to Zoloski. Damn.

Zoloski took my arm and guided me several feet away. "I'll see you when I get home."

"Where's your car?"

His gaze flickered toward Brown and he looked uncomfortable, as though his tie was too tight—he wasn't wearing one.

I felt a sharp stab of worry, and tried to squelch it.

"At the federal building. Brown can give me a lift."

I wanted to volunteer for taxi service, but was afraid of looking ridiculously, childishly jealous. Brown spent a lot of time with Zoloski, and I hadn't missed the undisguised lust for the Z-man in her big brown eyes.

Zoloski seemed to read my mind and my insecurity. "You sure you're okay?"

I tried to say something bright and sassy in return but could only blubber something about hating to find dead bodies. "Live one's, okay."

He kissed my cheek and lowered his voice, "I hope you're in bed when I get there...Go home, Sweetheart," he ended in his best Bogart voice.

Grinning, I obeyed.

Chapter 14

I AWOKE SOMETIME during the night. Light from the street streamed through the half-open mini-blinds. Zoloski's chest rose and fell in a slow, gentle rhythm, his peaceful face smoother and softer in sleep, almost boyish. I snuggled closer to his fuzzy chest. A soft sigh escaped his lips as his arm found my waist. Mohammed, the crowd of leering men, the dark silhouette of the running figure, all floated out of my mind as I sank into the Z-man's strong arms.

But the loving Z-man became the dratted cop by morning. At the dining room table, his grim expression telegraphed a bomb about to drop.

Despite the yellow tablecloth and fresh flowers, the smell of fresh coffee, my stomach tightened.

"I've got a warrant out for Lon's arrest," he said quietly. "He's not home. You know where he is?"

Waiting for me to pick him up. I choked down coffee and scalded my tongue. I coughed out, "You can't!" I ran to the sink for a gulp of water as panic twisted my brain into a pretzel. "He's innocent!"

"You don't know that, Blaize! And don't look at me like that. It's my job." He hiked an eyebrow as I sat back down, and took my hand. "Remember? Our little talk about not letting our jobs interfere with our relationship?"

Yeah, three days ago. It felt like a lifetime. I let him hold my hand, but couldn't return his affectionate squeeze. How long had he been sitting on this powder keg? "Is that what your *date* with Brown was about? Arresting Lon?" Or playing footsie?

Zoloski gave me his COP stare, softened only by the tiniest curve of his lips. "Yes. We'd planned to pick him up last night. Then you tripped over Mohammed." He took a bite of toast. Swallowed. "Just for clarity, I've got to remind you that it's illegal to withhold information. You were seen at Lon's yesterday afternoon." His eyes met mine. "Dammit, Blaize. Stay out of this." His expression spelled trouble with a capital "T".

Was our relationship in danger? Why did I always feel immune to the consequences of my actions until they came home to roost? More authority thumbing? Truth, justice, and the American Way should prevail—but I was old enough to know better—that scared me too. Lon's life was at stake here.

The Z-man waited, his arms crossed. "Talk." His green, green eyes gleamed with challenge.

I sighed, wondering what I should do.

"You know, if he runs there's no way he'll get bail."

"He's not running!" I snapped. "Someone's been watching Lon's place, following him, so he's been staying with friends," I admitted reluctantly. "I picked up his mail." I resisted the urge to pick up my teaspoon and drum it on the table. "How was I to know you had a warrant for his arrest?"

Zoloski pulled out his notebook. "Who's he staying with?"

"Curly and Moe."

He arched an eyebrow, but had the grace not to ask who the third stooge was. "Address?"

"I don't have it off the top of my head."

His look commanded, "get it," which he softened with "Blaize..." that could have been "please."

I rummaged through my purse and handed the scribbled address to him. "Amerol, Ken, Cain and Mohammed all invested in Anytime, Inc. didn't they?"

Not a flicker.

"Is the company a front for drug smuggling?"

"You know I'm not at liberty to discuss the case with you." His tone was annoyed.

"Is that Brown or you talking?"

"My Boss. Agent Brown. Take your pick." He didn't sound happy admitting it. But his tone lightened as he asked, "What about you? You've been a little selective about conversational topics the last few days."

He noticed! "I've been working..." I paused, thinking about Dimples O'Malley, and the rest of my escapade, resisting the words about Ken AKA Karla and the fake ID trailing through my mind. Whatever I discovered at "Karla's" address in Noe Valley could be important. But if I told Zoloski, he'd have to tell Ms. Centerfold. "Oh, I have a date with that paramedic Nicole Jackson—and possibly her partner—weight lifting at her club. You're invited."

The twist of Zoloski's lips told me he was not going to be sidetracked for long. "When?"

"Saturday. Nine a.m."

He narrowed his gaze, face thoughtful. "What do you know about her?"

His curiosity sparked mine—why was he interested? I verbally ticked off a list:

"She's a paramedic."

"Into weight-lifting."

"Transported me to the hospital."

"Lon too."

"She lives in Lon's complex."

"She and her partner knew Ken Woods, helped him change a tire or something."

I frowned. "Too many coincidences."

"You met her partner?"

"Yeah. Some guy. Al Martinez."

Zoloski's expression clouded as though mulling something over.

I thought about Martinez. He smelled like cop to me. I should know, I lived with one. Was that what was on Zoloski's mind?

He seemed to shut off his thoughts with a blink. "What's your theory about Ken's murder?"

I took a sip of coffee. My synapses snapped, crackled and popped with "They's":

They: Nicole Jackson and Al Martinez;

They: whoever was after Ken, according to Ken Woods lawyer/friend, Dimples.

They: Amerol and Cobra Face Cain.

"Theys" were coming out of the ground like worms after a thunderstorm. It was complicated. Too complicated. I sighed, unwilling to voice my suspicions. "I don't have a theory." Other than Amerol, which he didn't like. "You?"

His semi-smug expression said, yes, but he hedged, "Nothing concrete."

I returned to my earlier question. "Can you at least say whether Amerol is one of the investors?"

He sighed, long and deep like a far off siren. "If I get my butt canned I hope you're ready to support me in the style to which I've become accustomed."

"We can live in my office."

"Very generous," but he failed to repress a smile. "Yeah. Amerol is an investor."

Adrenalin. I was onto something, and he knew it. "Did Ken Woods invest too?"

Zoloski shook his head.

Damn. I'd been so sure. "Who owns the XXX club? Amerol?"

A spark of admiration. "Among others."

"Anytime, Inc.?" I shot out, the answer reflected in Zoloski's reluctant grin.

He stood, kissed my neck and said, "Can't put it off any longer, Blaize. Gotta call in." He picked up the phone, and turned away, ending the questions and conversation.

"You going to arrest Lon personally?"

Punching numbers with hard jabs, he asked, "You want me to?"

I hesitated. Would Lon talk about Ken's alias? About Dimples O'Malley? Not likely. I didn't like holding back from the Z-man; especially something that might be important to the case, but could I trust him? Sure, I could trust him—it was the COP I couldn't trust. Damn. I had a tough choice and literally had to live with the consequences. "Can I call and tell him you'll pick him up?"

Zoloski gestured at the phone, identified himself, asked if "Brown was around." His unpleasant tone reassured me. A second later, he covered the mouthpiece and said, "You sure he'll stay put?"

I nodded confidently, my insides doing flip-flops. Lon was anything but predictable these days.

"Okay." He turned away and talked into the phone, dictating Curly and Moe's address. "No, I'll bring him in. Be there in an hour or so. If Brown shows or calls, tell her I'll be in. But lose the address." A pause. Zoloski laughed. "Yeah, well my ass is hanging out already." He hung up. "Your turn."

Uncomfortable under the cool scrutiny of his emerald eyes, I dialed. Lon answered the phone. It was nearly eight—the time I was to pick him up—but he sounded fuzzy as though he'd just awakened. "You okay?"

"Hangover," he muttered. "Curly and Moe got me plastered."

Jeez, Louise. The man was blowing abstinence big time. "Are you coherent?" My words came out sharper than intended.

His voice sharpened too. "What's up?"

"They're going to arrest you. Zoloski's on his way to pick you up. You need to call a lawyer and have him meet you at the jail."

"Jesus." A long pause. "What about—" his voice dropped as though the phone were bugged, "Noe Valley?"

"Don't worry," I kept my eyes on the floor, afraid of what the Z-man might see if I looked up. "Call one of the lawyers I mentioned. Let *him* do the talking. I'll talk to you after you get out."

"Okay." Pause. "You really think I'll get bail?"

"Sure." I glanced at Zoloski and mouthed the word "bail?"

He gave a non-committal shrug.

I reassured Lon and hung up. "Can't you wait until Tuesday to arrest him?" After the holiday.

"No." No compromise there.

"You think he can get a bail hearing today?"

Zoloski put his arms around my shoulders and pulled me close. "Tonight probably."

"You think he'll be released?"

"If the judge doesn't consider him too big a risk."

"Doesn't the charge make a difference?"

Zoloski shrugged. "If the DA goes for second degree or manslaughter, he may have a better chance."

"Second degree—the killing is intentional but unplanned, without malice?"

Zoloski looked surprised. "Yeah. Average jail time of eight years for someone without priors." A twinge of sarcasm.

"What about manslaughter?"

"Probation, maybe? But in this case—" he shook his head. "Not with the hands chopped off..."

I pulled away. "But Ken was hit on the head first."

"*Probably* is the key word here," Zoloski said, looking unhappy. "Ken Woods *probably* would have died from the head wound."

I shuddered at the thought of being alive, even unconscious, and having my hands whacked from my arms. A jury would, too.

So much for dinner at Piatti's. Zoloski would *probably* work late, and I'd *probably* be running around to find someone else I could sacrifice to the police—like the real culprit.

Zoloski grabbed his gun and jacket. "Meet you at the restaurant at seven-thirty."

"If nothing holds you up."

He leaned over and covered my lips with his, the kiss tender and sweet. "Short of a national disaster I'll be there." His slow smile warmed me to the toes.

A few minutes later, after phoning my brother, I hit the freeway. My car door was repainted, good as new. Ian, smoking like a geyser, took my check, and mumbled, "You're a menace to vehicles." In parting, he added, "Business is slow these days, so if you have any more scrapes, come on over." His warm grin made the words meaningful. Like he cared more about me than the money. I gave him a quick hug.

Back in my baby, hauling butt toward San Francisco, I wasn't wearing flowers in my hair like the old song, but watching my rear-view mirror. Not that I noticed anything unusual.

By pretending I was an insanely aggressive driver in a Mac truck, I got around the City—*no problemo*. Even found a parking place on Steiner, near Noe Street. Almost lunchtime, but I couldn't eat until I'd satisfied my curiosity.

Karla Woods Johnson lived on the top floor of a three-story apartment building. Uncovered parking ran along one side of the nondescript chunk of terraced concrete. As I pushed open the lobby door I glimpsed a shadow at the corner of the building and paused. Paranoia? Or was somebody following me? I stepped inside, and waited. No one approached the door. After three minutes, feeling jumpy and silly, I knocked on the manager's door.

He was a slight, timid, near-sighted octogenarian, who squinted at my fake note from Karla allowing me access to the apartment. He reminded me of my grandfather and I felt unethical as we gabbed in the elevator.

"Such a sweet young woman. And her brother, so polite. Always checking to make sure she's okay, has everything she needs." He gave me a stern look. "Not many tenants like her nowadays."

Was he being funny? I couldn't tell.

The doors slid open to a stale smell and a long hall of worn brown carpet, three doors on each side, walls in need of paint. The manager led the way. "Down on the left. Hope she's enjoying her vacation."

"I'm sure of it." The place was quiet as a library. Everyone at work?

"Hawaii sounds great." He smiled. "Said she might find a job there. Told me to rent the place if she didn't show by the end of September." He turned the key. "Hope she comes back. She always pays on time, never bothers me." He smiled again. "A real gem."

Would he talk that way if he knew Karla was Ken? Had Ken really planned on Hawaii or had he decided to discontinue his charade and settle down with Lon?

I stepped inside, glimpsed a cozy living room, sectional couch, wild prints of women's faces on the walls. The manager hesitated until I put my hand out for the key. "Thanks a bunch," I said. "I just need to pick up a few things, then I'll return the key, okay?"

"Sure."

I closed the door, locked it and stepped into the living room, keeping my hands in my pockets. If and when the police found this place I didn't need my paw prints in it.

The fake leaves of a cherry tree brushed my shoulder as I moved to a bookcase and scanned titles. Paperback thrillers. *100 Years of Solitude* stood out between the host of novels. Magical realism. Lon had recommended it to me. Making my way through the fake foliage, I felt magically real, part of a magician's trick.

I turned, eying the dry ferns on two end tables, the open archway to the kitchen. An answering machine sat on the formica counter top, its red light blinking. Using a pen, I hit "check greeting", then rustled a notebook from my purse as it played Ken's recorded message.

A soft, breathy feminine voice said, "You've reached (415) 652-7277. Leave a message at the tone."

I copied the number down and punched "playback."

Beep. "Hey Karla, where've you been? I need to connect, you know? Call me." The machine kicked in the date and time. August 29, seven a.m., the day before Ken died.

Beep. A woman's voice. "This is Juanita Juarez. Did Xavier give you the money for the ID? Why haven't you called? Where is he? I'm at..."

I copied down her name and a local number as the machine spouted the date: August 30, 9:00 p.m.

The next three calls were heavy-breathing hang-ups.

As the machine rewound, I skimmed the rest of the barren, immaculate kitchen, then moved down the hall. The single bedroom was large for an apartment. I scooted past a desk and chair, around the king size bed to the open closet. Feeling unsettled, knowing I'd feel violated if someone went through my things, I told myself it was for Lon, pulled on my driving gloves and began rummaging through the women's wear. Karla liked clothes and had spared no expense in her attire. From a pink sequined evening gown to a more sedate black cocktail dress—with shoes to match—she had a wardrobe most women would die for.

Perhaps she had.

I felt uneasy, and the apartment was too quiet. I moved to the other closet, found business suits, dress shirts, ties, and a pair of expensive black shoes. I went through pockets, then checked under the bed, the dresser, and bathroom cabinets. *Nada*.

I saved the best for last: the desk. Opening the top drawer, scanning contents, hoping for something to identify the other key, I wondered where to look next. The Acura? Was it outside?

In the second drawer, I discovering a stack of bank statements.

Yeehaw! I copied down the account numbers, wrote down each bank, then did a ball-park calculation in my head. Twenty banks, twenty companies—probably bogus—a hundred grand or more per bank. A hot two mil.

I rummaged through more drawers, found a copy of Karla's rental agreement, and went back into the kitchen. Bank by bank, I dialed, entered the account numbers, his social security number, and requested the balance. Every account had been closed. Where was the money? Was that why Ken had been murdered?

As I replaced the statements, I noted one entry on top—for a safety deposit box. The money? I stuffed the rental agreement with Ken and Karla's signatures into my purse with my notebook, and eyed the bottom drawer. Locked.

I checked my watch. A half hour gone. It felt like four hours. I kept remembering that shadow in the parking lot. Time to skip. But I couldn't pull my eyes from the drawer.

I turned the bedroom inside out for the key, carefully replacing everything. I found it, along with what smelled like some fine marijuana, inside a tall vase of silk flowers. I sniffed the pot, memories of high school flooding my brain. Thank God I liked food now. My brain teased me with the notion I'd made the wrong decision.

As I jiggled the key into the lock, the phone rang. I jumped a mile, told myself to settle down and yanked open the drawer. It was full of audio tapes, wrapped in paper and banded together.

I scooped them into my purse, I'd already pushed my luck too far. After locking the drawer, I replaced the key and checked to make sure everything was as I found it.

A knock on the door nearly stopped my heart. "Ms. Alexander. It's the manager. Open the door, please."

Oh shit. I ran into the living room, took a deep breath to calm myself, and reached for the knob. Gloves! Using my teeth, I yanked them off.

"I don't understand what's taking so long." The manager's confidential voice clearly directed at someone on his side of the door froze my hand.

"Shhh..."

"I'll go down and get my other key."

I tried to see through the crack. Couldn't. Never a peephole when you needed one. Damn, damn, damn.

I crept quietly to the sliding glass door, winced as the lock clicked open. Heart pounding in my ears, I stepped onto the balcony. A guy in a suit stood on the corner under a bus sign. Nothing suspicious, so why was I so scared? "Shhh..." echoed in my mind. Good reason.

My hands grew clammy as I eyed the balcony below. From there I could drop to the ground—*maybe*. Gauging distances wasn't my strong point. I hesitated at the metal rail. I could break my neck, possibly walk away—or answer the door. No way, *José*. I swung my leg over the cold black metal.

Chapter 15

MY PURSE HIT THE parking lot blacktop with a heart stopping thud. How far up were three floors? Gripping the vertical bars, I swung my legs over the rail and stretched for the metal balcony rail below. Fear jangled my nerves. The toe of my shoe touched and I eased my grip on the bars, which immediately started slipping from my fingers. All my weight went on the right ball of my foot, the metal rail a balance beam digging into my metatarsal. I lost all purchase above and for a second waved my arms like a lop-sided bird on a wire. I sucked air and lurched inward, collapsing as I crashed to the balcony. One shoe sank as though I'd landed on soft mud. Lost a heel, but heaved a sigh of relief.

I stifled a groan as I scrambled to my feet. Below my purse looked forlorn. I swung my leg over the rail, lowered my torso over the edge—gripping the black bars and for once in my life grateful for all the chin-ups in the gym—and clung to the rail bars.

A muscle twinged as I strained to see the ground over my shoulder. Above, a sliding glass door opened. The manager's voice puzzled, "Where is she?"

Hell's Bells! I let go, and landed in a flower bed, my pumps sinking in the damp soil before I rolled forward to my hands and knees. I got up dirty, but in one piece, mutilated pansies everywhere. The man at the bus stop stared. Another small favor: the view of the third floor balcony was blocked by the second floor. Thanks, HP. I brushed off my pant legs, grabbed my purse and hobbled to my car, one leg now an inch and a half shorter than the other. I kicked off my lame shoes and started the car.

As I pulled onto Steiner Street, someone sprinted toward the car. "Wait!"

My hands whitened around the steering wheel as I leaned on the gas.

Cain looked like he could carve out my heart. Shaken, I skidded around the next corner, sped down several blocks and double-parked so my pulse could settle. A few tremors hit as I eyed my nyloned feet, my broken shoe. I pulled my gym bag from the back seat, tugged on my aerobic shoes and felt better.

But my brains felt scrambled.

A thought struck. Who'd left a message on Karla's machine regarding a fake ID? I pulled out my notebook, reread the message. Juanita Juarez had left a local number. Was Ken peddling fake ID's for Mohammed? It hardly seemed important. Other thoughts crowded in, like Ken's bank here in the City, his safety deposit box, the key in my purse. Should I call Zoloski and drop everything into his lap?

Yes, yes, yes. Impulsively, I pulled out my cellular. Nothing. Needed a recharge. I plugged it in the cigarette lighter and drove, swung down Noe Street, zigzagged a bit up the steep hill, and double-parked near a corner restaurant with a phone booth. Eyeballing the street and my car, I dialed.

I got Zoloski's voice mail. "I need to talk to you," I said in a calm voice. "I should be in my office," I checked my watch, "around three. I'll call back then."

I disconnected and fed more money into the slot, trying not to think about the tongue-lashing Zoloski might dish out.

"*Bueno*?" An older woman's voice answered, her tone cautious.

"May I speak to Juanita please?"

"*No comprendo...*" She spewed a long string of Spanish I figured meant, "call back later," or "you have the wrong number," or any myriad of things.

I racked my brain for the high school Spanish I'd once excelled at, finally said, "*Que tiempo volvera Juanita*?" trusting I'd got my verb and future tense right and she'd understand I wanted to know what time Juanita would return.

She said, "*A las seis...*"

"*Llamo despues seis,*" I call after six, I promised, hoping she got the gist. *Use it or lose it*, my brother always said.

Another long string of rapid Spanish. Was she talking to me, or someone else? The verbal blur ended in a murmured "*Si*," and a dial tone.

I hesitated, hating to admit that I'd either have to stay in San Francisco until six to talk to this woman, possibly later, and miss my dinner in Sac with Zoloski—and the soul-baring talk I planned to have in which I hoped we'd both put everything out on the table—or return to the City another day. Neither choice appealed. I'd had enough of narrow streets choked with cars and pedestrians who paid zero attention to traffic lights.

I wanted to hit the Golden Gate at a run, but Ken's bank was on the way and I couldn't let the opportunity pass. Somehow I knew if this thing went through Centerfold Brown and the government bureaucracy,

Lon would end up stinking in jail for weeks. I knew what Zoloski would say, *Better him than you,* but I couldn't stop myself from circling the bank.

I don't have to go in, I told myself as I snagged a parking place.

No sign of trouble, unless it was a young woman dressed in black leather, several rings piercing her nose, handing out flyers near the bank's front doors. A blond streak ran skunk-like down the center of her black hair. A scream for attention? You bet.

I sat in the car and argued with myself about *right* and *wrong and the letter of the law* versus *the intention of the law* as I practiced Karla Woods Johnson's signature. Forgery was an old childhood game—one I was good at—it didn't take long to get down the flowing curves and loops. I hesitated before I got out. Was I going too far for Lon? Absolutely, but like a true addict, I had to finish this.

With the box number seared in my brain, I skirted Skunk Woman, went inside, and scoped the joint before I lost my nerve. I zeroed in on the security area in the back, bypassed the deposit line, and smiled confidently at the bank officer. "I need to get into my deposit box."

He opened the door and stepped through, repeating my request to a starched matron. She had me sign the card, then checked it against the one on file. I crossed my legs to keep from shaking. Sheeee-it! Go directly to jail—do not pass go. I had to pee.

All business, the woman led me into the vault, found the box and asked for "my" key. I hefted it out—the box weighed almost as much as a sack of potatoes—and followed her to a cubicle.

A breath of relief whistled past my teeth when she closed the door. I opened the box, and froze, a mixture of fear and awe burning through my veins. Hundred dollar bills. Bundles of them! I pulled on my gloves, unwedged a bundle and made a quick count. Five grand per bundle. A hundred grand or more—a motive for murder if I'd ever heard of one. But where was the rest of the two million, and where had the money come from?

I put everything back, replaced the box and nearly set a record getting on the freeway. As I drove, I dumped the cassettes onto the passenger seat and slid one into the tape deck. Maybe it would explain the money.

A deep, male, heavily accented voice blared over the speakers. "Ken, where have you been?"

Mohammed? The Omar accent and tone was similar, but I'd only talked to the guy once.

Ken's voice: "I had a couple of clients in the City."

"Vic has some business he'd like you to handle. Tonight."

"Tonight?" Ken sounded anxious. "I'm in the middle of an audit. How about tomorrow?"

A long pause. "Eight o'clock tomorrow night." *Click.*

I imagined Ken hanging up, sweat dripping into his eyes. Something in the guy's tone and silence seemed threatening.

I popped out the tape and read the label: August 29. Holy Toledo! I almost drove over the car in front of me. Ian would have loved that! I'd hit the jackpot! Ken was supposed to meet with Amerol the night he was killed.

But Ken had been with Lon at 11:00—very much alive. Whatever the meeting with Amerol was about, Ken had been upset enough to get plastered.

I stuck in another tape. *Click.* "This is Ken Woods."

"You working late *again*?" Lon! Frustrated.

"Sorry, Lon. Can't help it. Got all this tax shit to file. The extension's about up." Ken sounded harried. "I swear I'll make it up to you in September. Take some time off...."

A heavy sigh. "Yeah. Right. See you later." Lon's disappointment hung in the air. Not on the best of terms?

Had Ken automatically taped all his phone conversations? More important: why?

I checked the label: August 26-28. I glanced at the bundles and wished I could hear them all at once. I put the first tape back in, wanting to hear the final part, and waited for it to rewind, ruminating about what I'd found so far:

1) Ken did tax work for Amerol. Amerol was one of the investors in Anytime, Inc.

2) Ken masqueraded as Karla Woods Johnson, using an ID from a club owned by Anytime, Inc.

3) Ken had over a hundred grand in the bank, maybe another two mil stashed somewhere else.

The toll bridge loomed ahead and I rummaged in a side pocket, slowed to a stop, paid the buck, and drove on. My checklist rolled on too.

4) Ken might have been securing fake ID's for illegal aliens— pure conjecture—but possible—not that it would pay millions. Would Juanita Juarez and her brother know anything worthwhile?

5) According to Dimples, Ken knew he was in danger.

6) The FBI was after something or they wouldn't be involved in the murder investigation. Drugs?

7) Al Martinez and Nicole Jackson were after something too. Maybe Zoloski knew and would tell me after I plied him with food, wine, and me...

A smile tugged at my lips. My mental list burned with thoughts of the Z-man.

The tape clicked on with an unfamiliar voice: "Ken?"

"Yeah?"

"We need to see you. *Now.*"

We? Who, I wondered.

"I don't think I can do this...."

Ken's obvious reluctance gave me goosebumps.

"Just think about the money you're being paid..."

Ahah!

"We'll be here until six. Make sure you're not followed." *Click. Click.*

"Ken, where have you been?" The heavy accent, I listened to earlier.

"I had a couple of clients in the City."

"Vic has some business he'd like you to take care of. Tonight."

"Tonight?"

Now I knew why Ken sounded so anxious—someone else wanted to see him too.

"I'm in the middle of an audit. How about tomorrow?"

The long unhappy pause.

"Eight o'clock tomorrow night." *Click.*

The rest of the tape was blank. My stomach growled. One-fifteen. I was near Fairfield, could feel the Sacramento heat—at least 100 degrees coming at me. Crawdad's sounded good for lunch, I could catch the river breeze, if there was one, and talk to the bartender. Time to tie up loose ends. Trent knew more than he'd said when I showed him the picture.

The place was crowded with Friday afternoon yuppies; a few boats tied at the dock. I sat at an inside table, ordered a sandwich, then moseyed over to the bar. "Hey, Trent, how's it goin'?"

He smiled. "Good, Blaize. Get you something?"

"Virgin Pina Colada."

He nodded, started to fix the drink, then glanced back over his shoulder as the grinder roared to life, pulverizing the ice. "Ross was looking for you."

Oh joy. What did he want? Running out of babes to pay the bar tab? I didn't ask, Trent didn't seem to expect it.

He served another customer then finished the creation for me. I paid him, chatted, then brought up Ken and the photograph. "Did you know the guys he was with? Dressed in business suits."

"I already talked to the police." His tone was polite, cautious.

"Detective Zoloski?"

"No. A woman." He hiked an eyebrow. "Great looking babe with a nasty attitude."

I stifled a smile. "Brown?"

He nodded.

My sandwich arrived, but I ignored it. "What did you tell her?"

He hesitated.

I smiled earnestly. "There's no law against talking."

"Ken came in that day looking on top of the world. Excited. Asked me to take a shot of the group when things got busy and they wouldn't notice. Said it was a surprise." He frowned. "After his friends left, he had a couple double's. Said 'Shit', a few times. Something happened, he looked worried. That's it."

"So why didn't you tell me this before?"

A shrug and a smile. "Why get involved?"

"Did you recognize anyone in the picture?"

He paused, fixed a drink, handed it off, turned back to me. We went back a long ways—to the days when I was dragging Ross from the bar at closing. Was he remembering too? He shrugged. "I guess I can tell you. I didn't want to say anything because the guy's loaded—heard it's not healthy to get on his bad side. Know what I mean?"

I sipped my drink, my eyes answering "yes." The drink tasted sweet and coconutty. Ahhh.

"Mr. Amerol—owns a chunk of real estate downtown."

"Thanks." Confirmation went down as slick as the colada. Still, didn't prove much. The five men in the picture knew each other. I didn't have the picture—didn't have proof Anytime, Inc. existed anymore...And Zoloski had arrested Lon. I quizzed Trent for another minute, got nothing more, and on the way out inhaled my turkey on sourdough.

I drove to my office, agonized over whether to leave the tapes in my trunk or take them upstairs. I left them. I needed to talk to the Z-man. And Lon, who I hoped was out on bail. I had a feeling, like everything else on Labor Day Weekend, it would take longer to manage and he'd be stuck inside til Tuesday.

My answering machine light was blinking when I walked in. I ignored it and dialed Homicide, thinking about the tapes. Could I blitz through them before dinner?

"Detective Zoloski," he sounded wired.

"You mean you haven't been shit-canned yet?" I teased, imagining a smile.

"Hey, Blaize. Nice timing. I was just going to call." *Crunch, crunch.*

"Late lunch?"

"Yeah."

"You pick up Lon?"

A slow, "Yeah."

"Did he make bail?"

"His lawyer was a royal pain in the ass."

What did I miss?

"Bail was denied. The DA considers him a risk. Lawyer's requested another bail hearing for Tuesday."

"Great," I dripped sarcasm. "So he gets to spend the holiday behind bars?"

A pause. "Sorry, Sweetheart." Bogie voiced. "It wasn't my call."

In other words someone higher up. Brown? I sighed, wishing I could give a swift kick to her little playboy butt. "What was he charged with?"

A hesitation. "First degree—but that'll change. Don't worry."

I sucked in my breath. "Can I visit him?"

A longer pause. "I'll meet you in front of the jail. Fifteen minutes."

I eyed my clock. 3:10. "Okay." I heard the scrunch of paper. "Thanks," I murmured.

"Save it for tonight," he murmured playfully.

My response was half-hearted, my thoughts with Lon. I picked up my keys and headed out.

The smell of a jail is half hospital, half human misery. The feel is worse than an elevator stuck between floors. The sound of the locks, the sensation of being closed in grated on my nerves—and I was a visitor.

Zoloski arranged for me to see Lon in a holding cell. It looked like an over-sized shower stall, beige paint on concrete block, no window, metal toilet with no seat, cement floor with a drain, and a plastic-covered mattress that looked comfortable as a bed of nails. I paced and waited, goosebumps rippling up my arms. How could Zoloski stand this part of his job? "How can you stand to listen to people pour out their misery and pain day after day," he'd once come back with.

The door squeaked slightly and Lon shuffled in. He looked like Robert Redford put through a meat grinder: faded tan, eyes shadowed and red. I stretched my lips into a smile as we hugged.

"I feel like a mole," he joked.

My stomach tightened. "You gonna be okay?"

"Hey, I gotta great lawyer, guy by the name of Brian Jensen—only charging me a few grand to handle the preliminary—and I get to mortgage everything I own for bail—if I get it."

I stepped back, read the questions in his eyes, but knew there were cameras watching. Listening too? "We'll talk when you're free," I promised. "Would you like me to drop off some books, personal items?"

He shook his head. "My lawyer's done that. He wants to talk to you—before Tuesday. I gave him your number."

"Okay." I tucked his lawyer's name in my mind. "Anything I can do right now?"

"Short of a miracle? No." He reached for me again and we hugged. "This is hell, Blaize," he whispered.

"Shhh...I've got a lead—a good one," I whispered back, patting him awkwardly. "Hang in there." I took a deep breath and stepped toward the door. "I'll see you tomorrow, okay?"

He brightened. "Great."

I rapped on the metal. Two uniforms ushered Lon out, and Zoloski guided me outside, his gaze concerned. Downtown never smelled so good. Nor did Zoloski. He wrapped an arm around me and I inhaled. Next thing I knew we were kissing. The kind of hot, melting kisses we did in private—usually. Was being incarcerated good for the libido? Or did I just need reassurance I was alive and free?

Someone whistled from a passing car. Zoloski pulled away, his expression reluctant.

"We've got to talk," I said.

He walked me to my car—about thirty feet. "Can't right now."

"It's important."

"I'm sorry about Lon—but I can't change things."

I thought about my trip to the City, the tapes. "It's not that."

"If I had time, I'd take you home, *talk*, then spend some time following up on...He traced my lips with his fingertip. Despite my worry about Lon, I felt a thrill of delight spiral down my spine. What the man could do..."Dinner, okay?" he said.

Although he didn't know it, he was giving me time to dig holes in his case. Not conducive to foreplay.

"See you soon," he murmured, his lips brushing my forehead.

I took off. Time to stifle my hormones and listen to those tapes.

Chapter 16

SECURE AT HOME, in the den/office space I shared with Zoloski—I
organized the tapes in chronological order. Ken had obviously been
taping his conversations for the past seven months. I jotted a list:
    February (1 tape)
    March (1 tape)
    April (2 tapes)
    May (2 tapes)
    June (3 tapes)
    July (3 tapes)
    August (4 tapes)

Sixteen total. I stuck February in the tape deck, leaned back in my
padded chair and eyed Zoloski's favorite wildlife print, a Siberian tiger.
The dark wall paneling made the office feel like a hibernation hole. I
had a brief thought about painting the walls to match the tiger.
    Click. "Ken Woods."
    "The boss likes your work." Mohammed? "He'd like to talk with
you further. Tonight."
    "I thought you said this was a one-time deal!" There was pure
panic in Ken's voice.
    "It is, it is..." A soothing tone. "Don't worry. We just want to
talk."
    A pause. "Okay."
    "Ten o'clock." *Click.*
    The tape hummed on. I paced the room, antsy, checking the time,
wanting to fast-forward, afraid I'd miss something if I did. Once I gave
the tapes to Zoloski, it wasn't likely I would hear them again.
    Click. "Ken Woods."
    "Hey Ken, this is Lon. I'm running late, but how about a quick
cup of coffee at the Weatherspoon?"
    "Ah, sure. Six-thirty-ish?"
    "Yeah." A pause. "Bye."
    "Bye." *Click.*
    They had met in January. This was the "slow-and-easy" Lon had
mentioned. Another long hum of tape rolled by. Frustrated, I stretched

muscles and paced.

5:15. If I cut to the wire, I had two hours until my dinner date with the Z-man, and I had fifteen hours of tape staring me in the face. Damn. I was going to have to speed through and take my chances.

I ran through the rest of February. No more mysterious calls. The March tape yielded one revealing conversation:

"Ken Woods."

"Hey Ken, the office has a favor to ask, if you could come by." Cobra Face? A stab-in-the-dark. I could barely recall our conversation in the elevator, the pitch of his voice, the faint accent.

"I'm working late." An excuse?

"It'll be worth your while." A hard edge said he could make it easy or difficult, but those were the only choices. The tone reminded me of a government bureaucrat—the kind who likes to play God.

A lengthy pause. I paced around my chair like a dog on a short leash.

"The bureau would *really appreciate* your time."

I stopped. *The bureau*? As in FBI? My brain synapses overloaded. Couldn't be Cain. Was Ken on the payroll? The man's conciliatory carrot brought images of a packet of hundred dollar bills—five grand worth. Did this explain Centerfold Brown's involvement? Had they hooked Ken into something, or caught him in an illegal activity and used it to gain cooperation? Either way, I felt stunned. How much did Zoloski know? A knot tightened in my stomach.

I dialed his work number, got his voice mail. "It's Blaize. We *really* have to talk. Don't be late to dinner."

Fast-forwarding through March took ten excruciatingly long minutes. I jotted down notes. 6:30 arrived as I spun through April and May, heard more "meet me here or there" calls from the voices I now assumed were from an FBI contact and Mohammed. Who was the contact? No idea.

I flipped through my notebook—everything I'd written down at Ken's apartment. No clues leaped out at me. But the name Juanita Juarez did. I wanted to find out what she knew. I dialed. No answer. No message machine.

Back to the tapes.

June gave me another shock.

"...this conversation is being taped isn't it?" Mohammed's baritone voice sounded pissed, like he *knew* it was. Taping a personal conversation without consent was a legal no-no, and people in Mohammed's line of work wouldn't take such lapses in etiquette lightly. The thought dried my mouth.

"No, of course not!" Ken snapped so indignantly, I believed him—and I was listening to the tape! Good Golly Miss Molly. I was a therapist, good at picking out "bullshit", but Ken was convincing.

Was Ken sweating? I was.

"Okay," Mohammed said, his voice hard. "If I give you everything, the FBI won't prosecute—that's the deal, right?"

Jeez, Louise. Ken was in cahoots with the FBI.

"That's what they said," Ken assured.

"If you're lying—I'll cut out your heart and drink your blood."

Eeewww. Was this Middle-East Macho or what? Mohammed with the Omar Eyes was taking on new dimensions—those of a dead Freddy Kruger.

"Hey, I'm just relaying the message." A pause. I could hear Ken take a drink. "Brown said she wants to see it all—everything you've got."

Brown! I wanted to shout in triumph. That nailed her and the FBI.

"Not before next month. When my cousin is out of town. I will call." *Click.*

6:53. Seven more minutes, then zip through the shower and jump into something spiffy, or I'd be late. I popped out the last June tape and snapped in July. Fast-forward, play, listen, fast-forward, play, listen. Nothing but work-related calls on the next two tapes.

I popped in the third, and glanced at my watch. Thirty seconds left. I caught one call in the middle of my fast-forwarding mania.

"You said he'd deliver! Where the *hell* is he? What the hell did you tell him?" A new voice, vaguely familiar, but I couldn't place it.

"He said he would call," Ken responded, his voice almost a squeak. "Give him time. He can't just walk out with the books whenever he likes. He'll come through." I heard *snow job.*

"He'd better, Kenny-boy, or you're going down." *Click.* My heart soared. Things were looking better for Lon all the time.

I scribbled a few final notes and stuck the notebook in my purse along with the tapes. I'd listen to the last three in the car.

After a pit-stop in the bathroom, I threw on an electric blue silk dress, floral print jacket, high heels, and flew out the door.

THE FIRST AUGUST conversation between Ken and his FBI contact held more threats. On the second, Ken offered Mohammed assurances, promising he wouldn't be prosecuted—and Mohammed stalled. I banded the tape with the others, and dashed into Piatti's.

Zoloski was at the bar, dressed in a snazzy work suit, and looking relaxed as he jawed with the bartender. He flashed me a dazzling smile and slid his arm around my waist. "You're turning every head in the joint." He kissed my cheek. "Want a drink?"

"Gin and tonic, tall, double the lime."

Zoloski's eyebrows rose. "Heavy afternoon?"

"You could say that."

His eyebrows danced. "We'll have to do something about that." He looked frisky. I hoped my guilty admissions wouldn't dampen his ardor. He was turning a few heads too, and I liked the idea of taking him home for dessert.

We sat together at the bar and studied a menu. The air was filled with the rich, heady smell of Italian cuisine.

"Want to share?" he asked.

I nodded and we agreed on antipasta, Mezzelune di Fagioli con Gamberi (half-moon shaped ravioli filled with white beans, basil and parmesan cheese served with sauteed shrimp); and Pane all'aglio (garlic bread). My gaze swept down the menu and up the other side. "How about *Pappardelle Fantasia*?" I read, salivating over fettuccine with shrimp, white wine and other goodies.

Zoloski nodded. "*Verdure alla Griglia*?"

My gaze skidded from his smoldering eyes to another tasty *estraviganza*: grilled seasonal vegetables with whole roasted garlic, grilled polenta and lemon. "We'll reek of garlic." I smiled.

Zoloski's eyebrows danced again, the curve of his lips seductive. "As long as we reek together, Sweetheart."

My heart did the old pitter-pat, but I glanced away feeling an anchor—the tapes—in my purse.

The Maitre'd showed us to a booth in the back corner. Quiet, romantic candlelight, far from the kitchen clatter. I set my purse on the banquette, and asked about his afternoon.

His looked me in the eyes. "Now that we've arrested Lon, the heat's off. Sorry, but the evidence is strong. The DA has a good case. They're pushing for a quick preliminary hearing. Maybe next week."

Then why was he tapping his hands on the table? I gave him a professional look. "All the evidence is circumstantial. He didn't do it."

The tapping stopped. Zoloski's expression challenged mine. "Yeah? Can you prove that?"

I nodded. Surprise lit his eyes and I wondered if it would turn to anger. If another cop had done what I had—discovered what I had—the

Z-man would run with it. But me? I pulled the tapes from my purse.

He read, "February," gave me a piercing look. "What the hell is this?"

"Ken Woods, AKA Karla Woods Johnson, had an apartment in San Francisco. The tapes were stashed there." A small knot formed in my stomach. I wanted to quit while I was ahead. "I found them today." Zoloski looked about to snarl something and I rolled on fast, like a freight train running downhill—not wanting to stop til I was finished. "I've listened to most of them. They implicate several people, *not Lon*."

Zoloski glanced around the restaurant, then handed the tapes back to me. "Put 'em back in your purse. Now." His jaw worked. PO'd. Big time. "Why didn't you tell me about the lawyer, let me follow it up?"

"Lon asked *me* for help. I'm his *friend*. I don't report to Brown." *And I wanted to do it myself.*

The waiter arrived.

Zoloski's glare chased him away, then he turned to me, "How much are you willing to do for a *friend* behind my back?" His voice was low, but anger flared in his eyes.

"Whatever it takes!" I snapped, regretting it instantly. Damn, I could throttle his ex-wife.

His gaze narrowed from the jab, but no words came. He took a long drink of water, set it down carefully, then said through clenched teeth, "Talk to me, dammit—and *don't* leave anything out."

With a fifty pound weight in my stomach, I spewed out my activities for the last four days, the whole *shmeer*.

Zoloski's lips disappeared a little more with each additional admission, his face growing redder. "You forged Ken's signature?"

"I didn't take anything," I protested, feeling worse than a kid about to be grounded for the rest of her life.

"Jesus Christ!" He slapped the table, rattling the dishes.

The waiter hovered at a safe distance and Zoloski waved him over. "A double martini," he ordered. The waiter scurried away. I wanted to go with him.

Zoloski trained his furious green eyes on me again. "Where's the key to the deposit box now?"

I pointed to my purse.

Zoloski glared. "Have you gone nuts? Do you know what position you've put me in?" His tone would have skinned me alive if it'd been a knife. "You care that much about Lon?" Pain and anger rang in the question.

Yes, I care about Lon, I thought—but my love of solving puzzles, being in on the action, had brought me here.

He held up a hand to stop me from saying anything. "Good ol' Lon." He paused.

I bit back a comment about good ol' Brown.

"You realize you might have just hung him? Tampering with the evidence?"

Shit. Just what I needed—a guilt trip. I was not going to defend myself.

The waiter brought the martini and Zoloski downed it in one gulp. "Another," he ordered before the man could get out of earshot.

The waiter threw a cautious look my way. "I'm fine," I cracked. Just go away.

"You are not fine," Zoloski said in a seething voice. "You are wild, unpredictable, and out of control to the point of getting your neck chopped. And mine. Brown is going to bust your butt. What do you expect me to do? Pull a frigging hat trick?"

I felt like a four year-old, hoping he'd have that mystical, magical inspiration. Instead, his eyes looked lethal.

"Look," I said, "I know I took you by surprise, dumping all this in your lap, but..."

He interrupted. "Surprise is an understatement."

A chill worked its way down my arms. Was this it? Was he calling it quits? *Sayonara,* Babe. Didn't he know I would dive over Niagara Falls for him?

His second double-martini arrived, but he pushed it away, his silence worse than the tirade.

The thought of food nauseated me. "Check, please."

Zoloski gave me a dark smile. "Thanks for the meal, Blaize. Best damn food I never ate." I couldn't look at him, at the veil across his eyes. He'd gone to some other planet and I wasn't there. If Men were from Mars and Women from Venus, where was the bridge?

The therapist in me blurted, "I know I pushed things." Please, a glimmer of understanding.

He stood. "I think it's called *trust.* Let's talk at *home.*"

I could have broken icicles off the words. Maybe he intended to pack my bags.

What I would've given for a chocolate fudge cake, a pack of cigarettes and a steamy romance novel to bury my head in.

I LEAD-FOOTED THE gas, Zoloski's Jag keeping pace behind. The balmy night air clung as I drug myself to the door. Zoloski had it open before I found the key. The air-conditioning hit me like a bucket of cold water as I dropped to the couch. Zoloski tossed his jacket and gun on a chair, and sat at the other end, his expression unfathomable. Memorizing my features before he banished me? "You really know how to push my buttons." His foot swiveled on the carpet.

The thought of moving back to an apartment alone sucked the air from my lungs like a black hole in space. My own place had seemed inviting when I was angry at him, but it sure as hell didn't now. I forced myself to meet his eyes, fixed my face into a professional mask of calm, churning waters beneath.

His gaze narrowed. "You've put me in a hell of a fix! I can turn you in or risk my career trying to get you out of this mess. I won't ever see another promotion if I try to cover this up and Brown finds out."

At the mention of Brown, the angry kid in me wanted to say, "Fuck it, don't do me any favors!" I took a breath and struggled for words, emotions swirling in my gut. "I don't want you to stick your neck out, Stephanos. Arrest me, or whatever, but don't risk your job." A lump formed in my throat. "You love it. And I don't know if we could weather that storm." I meant every word. "I'd rather sink on my own than take you with me."

My words took the wind out of his sails. He stared.

In the silence, a bunch of "shoulds" ran through my head. I shoved them back into a dark hole. But I knew, sooner or later, my reluctance to trust him to be there, would surface again. How could I trust my friends, but not my lover? I had the sense I was following in my mother's footsteps and that scared me. All I need is a willingness to trust, I told myself. Step three in recovery. It would come. But when?

He stood and paced, long furious strides from one end of the room to the other and back.

My eyelids felt like sandpaper. Was this what battle fatigue felt like? I'd said everything I could say. The rest was up to him. Still, catastrophic fantasies swept through my mind: Zoloski turning me over to Brown; jail walls closing around me in a sterile claustrophobic choke hold; my career going down the tubes; Zoloski being skipped over for his next promotion, and the next; refusing to talk to me again; Brown moving in...

The last swarm through my brain with vivid mental pictures. Abruptly, I realized the Z-man had stopped pacing, was watching me. He pulled a notepad and pen from his jacket and sat down beside me. "Go over everything you've done. Date, place, time, everything for the last week."

I did.

When he finally finished writing, he looked semi-human, like maybe my story had some validity if I could tell it twice in a row. "You've listened to all the tapes?"

A cease fire? A shot of relief flooded through me as I shook my head. "I fast-forwarded, got the gist of conversations, then moved on. I listened to important parts." I read my notes out loud while he scribbled.

My voice cracked, and I prayed he'd spent all his bullets.

He stood and stretched. I remembered the last time he'd held me, wanted him to hold me now, to say "We're a team," like he sometimes did when I grumbled about housework. But I was drained, not into risking a turn down. The trust issue had yet to be broached. "You want me to move out?" I rasped—as though that was the answer. I wanted him to stick the stake through my heart and get it over with.

He stared down at me. Working out logistics? He shook his head slowly, like a judge uncertain of the best sentence. "Let's talk later."

Later, as in "I'll give you a call?" I didn't want to wait. "I need to know where I stand."

"In the morning..." Zoloski smiled, a slow, quirky grin that made me tingle in all the right places. "After we listen to the tapes."

We? A fluttering hope.

He leaned down. "Before we meet Jackson and Martinez at the gym."

We again. Tension dropped from my shoulders. A thought slid from my lips: "They're not really paramedics, are they?"

He brushed his lips against my ear, sending heat down my back and relief through my veins. "Why don't we ask them...?"

We as in a team?

He kissed me before I could ask.

I forgot the question.

WE TURNED THE bed sheets into a cyclone with hot and heavy passion, talked a bit, then dozed off for a few minutes. I awakened to Zoloski's tender gaze, his green, green eyes dark under the dim glow of the night lamp.

He ran a finger down my cheek. "I'm wide awake."

I wasn't. Yet a thrill of delight spread warmth down my middle. We made love again, a slow dance this time that left me spent. Zoloski surprised me by kissing my forehead and sliding out of bed. "I'll be in the office."

Listening to the tapes. I rolled over and tried to sleep, but couldn't. Too many worries niggled at my brain. What I needed was a nice 2:00 a.m. shower to put me over the edge.

Water rushing in my ears, I heard the phone ring, then break off. Zoloski must have picked it up.

I turned off the spray and stepped into steamy air. Who would call in the middle of the night? Centerfold's sharp eyes and patrician nose came to mind. I padded into the office in a bath sheet toga, goosebumps on my arms and legs, water dripping uncomfortably down my neck. Still on the phone, Zoloski swiveled toward me as I entered. Besides the smell of sex, he wore only a pair of red briefs. My favorite color. His eyebrows rose. A flush worked its way up my neck. Sometimes our wicked minds worked alike.

The gleam in his eyes turned somber. "You found what?" A pause. "Where?" A longer pause. "No, I'm glad you called. No, I'll talk to Brown." He glanced at me, a little frown of concern wrinkling his brow. Whatever he'd learned wasn't good. "Look, I've got a meeting in the morning I can't break. Tell her one o'clock."

I shifted. He was meeting Brown at one on a Saturday—his day off? Questions shot through my brain like a handful of darts.

"Uh-huh, yeah." He jotted something on his desk pad. "Yeah. See ya."

He got up and guided me back to the bedroom. More questions sizzled in my brain, but I held my tongue.

"That was a buddy of mine."

I sank onto the bed.

He followed. "They found Ken's hands—and teeth."

I gasped.

Zoloski slipped his arm around my shoulders. "In Lon's gym locker."

Chapter 17

SOMETIME BEFORE dawn, Zoloski rubbed my back and I got a few hours sleep. But dreams of Lon as a magician on stage in the Castro intruded. In a black satin cape, the scarlet lining splashed against a black tux, he tried repeatedly to pull a white rabbit from a top hat. Lost his hands every time.

Throughout the act, I, his scantily dressed assistant—with a military crew cut and whispery Marilyn Monroe voice—smiled and smiled, exposing more and more of my toothless gums. Teeth rolled on my tongue like marbles, blood caught in my throat. The bitter taste lingered as I woke—alone in bed.

"Stephanos?"

No answer. I pulled on gym clothes, my mind reeling with images of Ken's hands, his teeth—Lon's locker. Who else knew the combination?

"Stephanos!" I called louder.

A grunt from the office.

The clock read 9:00 a.m. Just enough time to scarf a bagel, juice, and coffee. Damn the dream. It lingered like a hangover. Food gagged me.

Lon belonged to the same chain of gyms I did. He frequented a plush, mid-town branch on Alhambra, while the Z-man and I used the Carmichael version. In search of a hug, I drew Zoloski into my arms as the last tape clicked off. I smiled up at him, loving the dark hair that curled up at the nape of his neck, the stray grey strands, the sharp sparkle of his emerald eyes. Somewhere between sleep, the tapes, and the phone call our conversation about "the future" had gotten shoved to a back burner. Now? "Why don't we cancel the workout with Nicole Jackson?" *Talk.*

Zoloski's arms warmed my back. We both wore baggy gym shorts, tank tops, and cross-trainers. "No point. Lab boys won't know anything yet."

He thought I was asking about Lon's locker. Did he plan to take me with him?

He gave me a distracted kiss on the forehead. "I just want to take a look around, see how easy it would be to break into..." Closing his notepad, he crammed tapes, paper, and a 9 mm Glock into his gym bag. "Let's go."

I didn't correct his assumption, sensing this wasn't the time for a conversation about our relationship, and our trust issues. Yet his distracted air told me he was holding back. As we walked to the car, anxiety twinged. "You going to give the tapes to Brown?"

"Yeah. When I figure out what to say to save your ass and mine from my boss' meat grinder."

I left that alone. "I'd like to tag along when you visit Lon's club."

"We'll see," his tone non-committal as we climbed in the car. "I may go to the Bay area tonight, check out Ken's apartment." His tone said he knew something already.

I waited.

"I called a friend in the City, had him run O'Malley through the computer. He's got a record trafficking heroin."

Dimples? He'd seemed so cute and harmless.

"My friend's going to pick him up and question him."

"Then what?"

A shrug. "I'll check out the banks, the Juanita Juarez woman, cover all the bases. Probably stay over a night, maybe two."

In the three months we'd lived together we'd always made it home, even if only for a snuggle. Jeez, Louise. A punch in the stomach would have hurt less than his casual "one night, maybe two." How many times had Ross talked about buddies of his, cops, that had one-night-stands when they were out of town? I squelched the thought. Ross and Zoloski were miles apart.

I told myself gratitude was more in order. He was following my leads—leads which might clear Lon. I owed him. "A day or two? Sure." I would achieve "casual" if it killed me. I'd take in a movie, visit Lon in jail. Plenty of ways to anesthetize abandonment. Without a quiver in my voice, I said, "You want to tackle Martinez while I take Jackson? Divide and conquer?"

He threw me a sideways glance. "You volunteering for detective work?"

Oh Shit. "How about helpful sidekick?"

He snorted, but his face softened. I could almost see his mind shifting gears as fast as the Jag. "You keep Martinez out of earshot while I talk to Nicole Jackson."

"Just *talk?*" I teased, the knot in my stomach loosening a notch.

Zoloski cast me an assessing look as warm morning air rushed past my face. I almost missed his wink. "Just wiggle that little behind.

Keep him busy. And remember you're just gathering information to pass on—to me."

The wink took the sting out the reprimand, and melted the rest of my fear. "Flirt."

He grinned, softening the chiseled lines of his face. "You look so great he won't be able to think straight," he said.

That warmed me more. "You mean he won't be thinking with his head?"

Zoloski laughed. "Only the little one," he said.

I flexed my biceps, showing off the definition. "Great, huh?"

A wicked smirk. "He won't be looking at your arms, Sweetheart."

NICOLE JACKSON, AKA Ms. Olympia, was at the check-in counter chatting with the young stud behind it. Her black exercise bra-top outlined a shapely bust with lots of cleavage, and her gym shorts emphasized her Scarlett O'hara waistline. "You both made it! Great!" She smiled and shook Zoloski's hand. At thirty-one, I felt like Methuselah's sister, way overdressed, too white, too tall. If Martinez was supposed to be ogling my butt, what would Zoloski be watching?

I cranked a few affirmations, straightened my spine and shook her hand. "Where's Al?" I asked, sweeping the area for her stocky cohort.

She frowned. "Not here yet. Come on, I'll show you around."

Zoloski said he'd meet us in the weight room. I followed Nicole into the ladies' locker area. Ah, air freshener and sweat! I stashed my bag, and trailed her to the "real" gym—barbells, benches, free weights and BO.

Nicole sat on the floor and leaned over her legs, stretching the hamstrings. "You and the Detective been together long?"

Technically, three months. "Six months," From the day we met to now. I eyed the Nautilus machines across the hall—my usual stomping grounds when Zoloski and I weren't lifting together.

"He's a cutie." She gave me a friendly smile.

I stretched my arms over my head. "I know. You involved with anyone?"

"Well... Al and I have gone out a few times. But we work together, so I don't know... and I have a little girl..."

The kid surprised me. "Oh, yeah?" She didn't look old enough.

Her dark eyes warmed. "She's five and smart as a whip."

"Great," I murmured, wondering if I'd ever have one. I pushed the thought away. "Had your condo long?"

She frowned. "Actually it's Al's. He's house-sitting. A friend of his is letting us stay the summer—helps out on the rent." She radiated sincerity. No way, José, too many coincidences—from my ambulance ride to Lon's rescue. Where was Zoloski?

Speak of the devil. He was coming through the door, Al beside him, the two looking like Mutt and Jeff. Although well put together in his crotch-cutting gym shorts, Martinez was still a shrimp next to the Z-man—albeit a strong one.

"I see you met." I extended my hand to Al. His grip was warm and firm.

Al nodded. "In the locker room." His pit bull expression and intense gaze moved from me to Nicole. "Hey, Nick, you up today?"

She got to her feet and gave him a brief hug. "Good enough to bust your chops."

"Nick's the national power lifting champion for her weight class," Al boasted. He rattled off statistics.

I was impressed and said so.

Nicole, all of five-one, shrugged as though bench-pressing 195 was no big deal for someone who weighed 114.

Zoloski echoed my compliment, fixed her with a wipe-out grin. "Spot me while I do squats?" Charm rolled off his tongue in waves.

She looked pleased. "Sure." They walked off together.

Mustering enthusiasm, I tore my gaze from Zoloski's backside and fixed on Al. "Need a spotter?"

He hiked an eyebrow and gestured toward the bench. "Sure. Why don't you start?"

Tomorrow morning I would regret this. The bar was a cold, heavy 45 pounds. I warmed up with ten reps, then moved to 65 and did five more. He added 50 pounds and did ten. As I took the weight, I asked him how he liked living by Garden Highway.

"Great. Great place." His gaze slid down my torso.

I felt underdressed, but smiled and pressed 95. "How do you like your job?"

"Fine."

A man of few words. The twelve-step definition for FINE ran through my brain: fucked up, insecure, neurotic, and evasive.

He chatted about the job while I exhaled like a vacuum cleaner in reverse with each lift. By the tenth rep, my teeth were locked, my pecs and arms straining against the weight.

"How long you been a paramedic?" I grunted as I replaced the bar.

"Long enough." He started on his next set, hissing like a snake.

The set went fast. He sat up, muscles bulging, veins tracing down each arm, sweat glistening on his chest. "Nick and I work well together." His eyes did another sight-seeing tour over my hills and valleys.

Yeah, right. Real well. I reduced the weight to 125, and lay back on the bench. No pain, no gain. I hissed out four reps. He looked impressed. After all, I was still going strong. Ha! Ha!

In between the next set, I learned Al was single, no kids, didn't want to talk about any specifics of his job, and had been working with Nicole since June. They agreed on that at least.

I spotted him at 220. He spotted me at 135, his body brushing mine at every opportunity. Sweating like a pig and smelling worse, I made one rep alone, three more with help, then died.

Before I could talk myself out of it, I leaned over Al as he pressed 250, and whispered, "You're a cop, huh?" like I knew he was.

The bar slipped sideways and I grabbed the end. Better than a lie-detector test?

He shoved it back into its carriage with a clang and sat up. "I'm a paramedic."

And I'm Little Orphan Annie. I tilted my head and gave him my best "you can trust me," look. "Sure..."

His light brown eyes measured mine.

"I bet you have ID."

He leaned forward, his body moving like a well-oiled machine, nothing left to the imagination. "Not on me." A pause. "Wanna search?"

I was right! Confirmation shone in his expression—a distinct invitation glimmering in his deep set eyes. "You've been lucky so far, Blaize. Why don't you leave the investigation to pros?"

My jaw dropped. It was just what Zoloski would say, but Martinez' words sounded as much come-on as threat. I dredged up a flirtatious expression. "You were on the scene before Ken was murdered—as a paramedic. Cool."

He glanced toward the doorway. "Why don't we talk later? You swim?"

I stretched out a leg, pressing my backside in the air—a good hamstring stretch and a better tease. "Love to swim. What time?"

He grinned. "This afternoon. Four. Meet me at my condo. Number 242. We'll go for a dip...and talk."

I had the distinct feeling he was looking to dip his stick. Fat chance. But I nodded. More questions tangled my tongue as I followed his gaze. Zoloski was striding towards us, his expression affable, but the muscles along the side of his neck were tight. "Nicole's finishing her warm-down..." his tone rang with enthusiastic admiration. A pause, his gaze traveling to Al. "Blaize and I are going for coffee. Want to join us?"

We were?

Al shook his head. "Got errands to run." A darting glance my way. "Won't be free until this afternoon." He chatted for a few seconds, then picked up his towel and headed for the locker room.

The Z-man lowered his voice, "He was scoping you big time. What'd you find out?"

I hesitated, then muttered, "The guy's a cop and we have a four o'clock swim date. I think he wants to show me how to do mouth-to-mouth."

His eyebrows danced. "Oh?"

"This could be a break."

"A cop? How did you get that?"

I made a fist and flexed my biceps.

A smile cracked his lips.

I lowered my voice. "Nicole spill her guts?"

The smile broke into a grin. "Life story. I'll check her out."

I gave him a look. "You already did. Glued to her backside."

"I've been telling you for three months to stick with the free weights," he shot back. "Especially squats. Fringe bennies."

"As long as you keep yours monogamous," I warned.

His green eyes sparkled. He tapped the end of my nose with his index finger. "You too. You're not out of hot water yet. Remember that."

"Yessiree, Bob." Ah, sarcasm.

He ignored it, his face thoughtful. "I'll meet Martinez at four, on my way out of town. You stay home."

"Stay home?" I howled.

"After we get the layout of Lon's club and I meet with Brown, I'll drop you off."

Bribery.

On the way out—showered, blow-dried, fresh tank top and shorts, ready for Sac's noontime eighty-five degrees—I conjured up schemes to convince Zoloski to take me with him to meet Martinez, and afterwards, to San Francisco when he investigated my leads. "How about Teamwork with a capital T?" I said in my sexiest voice. "I could stay in your hotel room."

Zoloski groaned and shook his head. "Babe, you already owe me a helluva-lota favors."

I kissed him, a light, chaste public kiss that had potential. "I won't forget."

Chapter 18

LON'S LOCKER was near the far end of the hall, hidden from the front desk. In the corridor of freshly painted beige metal compartments, my imagination dripped blood from the bottom. The dream of bones rattling in my mouth returned and I shuddered. When Zoloski opened the locker, my breath froze. But it was empty except for smudges of fingerprint dust.

"Let's hope the lab can tell us more," Zoloski murmured as he closed away the odor of rot. He gave me a squeeze. "I'm going to speak to the manager, hang tight."

While he was gone I made a mental checklist of what I knew or suspected: someone wanted Lon framed for Ken's murder; the FBI had used Ken as a go-between to get evidence against someone—Amerol?; Ken was paid a ton of cash—I tried to think of where he might have stashed it.

Pit bull Martinez was involved, but I had no idea who he worked for.

Who was the woman named Juanita, who'd left a message on "Karla's" answering machine, asking about her brother, Xavier, and an ID? It didn't seem like it would have anything to do with Ken's murder...

"Lost in space?" Zoloski's voice startled me.

I jumped a mile. "Don't do that!"

He chuckled. "Sorry." The crinkles around his eyes evaporated into lines of purpose. He glanced at his watch. Mine said one-ten. Centerfold Brown was late.

The Z-man smoothed his dark blue tie. His creased pants, navy jacket, and white-on-white shirt looked sharp. Dressed for success or dressed for Brown?

She appeared on cue, her long-legged stride across the plush carpet combining a hint of "come hither" sashay with a bit of military determination. A frosty glance my way said any friendliness was an illusion.

She brought Zoloski into the cross hairs of her dark eyes. "We need to talk—alone." She gestured toward an empty child care room. I almost saluted, but decided that wouldn't help my case, or Zoloski's.

She closed the door in my face.

Through the window, I saw her scowl in my direction. I backed off and paced the hall, retracing my steps four times over, nodding and smiling at sweaty faces as they passed. Why was Brown so pissed? Had she found out about my escapade in San Francisco?

I'd rather go to jail, or even kiss the lady's playboy butt, than see Zoloski lose his job. Shit, the court would certainly take pity on a dumb yuppie like me. My inner voice squawked, "Yeah, once the lawyers clean you out." Bats fluttered in my stomach.

The deep rumble of Zoloski's voice stopped my ruinous ruminations. From an angle that would make it hard for Brown to spot me, I spied through the glass door panel. Zoloski's arms were crossed and he was glaring down at Ms. Centerfold. Smokin'!

Brown glared back, her arms crossed under her Barbie pontoon breasts. Her words snapped, audible even through the wall. "Don't think I won't nail your ass if the shit hits the fan, Stephanos. You *and* girl Friday."

Moi? Stephanos, not Steve? How long had *she* been calling him that? Ooh, that green showed up at the most unexpected times.

In two strides, Zoloski was at the door. I stepped away as he yanked it open. "I don't like threats." The tight lines around his eyes said "Go fuck yourself," which I liked, but his tone remained level. "I've cooperated with you every way I can." An edge of steel. "You're the one trying to cover up. You used Woods and got him killed." He paused. "You better keep that in mind. See you at the office Tuesday, Bunnie." He grabbed my arm, hurried me across the huge gleaming lobby—*Bunnie* bouncing in my ears—past the long expanse of juice bar delights, and out the door.

Wheels spun. She'd used Ken and got him killed...Holy Shit. Bunnie Brown? Her parents must have been dysfunctional.

My arm grew stiff under Zoloski's tense grip and I pried it loose. Thoughts snapped like rubber bands in a jangle of nerves. I stifled an inappropriate laugh.

He frowned. "You get the gist of that?"

"Yeah." Sort of. While fumbling for my sunglasses I race-walked to keep pace with his long strides. The pavement sizzled under my shoes—I felt it through my cross-trainers. "You keep the tapes away from the media and she keeps my ass out of hot water?"

A grunt of confirmation as he climbed into the Jag.

I waited until we were on the freeway. "Does she know about Ken's apartment?"

A sidelong glance and a nod. "Claims she got an anonymous tip. Has the apartment staked out. I told her you ran because your overactive imagination had Ken's murderer at the door."

"But I thought he *was*!" I was pretty sure Cobra Face had attacked Lon in the Castro. I rummaged through my purse for a stick of gum. "Now what?"

He pressed down on the gas pedal and the car shot forward. "Brown wants you arrested for obstructing justice. I offered her the tapes instead."

My gum lost its flavor.

"We've got until Tuesday to come up with more. Once Brown gets the tapes they'll be buried under federal concrete, and we'll have lost our leverage."

Jeez, Louise! "But if Lon goes to trial, the FBI's involvement will come out..."

Zoloski's hands tightened on the wheel.

My jaw dropped, my brain making a gigantic leap based purely on Zoloski's angry expression. "It won't go to trial...This whole thing is a farce...she's using Lon..." To get someone else?

A quirky, half-angry look. "She denied it. But she's full of shit."

How reassuring—so what was the plan, man? Glad for Lon, I waited, hoping the Z-man would offer it up instead of making me pry it from his lips. He took the 10th street offramp and headed down Broadway to South Land Park, Sacramento's oldest subdivision. Nice real estate. Old colonial, Victorian, and Spanish style homes on lush green chunks of land, mid-priced at 300 grand. Most of the Democrats live here while the Republicans camp out in Carmichael, or at least that was the political scuttlebutt. We passed Curly and Moe's. I couldn't stand the silence. "Where're we going?"

"My boss is keeping the tapes safe until we turn them over to Brown. He's going to make copies. Insurance."

"Has someone followed up on Anytime, Inc., the other investors?"

Zoloski snorted. "No shit, Sherlock."

That shut me up.

He pulled into a large, brick-paved circular drive and rolled to a stop near a long row of steps that seemed to unfurl from the three-story colonial's double doors. "Stay here."

I saw his arm bend as he climbed the wide steps, imagined him straightening his tie. Now I knew why he'd dressed up. The door opened and he disappeared inside.

I drummed my fingernails on the dash, plugged in Clapton's blues cassette and tried to drown out my fears. What I really wanted was a cigarette. To inhale the nicotine, feel the dizzying rush.... I got out of the car and walked along the edge of the drive, grateful for the shade of oaks and sycamores—gnarled and twisted after a hundred years of baking and flooding, baking and flooding. Made me think of myself and other addicts. No matter how we looked on the outside, without some kind of recovery process we were gnarled and twisted on the inside. I eyed the distance around the drive, about an eighth of a mile, and started a fast walk.

Two miles later, Zoloski came out, his stride more relaxed. "I thought I told you to stay in the car." Half a snarl.

"My butt got tired." I snapped before I caught the curve of his lips and realized he was teasing. I dropped into the bucket seat. Sweat dripped down my blue cotton tank top, collecting at my waistband. But my endorphins had kicked in. I felt great...The engine roared, Clapton blared, and I hastened to turn the music down. "What'd he say?"

A wary look. "He said to ship you off to Canada or block out visiting days on my calendar."

I wasn't sure if he was kidding.

AT HOME, ZOLOSKI enlightened me over a lunch of szechuan shrimp and broccoli. "This is the plan." He tapped his finger on the dining room table, indicating there would be no deviation. "You come with me to visit Martinez, a Fed by the way."

I shoveled a mouthful of shrimp to stifle a question.

He read my mind. "The brass decided I should know he's a good guy. He also said I should keep you under surveillance, and the cheapest way to do that is to keep you with me."

I couldn't squelch a rush of excitement.

It must have showed, he looked pained. "This is no joy ride. Brown's after Amerol for money laundering. Big money."

Drugs? "And you think Ken tried to rip off a couple million?"

"It's possible."

Damn, sometimes Zoloski gave me more information than I ever thought I'd get, other times he had lips tighter than plastic wrap stretched over a bowl. "So Amerol could have a motive for murder?"

A shrug.

"Does Martinez work for Brown?"

"I'm not sure. He may have his own agenda. The boss wasn't exactly enlightening about that. Could be the drugs," he speculated, "could be tax fraud...And he's interested in you too." His tone definitely inferred a question: Did you tell me everything? Shades of his ex-AGAIN. At least he didn't say it.

I reached across the table and put my hand over his.

A long, intimate look passed between us, promising a future that I both wanted and was frightened of. He went to the stove, his movements a bit stiff as though the emotions made him uncomfortable too. He poured more coffee and returned, his expression and tone all business. "The shit doesn't hit the fan until Tuesday, Sweetheart. Let's get to work." The air was heavy with warm fuzzies.

"Let's," I murmured. I had never felt more loved.

ZOLOSKI SPENT THE next hour on the phone. Rather than eavesdrop, or give in to the urge to suck on a cancer stick, I mowed the lawn. All the physical exercise was either going to kill me or turn me into Godzilla. I showered, again.

Zoloski was off the phone when I sashayed by in a flowing skirt and matching purple top. His notebook lay open on the desk, illegible scrawls slanted across the page. I sat on his lap. His arms snaked around my waist, his warm breath tickling my ear. "You want to read it," he whispered, "go ahead."

Damn. "Nicole Jackson? Fire? Four?" The rest was chicken scratch.

"A buddy of mine in the fire department says she checks out. Been a paramedic four years, excellent record."

"A cover?"

Zoloski hee-hawed. "You watch too many movies, Sweetheart."

"What about Martinez?"

"All right. There are exceptions."

I studied Zoloski's chicken scratch. "He and Brown know each other?"

A reluctant, "Yeah."

How well? The image of Brown and Martinez in a clinch seemed a perfect match. Adonis and Venus. I almost laughed. I gave Zoloski a peck on the cheek, started to stand and he pulled me back, lips nuzzling my neck. "Ready to go?"

"Ummm...yes."

He twisted his wrist. "Damn. No time for favors."

"Later, Big Guy," a lousy French accent.

He disappeared into the bedroom and returned with a full duffle bag. It matched my blue one, only his was pink. A sale I couldn't pass up. At the time, he'd guffawed over my color choices, then surprised me by choosing the pink one. Probably because I'd held out the blue. I made a mental note to surprise him again when this was over. Later, Gator.

On the freeway, I remembered my promise to Lon. "I'd like to stop by the jail for a few minutes."

A hesitation. "Okay." His tone was even. "Ten minutes long enough?"

"Yes."

He added in a conversational tone. "He'll be all right. Don't worry."

"What do you think's going to happen at Lon's hearing?"

"Don't know." A thoughtful pause. "My guess is Brown's using Lon's arrest to put her quarry at ease."

Her's but not your's, I wondered, not sure I wanted the answer. "Amerol?"

"Or one of his buddies—someone involved in Anytime, Inc."

With icy clarity I recalled Amerol's flat, shark eyes. "If Brown was using Ken to get evidence against Amerol, then Amerol had every reason to murder him."

Zoloski cocked his head, but said nothing. The silence irritated me, I wanted confirmation.

"Do Amerol and Cain have alibis?"

"Both men have alibis for the approximate time of Ken's death. And Amerol has an airtight one for the time Mohammed was killed."

I thought of the tapes. "Maybe Mohammed murdered Ken on Amerol's say so, then Cain murdered Mohammed to keep him from talking. I don't see Amerol hesitating to knock off a distant cousin. Especially one who was willing to spill his guts to the FBI."

He shot another look at me. "There's another way to look at this." His expression said I wasn't going to like it. "If Lon learned of Ken's alter ego, and knew Ken was helping the FBI, Lon could have planned the murder and stolen the money.

No way.

"Maybe Ol' Dimples whacked off Ken's hands and yanked his teeth, helped Lon out, then dumped them in Lon's locker." He snapped his fingers. "Now he gets all the money."

Murder in the first? I thought, unsettled by the way the pieces could be fitted together. "No. You didn't see his face when we were in the Castro, Stephanos. The men who chased us were damn real. It wasn't an act. He was scared, hurt. He couldn't have planned this."

No comment.

My stomach clenched like an angry fist as Zoloski pulled up to the curb in front of the new jail, which would probably be called "new" for the next ten years.

He stopped me as I started to get out. "If you're right, Cain murdered Mohammed, and Mohammed murdered Ken, then you could be next. You saw the photograph of the men together at Crawdads. You've heard the tapes." His grip tightened, matching the lines around his eyes. "You keep digging and you may find yourself in a hole you can't climb out of. And damn it Blaize, I don't want to get that call."

His tone shook me before I realized he was probably trying to scare me. "I'm a big girl, Stephanos," I reminded him, then added in a teasing tone, "And I'm working with you now."

He shook his head. "I'm not Superman, Blaize. Can't catch bullets in my teeth or leap tall buildings. Remember that."

Time to switch subjects. "Do you think more than one federal agency is involved?"

His expression implied either he was deciding how much to tell me, or considering the idea. "Sure. Depends on what illegal activities we're talking about." We walked up the steps, nods of recognition and hellos directed at Zoloski as we passed. "The DEA would be interested in the drug angle..."

Drug Enforcement Agency.

"...the FBI in money laundering. Both are under the Justice Department. Treasury, would be interested in unreported income. Every department has their own agenda."

I mulled that over as we moved through the sallyport. "You going to talk to Lon, too?"

"No." He looked uncomfortable. "I've got his statement." Would the two men ever be friends? His expression said, "Not likely." Powerlessness—I reminded myself of the first step. I was powerless over Zoloski's feelings.

On that note, I went inside. My meeting with Lon was quick, but not painless. I hated seeing his despair, his blue eyes tired, his handsomeness dimmed. I wanted to tell him about the tapes, but wasn't sure who might be listening. I settled for, "Buck up, things are ripping along. You'll be out in two days."

He gave me a weak, unconvinced smile.

And then I was breathing fresh air outside, Zoloski beside me. "Everything okay?" he asked as we climbed back in the car.

"Hunky dorey." I regretted the compulsive sarcasm as soon as I said it. I picked up the cellular and dialed Lon's lawyer. Surprisingly he answered.

"Brian Jensen." A gruff voice with a likeable streak.

"Blaize McCue. Lon said you wanted to talk to me?"

"Yes." Papers rustled. We made a date for Tuesday, eight a.m.

"What are you planning to say to him?" Zoloski asked.

I shook my head. "Nothing. He wants to talk. I'll listen." If Brown was after Amerol, she knew Lon was innocent—he would be released. No matter what the Z-man thought.

Zoloski switched on music, but after one song turned it off. "Okay, this is how we play Martinez."

In the eight minute drive from the jail to the condominium complex, he covered the script. He should have been a director—I'd be his oscar-winning star. Or fall flat on my face...

Chapter19

I TRIED TO imagine myself in steel-tipped boots, swaggering like a real ball-buster as Zoloski and I strode past the swimming pool. Weeping willows swished in the breeze, casting lacy shadows across the cement. The smell of the river teased my nose and made me wish my feet in its cold waters. Freeway traffic droned in the distance, its regular rhythm soothing—except for my pounding heart and dry throat.

Zoloski cocked his head, his gaze quizzical, "You ready?"

No. My stomach was twisting with pre-performance jitters. "Ready Freddy." I led the way up the stairs, noting Martinez' condo was across from Lon's and in a good position to see who came or went. What had he seen the night Ken died? Anything? Or was he off playing ambulance driver as he claimed. Jackson had confirmed it, but she was probably in on the game.

I knocked on his door, half-expecting Martinez not to answer if he spied Zoloski—but the door swung open with a flourish. Martinez was not in a swimsuit, but a power suit. White silk jacket and slacks, about two grand worth. Blood red shirt, open at the neck. No tie. Fed's were obviously making money these days.

"Blaize. Detective Zoloski, what a surprise! Come in." A glint of amusement showed as our eyes met and I realized he'd expected Zoloski! Centerfold Brown's doing, no doubt. He gestured toward the living room, then shot another look at me, his lips stuck in a smirky half-smile that disguised his thoughts.

Everything, from his clothes to the living room and what I could see of the kitchen, gleamed. Since "Good Cop, Bad Cop" now seemed far-fetched, considering Martinez was not thrown-off or on-edge, I wondered what to do. My feet sank into the plush cocoa carpet as I followed Zoloski and dropped beside him on the dark leather couch.

An uncomfortably tense silence settled into me, and I surveyed the living room—laid out exactly like Lon's. Martinez and Zoloski both wore masks of control, plastic all the way. They were good at that. But hey, I could keep a damn straight face even if I felt like jumping out of my skin.

Zoloski glanced around. "Paid for by the taxpayers?"

A prize-winning smile blazed across Martinez' face. "Gotta look the part."

Zoloski leaned forward. "And what part is that?"

Martinez' hiked an eyebrow. "I assume you've been briefed." An image of two prize-fighters dancing around each other in the ring came to mind as he slipped his hand inside his jacket, pulled a federal ID.

Zoloski tensed—automatic reaction in a cop.

Martinez tossed it on the coffee table. "This ought to answer your question."

Zoloski picked it up, scanned it, turned it so I got a peek of TREASURY, then dropped it back on the table.

Martinez was not the kind of guy I pictured in the ranks of the IRS. I couldn't imagine him satisfied amidst bank statements or tax records.

He sat back, pulled a pack of Camels from his jacket and offered me one.

Like Pavlov's dog, I salivated, but conjured up thoughts of black lungs, bronchitis, smelly clothes, and bad breath. I shook my head. "I quit." Then grinned nicely, "But go ahead."

He flashed another thousand-dollar pit bull smile, the arrogant line of his jaw annoying me, then put the pack on the table. "Now that we know we're on the same side, maybe we can exchange some information?"

Zoloski stood abruptly. "Mind if I get a glass of water?"

What was he doing?

Martinez waved a hand toward the kitchen. "*Mi casa es su casa.* The glasses are in the cupboard on the right."

I watched Zoloski glide around the corner, heard the cupboard open. This wasn't in the script.

I smiled at Martinez. "Where's Nicole?"

He shrugged. "Took her little girl to her parents. Won't be back until tomorrow." He leaned forward, his voice soft. "I liked your act this morning. You ever want to play, give me a call."

The rotten son of a bitch! My cheeks burned. "You talk like that to Bunnie Brown?"

His eyebrows rose all innocence. "Who?"

"Oh come on, you and Brown are tight—both feds. She called and told you we were coming, didn't she?" I had my steel-toed boots back on.

He smirked, arrogance reeking from his pores. "She mentioned it." His gaze slid up my leg.

I was about to kick his balls. What was taking Zoloski so long, a drawer-by-drawer search? At last I heard the tap water run. I glanced around the room, gaze skidding from the framed print of a red Ferrari superimposed over a woman's nude silhouette, to a surrealistic print of what looked liked blood-spattered roses. Lousy taste in art.

"Looks like you got a nasty cut." Martinez said.

My hand fell to the thin red line above my ankle—another souvenir of Mac the Knife. An uneasy quiver shot through me. How much did Martinez know about that? Did he have a file with my name on it? Feeling defensive and vulnerable, I lashed out with a "fuck-you" smile. "You shoulda' seen the other guy. I blew his balls off."

His gaze narrowed. "Ouch." His smile challenged me, the stakes unnamed.

Tension hung there beside his warm, benign expression. Unpleasant goosebumps ran down my arms and I went from hot to cold in two seconds. "I'd like to use the restroom," I said, standing, acutely aware of his eyes all over me, a placid half-smile on his lips. I nearly collided with Zoloski. God, the three stooges—me in the middle, the Z-man and Martinez as book ends. I hurried down the hall and closed the door.

I ran water, cooled my face and brought myself under control. Returning to the living room, I passed the master bedroom and peeked in. Red satin bedspread, red carpet, red curtains, a photograph of a naked woman over the bed. Not Nicole and her daughter's room. But the next room, striped pastels could have been. Yet everything was so neat, I wondered if Nicole really lived here. Other than a stuffed animal on the bed, I saw no mess, no clutter—what I always connected with kids.

I detoured through the kitchen and glanced out the window. Perfect view of Lon's apartment. Straightening, smoothing my shorts, I wondered what Zoloski had learned while I was in the bathroom. Readying myself for another go round with Martinez' roving eyes, I strode back in.

Martinez was leaning toward Zoloski, a cocksure glimmer in his expression. As I entered, their conversation stalled.

Martinez eyed me like a rare steak and I could see Zoloski's shoulders tense, his hands tighten.

"So what'd I miss?" I quipped like a professional negotiator.

Zoloski glared as though I'd ruined some macho fun.

Martinez leaned back against the couch and crossed his arms.

"Al, here, was just about to tell me why he has Lon's apartment staked out," Zoloski said with a hard stare. "Then maybe we'll deal."

An elegant, yet derisive snort. "Nice try. First, why don't you give me the tapes Blaize ripped off. First time I've seen a city cop use his girlfriend for B and E by the way."

Oh shit. Someone needed to tell Brown that loose lips sank ships—mine. "We don't have them," I said as I sank back into my previous indentation.

Zoloski threw me a sideways glance that said, *Clam up, this is my party.*

I crossed my arms.

Martinez kept his eyes on me. "Who does?"

I stared over his shoulder at the Ferrari.

He turned to Zoloski. "You've heard 'em?"

Silence.

A sigh from Martinez. "Woods worked for Brown. I originally moved in here to watch him."

As if we didn't know. Yet he had the upper hand, why was he telling us this? "A paid informant?" I ventured.

He shrugged. "Ken was gathering information and passing it on."

Zoloski nodded thoughtfully, his shoe tapping softly on the carpet. "On Anytime, Inc."

Martinez contributed back, "I got involved when we found out taxes weren't being paid."

I still found it hard to believe the guy was Treasury. He didn't fit my image of an IRS wimp—didn't come close. I recalled Ken's persuasive voice, coaxing Mohammed to give him the books. "Like Capone?"

Martinez gave me a look of admiration that made Zoloski's lips turn down. Uh-oh.

Zoloski interjected, "So you're angle is tax fraud, Browns' is money laundering. What about drugs? Who's with DEA?"

Martinez sat up. "I don't know about any drugs, or DEA. Did Brown tell you that?"

"Just brainstorming here. I'm homicide. Last in the information line from the Feds."

"Maybe you should work on Brown." Martinez gave me a look that said he'd like to "work" on me.

Zoloski's green, green eyes flashed and I wondered how much more he'd take before he flattened Martinez and got himself in a big heap of trouble. I got a brief thrill from the mental image of Martinez flat on his back, out cold, before it vanished into worry for Zoloski and his job. "Who's the target?" Zoloski asked in a carefully neutral tone.

"Amerol?"

Martinez softened his voice. "That's none of your concern." His relaxed posture emphasized the control. "You fuck up my case, Detective, I could get angry."

The understatement vibrated with possibilities.

Zoloski's fingers curled as he stared back. "That a threat?"

Martinez slowly shook his head. "Just sharing my feelings, Steve. That's all."

Zoloski hated being called Steve. He stood up and started for the door.

I hung back. The only kind of feelings Martinez had were connected to his groin, but I was willing to play along with innuendos—for information. "Did you see Ken Woods leave the apartment the night he was killed?"

Martinez looked me straight in the eyes and shook his head. "I was working with Nick that night." *Working*, as in sex? He pulled a card from his pocket and slipped it into my hand, the challenge back in his light brown irises.

Zoloski opened the door and glanced back.

I palmed the card, hoping the Z-man hadn't seen. Attacking a federal agent would not help his career.

Martinez extended his hand to Zoloski. "No hard feelings."

Zoloski ignored it. "I want a statement. Downtown. My office. Monday morning, eight o'clock. Don't make me pick you up."

Martinez barely flinched, then drew his tanned face back into bland lines. "You sure you want to drag your girlfriend into this?"

"She's covered."

I was?

"I can be there at nine." Martinez' capitulation surprised me.

"I said eight." Zoloski guided me out to the landing. I took the stairs at a half-trot, the Z-man on my heels. I didn't relax until we were in the car. Martinez, a good-guy Fed. It didn't seem possible. "What do you hope to gain by questioning him?"

Zoloski revved the engine and the car shot forward. "He knows a lot more than he's letting on. I'm going to see what I can squeeze out."

"I thought we were going to do that now. Why did you back off?"

"He was too prepared. I want him to stew over the tapes. Get nervous. Him *and* Brown. Anyway, Sweetheart," he said in his Bogart voice, "You're not a cop, remember?"

I ignored it. "Everyone involved in this case is involved from a different angle?"

Zoloski nodded.

"So now you believe Amerol is behind Ken's death?"

A speculative look. "Lets just say it's a definite possibility."

Why didn't that make me feel better?

OUR FIRST STOP in San Francisco was north of Market Street, in the Tenderloin district. A rough area I wouldn't want to walk through alone, day or night. Women in plunging necklines and high hemmed Spandex dotted the sidewalk like cheap confetti. A collision of Mardi Gras and human misery.

I phoned Juanita Juarez, reassured her I was a friend of Ken and Karla's. She spoke fluent English and knew both Ken and Karla. She gave me directions to her apartment. I dug through my purse for a pen and took a peek at the card from Martinez. He had scrawled the words "Call me!" Like hell.

The tenement housing where Juanita lived wasn't Tijuana cardboard, but it wasn't far ahead. Puke green threads too bare to earn the name carpet led the way to her door. I knocked. A dead bolt clicked.

The door opened a chained two inches.

I identified myself and Zoloski.

She let us in—an overflowing figure covered in black from head to toe. Long ebony hair hung to her waist. Wide frightened eyes flickered with uncertainty. She looked all of twenty. She ushered us into the clean, but worn living room.

"Juanita—" An ancient, frail figure appeared from what must have been the kitchen, the smell of spicy enchiladas wafting from her clothes.

"*Mi abuela*, my grandmother." Juanita murmured.

In a querulous, questioning tone, a long flurry of Spanish flowed from the old woman's lips. Juanita answered in kind and I caught the names Ken, and Xavier. Her brother? Boyfriend?

My gaze fixed on the far wall of family pictures—everything from old black-and-whites to the formal color pictures of high school graduations. Juanita's smiling face beamed back at me. I crossed the room, taking in faces and features, and fixing on one that bothered me. He was small, fairer-skinned than any of the others, same dark hair and liquid eyes. Nice even features—good-looking.

Zoloski joined me. We looked at each other.

"You thinking what I'm thinking?" I asked.

He took a picture from the wall and studied the face. "Yes."

"*Mi hermano*, my brother, Xavier," Juanita murmured.

The muscles tightened in my back, moving toward my shoulders. Xavier Juarez could have been Ken's younger brother. It was one of those weird coincidences—everybody has a double, I'd been told once. With all his teeth missing, he would pass for Ken. Was that what happened to all the money? Did Xavier have it? I fixed on a statue of the Virgin Mary, a crocheted white doily beneath it.

Zoloski did the talking and I was impressed. He left me behind, speaking Spanish almost as well as he did Polish and Greek. Whatever he said seemed to inspire the women's trust.

We left with the photograph. Juanita stopped Zoloski just outside the door. "*Mi hermano es muerto.* No?"

What? *Her* brother was dead. She was asking for confirmation. How had I missed that? My God, everybody was turning up dead, everybody connected to Ken Woods. Or...a thought snagged my brain, snapping a different picture. Had Lon identified the wrong corpse? Was Ken alive?

Zoloski was saying, "I'll call you."

Juanita stepped back inside, tears rolling down her cheeks. The door closed.

"Stephanos, there isn't two candidates for Ken Woods in the morgue is there?"

"No."

"If her brother's under a sheet, where the hell is Ken?"

Zoloski gave me a grim look. "The lab hasn't identified the teeth and hands yet...You think Lon could have ID'd Xavier Juarez as Ken?" He gave me a look I didn't like. "Hard to believe—for guys that close."

A momentary stab of desire for a box of fudge cupcakes struck. I ground my teeth. Had Lon been feeding me crap and calling it caviar?

I dug through my purse like a dog desperate to chomp a bone, pulled out my emergency pack of cigarettes, tore off the wrapper and stuck a cancer stick in my mouth. What the hell, I'm not perfect. Zoloski knew that by now.

He said nothing.

Naturally, I couldn't find matches!

The Z-man grinned.

Chapter 20

ON THE WAY to Ken/Karla's apartment, Zoloski was quiet and thoughtful. I was in shock.

Vanna White and Wheel of Fortune blared from the manager's office walls. Zoloski rapped on the door. Tenants could scream their heads off and not be heard. Zoloski rapped harder, bringing an abrupt silence.

The door squeaked open. The manager scowled at me, but his voice went from angry to sugary when Zoloski flashed his badge. "I need to see Karla Johnson's apartment."

One barbed look snaked my direction, then we were in the elevator. Small, stubby, wrinkled clothes, a rumpled fringe of hair, he looked like he might have been asleep in front of the boob tube.

As the old man unlocked the door, Zoloski asked, "Who's been inside in the last two days?"

The manager frowned at me. "Since *she* jumped off the deck?" Like I was some kind of disease. The scowl disappeared. "Karla's boyfriend. He came back right after you run off."

"Boyfriend?" I repeated.

"That nice lawyer fella."

Dimples?

"And the other officer, Detective Cain."

My pulse did a tap dance shuffle. Cobra Face Cain impersonating an officer. Zoloski threw me a sidelong look which I returned.

I chimed in, "Five-ten, black hair? Faint accent?"

The man bobbed his head. "That's him. Nice officer—even if he is one of them Turks. Say, is Karla in some kind of trouble?"

While scribbling in his notebook, Zoloski said, "Routine inquiry," dismissed the manager with a "thanks" and opened the door.

I gasped. Someone had ripped apart the couch and love seat, and broken every piece of crockery in the place.

Zoloski tapped my elbow. "Don't touch anything."

"What's to touch?" I was glad I'd lifted the tape from the answering machine, because it looked like the wreck of the Hesperus. I followed Zoloski into the bedroom. The antique desk where I'd found the tapes was firewood.

With his pen, Zoloski moved some of the papers strewn across the carpet. I peered at the ripped mattress, and shuddered. Dimples? Cain? Whoever had done this liked destroying things... enjoyed it...Did he get his jollies chopping off hands and yanking teeth?

Jeez, Louise. My money on Cain, I was glad I wasn't Abel.

I bent and sifted through what remained of the vase. No desk key.

"Blaize."

I tiptoed through the mess and crouched beside him. He lifted a piece of paper so I could see the writing beneath a fine layer of white powder. Arabic? Zoloski touched his finger to it, then to his tongue. "Heroin."

Drugs. "You think Cain was searching for a stash, or the tapes?"

"Both." Carefully, he picked the paper up by one edge and slipped it inside his jacket pocket.

My gaze fixed on a curious red wire running along the floor. I slid my pencil under it.

"Blaize." A strange ripple in Zoloski's voice.

I turned, moving the wire a fraction of an inch. "Yes?"

Click.

Zoloski's eyes widened.

I had a sense of slow motion as he jerked me to my feet. Panic. "Trip wire..."

He pulled me toward the front door, the carpet flashing beneath my shoes.

A roar filled my ears. The blast threw me through the air like Superwoman. Zoloski hit the wall with a resounding CRACK! I slammed into him and landed on top.

I sucked for air, couldn't breathe, felt like a scarecrow blown upside down, and crushed beneath a tractor. The building shuddered and groaned, or was it me? I scrambled to my feet as flames erupted from Ken's apartment, snapping at my heels. Choking black smoke billowed overhead.

"Stephanos!" I shook him. His head lolled to one side. My heart lurched. No! I dug my fingers under his armpits and lurched and dragged him into the hall.

"Don't you die on me, damn it!" Heavy black smoke enveloped us. I had no idea where the stairway was, or even if one existed. Coughing, eyes burning, I fumbled down the hall, found a door at the end and shoved. Didn't budge! A zillion layers of paint held it in place. Damn, damn, damn! Heart pounding, ears ringing, I ran back the other way to the elevator and hit the button. Please, please work.

The doors slid open. Thanks, HP. I pulled the emergency stop, then ran for Zoloski. He moaned and tried to roll away from the heat. Alive!

I crouched, looped his arm over my shoulder and pulled. "Here we go, Big Guy." His eyes closed and he sank back to the carpet. Damn! I yanked him across my shoulders in a fireman's hold. Six foot two, eyes of green, weighs more than a Nautilus machine...Where the hell did that come from?

I staggered into the elevator, tried to ease him to the floor, and dropped him. The back of his head hit the wall and his eyes fluttered. I jabbed the button.

The elevator dropped. My head reeled, and my back twinged in all the wrong places. The doors slid open on the first floor. I gulped air, bubbles of relief bursting in my chest.

Zoloski winced. "What the hell?" He lurched to his feet, stumbled, caught the edge of the door and held himself upright. He looked at me and laughed.

"What's so damn funny?"

He pointed to my blouse. "Must be ash Saturday."

I glanced down. My flowing silk was no longer royal purple, but a blackened matte, no hint of its original splendor. A hundred, fifty bucks up in smoke. But I laughed. Ears buzzing, skin burnt, eyes smarting, I'd never felt better. "You okay?"

"Yeah," he mumbled, the mixture of humor and pain giving his face a comical mask. "You?"

"Yes."

Sirens screamed like fast-approaching demons. Drunk with relief, I wrapped his arm over my shoulder and staggered to the outside steps. Fresh air! A firemen raced by. "Anybody else inside?"

"Don't know," I yelled above the din.

"You two okay?" Another asked.

The answer died on my lips as I stared across the parking lot. The Jag's long sleek hood wore a camouflage of glass and wood—fallout from the explosion. Zoloski saw it too and the blood left his face. "Goddamnit!"

We removed the plaster and wood, then carefully picked off the glass. "Not as bad as it looked," I murmured encouragingly.

Zoloski shot me a sour look. "You didn't spend the last two years of your life slaving over this baby."

All of a sudden I realized how close we'd come to that long dark tunnel with the light at the end.

Zoloski grabbed me as I sank toward the pavement. "Blaize?" He supported my weight.

"I'm just having a bit of aftershock," I murmured.

"I'm here. We're both okay." His heart pounded against my ear. I trembled and he kissed my forehead and brushed back my hair tenderly. Then he did a double-take, studying it as it fell through his fingers. "I think you just got a hair cut."

For some reason it struck me as extremely funny and I laughed until my sides ached. He laughed too.

The next hour passed in a blur of firemen, water-gushing hoses, and frantic renters screaming about everything going up in smoke, and policemen with questions, questions, questions. Zoloski called a friend on the force and we got a ride downtown. While we waited, Dimples was brought in.

His lower jaw dropped halfway around the world when he saw me. Shock coupled with guilt flared in his cute brown eyes. I started toward him, ready to strangle out a confession. Zoloski grabbed me, sat me down. "This is my job. You wait here."

Damn, but I envied Zoloski as he escorted Dimples into a side room. I wanted to be in there firing questions and making the guy sweat. Twenty minutes later Zoloski returned with a satisfied grin. "Asshole was looking for the stash, but didn't know where Ken lived and couldn't get the bartender, Max, at the Pink Flamingo, to give him the envelope. Evidently Max was very partial to Kenny and his money." Disgust and sarcasm dominated Zoloski's tone. "So O'Malley set Lon up to be ambushed at the Pink Flamingo, which didn't work. But he had Lon's address. He followed you back here. And after you left, he returned, searched the place and left a present."

"Why, if he found what he was after?"

"Wipe out any incriminating evidence."

"If he'd do that he could have killed Juarez."

Zoloski looked too wiped out to answer.

Were my suspicions about Amerol and Cain off track? I felt too wrung out to process information without help. Smelling like burnt hair, bedraggled and tired, the sun setting in a spectacular splash of purple, and red, we climbed into the Jag and zoomed for home. Head on Zoloski's shoulder, sleep tugged at my eyelids and melted my thoughts to syrup. I dozed off, only to snap awake ten minutes later. "What about the bank?"

A grunt that said, *You're kidding.* "Need a court order before I can do anything about that. I'll drive back Monday afternoon."

Unhappiness underscored every word. His new suit ruined? The car? The destruction of evidence? Couldn't get worse, I thought.

It could. At home.

Zoloski shoved open the door, exposing a view of wreckage akin to the latest LA earthquake.

His jaw dropped. "Goddamn, son-of-a-bitch..." His hands clenched and unclenched as he stepped through the hurricane in the living room, to the tornado in the den. He came to a standstill at the door of the master bedroom.

At least the bed was in one piece, I thought as I numbly sank down against the mattress. I bent and extracted a pair of walking shorts and a T-shirt from the mess.

"What are you doing?"

I held up my blackened skirt. "Goodwill won't take this thing." I pulled on the shorts.

Zoloski shook his head. "I think women are from another universe," he murmured. A smile tugged at his lips. "But I like the view."

Warmth flooded my veins. How in the midst of chaos could we be half-smiling? Still glad to be alive? "I think your testosterone level is out of control. Or maybe it's mine."

His eyes promised mad, passionate, love—later.

The lines of his face hardened as he stared at the watercolor that hung over the bed. Crisp, bright, colors of the ocean, a profusion of sailboats spread across the bay, lay twisted in a broken frame. A jagged slash ran down the center. We'd bought it together to celebrate my moving in.

He pulled the cellular phone from his jacket pocket and began jabbing buttons. "...Get some people over here now! I want everything dusted for prints!" He disconnected, and looked at me.

"Cain?" I ventured. If he knew about the tapes he'd be motivated to get them back for Amerol. I said as much, but Zoloski didn't seem to hear. "Look at the bright side." *Ha*, my inner voice scoffed, matching the look on Zoloski's face.

I followed him down the hall. "At least they didn't get the tapes...." I trailed off, staring at the disaster in the kitchen. A skier's paradise of floury powder that would be a two day nightmare of cleaning.

And then I saw my painting—what was left of it. My one artistic endeavor from college that I'd contributed to Zoloski's decor. I'd called it "The Bell Jar" and yes it was a dark, brooding painting like Sylvia

Plath's life—but it represented a darkness in my soul that recovery had eased. Tears pricked my eyes. I picked it up.

The Z-man murmured something and hugged me.

I felt eight years old again—after my brother had burned all my toys—by mistake. Resolutely, I carried the mangled canvas out front to the garbage can and shoved it in. By the time I got back I wanted to put my hand through a wall.

Zoloski drew me to the door. "Since you're dressed in clean clothes, go pick up some take-out, I'll stay here."

I gaped. "You're hungry?" My stomach burned like a flame-thrower.

He studied the street. "Yeah."

Now what? Just trying to distract me from my pain? Why didn't I believe it? The tightness around his eyes? The line of his mouth? Was he planning to slam his fist through the walls, haul Cain's ass in for questioning? "Will you be here when I get back?"

His face softened, but his gaze skittered away. "Should be."

A half-assed answer if I ever heard one. "Leave a note on the fridge."

His lips curved. "Go," he said as a police car pulled into the drive.

"This is not teamwork," I protested.

He leaned in the window. "No, it's detective work. Go."

I sped to the nearest Chinese take-out, ordered broccoli shrimp and kung-pao chicken, and raced back. The police car was gone, Zoloski's Jag still in the drive—he hadn't left. Relief. Until I opened the front door.

Two cops were busy "dusting". The woman smiled. "Zoloski said you were bringing Chinese. How thoughtful."

I stifled a snarl and forced a smile. "I'll just leave it on the patio table, unless you've finished with the dining room?"

"Dining room's fine," the man chimed in. "We're almost through here. Just the bedroom and den left."

I set the bag on the table and dialed Zoloski's cellular. Fifty rings later I hung up. I eyed the cops. "Did Zoloski say when he'd be back?"

"A couple of hours," the man answered. "Said he'd send back the car if it was going to be longer."

"A robbery," the woman added.

Robbery or homicide? Did he know who did this?

"I'll be back," I promised, heading for the door. "Help yourselves to the food."

I DUG MY cellular from my purse while speeding on the freeway. Mario Andretti, watch out.

No sound when I punched the buttons. Dead batteries? I'd just charged the damn thing. It was obviously ready for the junk heap. I tossed the phone on the seat and gripped the steering wheel harder, images of Zoloski breathing down Cain's neck filling my head. I wanted to be there.

I pulled off on J street to use a phone. Got his voice mail. Damn! Now what?

I dialed Zoloski's cellular. No answer. I dialed home, got his voice on the machine. I tried Pat. Caught her at the missing person's desk. "Where is he?"

"Just a minute."

I tapped the side of the phone and waited.

"He's on a call. Convenience store robbery."

Not interrogating Cain? I felt disappointed, but I asked for the address. Maybe I could give him a lift home and we could still have dinner together, salvage something of this day.

"Thanks Pat. I owe you one."

A worried chuckle. "Try a hundred."

I promised dinner at Mace's, hung up, then hesitated. Zoloski wouldn't want me barging in on a robbery scene. But I had questions and I wanted to bounce more facts around. My brain was on automatic pilot. Where was Ken Woods?

On the way, I realized I hadn't told Lon I believed Xavier Juarez was in a grave marked with Ken's name. *Mañana.*

Settling back into the seat, foot heavy on the metal, I imagined Zoloski still wearing his blackened suit, inside the Seven-Eleven, talking to the owner who'd shot the robber.

Chapter 21

WHEN I PULLED into the gloomy, but busy parking lot, Zoloski looked as I'd imagined him—talking to the coroner, to the lab people, listening, jotting notes, completely absorbed. He looked up and scowled at my car. I wiggled my fingers at him through the windshield. Life is joy.

He zig-zagged past the people to join me as I opened the door.

"I thought you might need a ride home, and I have some ideas about Ken Woods."

His raised eyebrow said he knew a con job when he heard one. "I've got a ride home."

I crossed my arms. "I want to talk, not wait around at home for you to come through the door."

A skeptical look and a half-grin. "Okay, it's your butt. Plant it in the car and wait. I'll be out in an hour or so."

An hour!

He turned to go, then turned back, a big grin on his face. "Maybe you should go get your hair cut, then come back..."

"My hair?" I glanced in the mirror. Oh, hell. I'd lost an inch on one side, singed unevenly. I ran my fingers across the back, felt more jagged unevenness. Jolly great. I planted my backside on the pale grey leather, slammed the door and called, "See you in an hour," then, remembering I was in a parking lot with cops, sedately pulled onto Sutterville and headed down past the junior college headed toward a little hair studio near Broadway that I sometimes hit in desperation.

Forty-five minutes later, my hair now more layered and two inches above my shoulders, I returned to the parking lot. Zoloski was inside the store. I saw the back of his head, couldn't see who he was talking to. I turned on the inside light, and reached below the seat for a steamy romance—another of my stash.

But neither the heroine's hot exchanges with the hero, nor his bulging biceps, gripped me. Now that I'd taken care of my hair, the bomb explosion, Dimples, and all the facets of this case had my neck muscles tied in knots.

I sighed, took out a piece of paper and jotted down what I considered the facts to be now:

Ken Woods was:

(1) An informant for the FBI.

(2) Collecting evidence of money laundering against Anytime, Inc.; Amerol. Probably.

(3) Trying to convince Mohammed to help the FBI. Mohammed has a fake ID business going on the side, which Ken makes use of. Probably.

(4) Calling himself Karla Woods Johnson. Stashes cash there.

(5) Selling or transporting drugs? Probably.

(6) Dealing with Xavier Juarez. Probably.

I sat unblinking as pieces came together in an image of stark clarity and I seriously thought of Ken in the present tense—saw Ken as a murderer. An unpleasant question jogged my brain. Had Lon been duped, or was he up to his baby blues?

Was I completely off base about Amerol and Cain? Where did Martinez fit into the picture?

Tap, tap, tap. I jumped, almost put my head through the window.

Zoloski rapped on the glass again as I stilled my racing pulse. Frowning, I popped the lock and he climbed in.

I stifled a nasty comment about scaring the bejesus out of innocent females. The lines of his face were weary, the glimmer in his green eyes distant. He was far away. My Chinese dinner and brainstorming session were out.

I clicked on some background music and headed up I-80. He didn't notice as I whizzed past the Antelope offramp, past Riverside Blvd. and the blossoming city of Roseville, on up to Rocklin. Last thing I wanted to face was the Z-man's torn up house.

As I got off the freeway, Zoloski returned to the here-and-now. "Where're you going?"

I pulled into a hotel parking lot. Nice rooms, reasonable rates, breakfast included. Back in the annals of my pre-Zoloski history I'd spent a night here. The service had been great.

I got out and gave him the 'ol "hey fella, follow me for a good time" look.

A smile tugged at the corners of his lips as I signed in for a room with a king-size bed.

As we slid between the covers, skin-to-skin, he whispered, "I love you." A moment later, his breathing deepened.

No mad passion and no Q and A. Bummer days. I sighed and snuggled deeper into his arms, and listed questions in my head for our breakfast chat. I got to L—for Lying or Lon, before I sank into oblivion.

THE NEXT MORNING, Zoloski looked so sated and happy, I put my questions on hold for the road. Leaning back with a satisfied half-smile, his eyes sparkled with admiration.

"You look like the cat who ate the canary," I remarked as I hit the gas.

He grinned.

My face flamed.

"I like your hair," he said. "Short and sassy. Suits you."

Things were going too well to point out I was neither short nor sassy—in my opinion. I had a bunch of questions, starting way back with Mohammed's murder. "Was Mohammed killed with a similar knife to the one used on Ken's hands, uh, or Xavier's hands?" I blurted.

The grin vanished. "It's Sunday, day of rest and all that."

"We've had our *rest*. This is teamwork. You give, I give, and everybody's happy."

Zoloski raised an eyelid, groaned, and sat up. "You still owe me a few more favors, Sweetheart."

"Oh yeah?" I purred, running my hand up his thigh.

"Hey!" he howled, surprised.

I laughed, moved my hand back to the stick shift. "How about this? Ken Woods, AKA Karla Woods meets Xavier Juarez. Notices the resemblance between them. Cultivates friendship. Xavier needs an ID, asks Ken for help. Ken says no problem. In fact Xavier's played right into his scheme."

Zoloski's intent stare unsettled me. Did he think I was way off base or had I hit the nail on the head?

I plowed on. "He goes to DMV and applies for another license. A few weeks later, he gives it to Xavier. Now he's ready to disappear— no more Amerol or FBI problems. He murders Juarez and dumps the body. Two million plus just waiting to be spent."

Zoloski mulled it over, his gaze on the passing cars. "Except we have the corpse's hands and teeth." He looked at me. "And if they don't belong to Ken Woods, we'll know Tuesday. Ken would have burned them, or buried them, or dropped them in Lake Tahoe—some place where they'd never be recovered."

I pulled to the curb in front of Zoloski's house and looked at him. "So who put them in Lon's locker and why?"

Wheels turned. "Maybe Ken did. Maybe he lost his nerve and just wanted to dump them."

"Wouldn't Ken have needed help with the body—and everything? He wasn't a big guy." I couldn't keep the doubt out of my voice. Then I realized I'd just given Lon a subtle plug for the role of accomplice.

But Zoloski let it go with a shrug. "Why don't we chew on that while we clean?"

"First tell me once and for all, was the same knife used on Mohammed and Ken or his lookalike?" I followed him into the house.

"Once, and for all, maybe." His tone was grim, but I couldn't tell if it was from some inner vision of the murder scene or the disaster in the living room.

I told myself I'd paint some more pictures on my next vacation, and I could help Zoloski redecorate.

We started in the kitchen. I whooped when I found the expresso maker in one piece, and fixed some high octane caffeine. Stomachs warmed, brains stoked, vacuum roaring, we worked our way toward the master bedroom, finishing the task in time for dinner.

Zoloski threw together a pasta salad sprinkled with fat free cheese and we munched at the patio table. "You come up with any ideas?" I asked, swallowing the last salty noodle.

An enigmatic smile. "A few. Lets see what I get from the lab first."

I shot back a look of steely determination. I'd been patient. It was Sunday, going on Monday, I wanted facts.

"Whoever killed Mohammed wore gloves. The office was cleaned out. No files, no money, nothing." Zoloski got up and stacked the plates. I followed him inside. He ran water over the dishes and stacked them on the counter.

I found myself frowning.

"What?" he asked.

"You look good in the kitchen," I commented, half-meaning it, half-sarcasm. "A rare gem."

"Oh yeah?" He leaned against the counter. "Got a problem with the way I left the dishes?"

My back went up. "Why didn't you put them in the dishwasher?"

He crossed his arms. "Because it's tough to have a conversation over the noise. You know, if you want me to do something differently, you need to ask." His calm infuriated me. And so did the unreasonableness of my own expectations. Damn.

Zoloski finger-combed his hair. Dark, grey at the temples, it made him look like a Woodstocker gone conservative. "I'm going to work on the Jag."

That's right, *bail out.* I nodded.

He hiked an eyebrow, like "what, no protest?"

"Stephanos?"

He turned. "Yes."

I forced my gaze to meet his. "Asking's tough. I might have to hear NO. Somehow that equates to 'You don't love me.' I don't want to feel it."

The corners of his lips curled. He leaned over and kissed my cheek. "See ya in a while."

After he disappeared into the garage, I tapped my nails on the table, feeling useless, and wanting to do *something* to help Lon. I picked up the phone. Dialed.

Martinez answered.

"This is Blaize McCue."

"Hold on, I just walked in the door." I heard the murmur of voices, then silence. "Hello, Blaize?" He sounded friendly, a bit surprised.

"You wanted me to call," I reminded him.

"I wanted you to come to my place yesterday—alone."

"For a *swim*?"

A harsh laugh sounded in my ear, didn't sound like Martinez at all. "Okay, okay, so I came on a little strong. But I do have some information...." Soft breathing.

My gaze narrowed as though it would help me see through the phone line. "What?"

"Look, it's Lonnie boy's neck, not mine. You don't want to come over, fine."

I found my voice lowering to the same pitch as his. "What do you know?"

"More than Brown knows, that's for damn fucking sure." My vision of them in bed together evaporated.

"You have my attention. Talk to me."

A pause.

Considering options? What was he after? Somehow I didn't think it was a roll in the hay, or my unique counseling skills.

"My place. Wednesday night. Nine o'clock. The cop will work late. You'll be on your own. No wires, or no information." He hung up.

Now what? How did he know Zoloski would work late? I went into the garage. Zoloski couldn't hear me over the loud whir of his sander. I sat on the cement, watching my favorite hunk while thoughts roller-coastered through my brain. Would there be an emergency tomorrow night?

Lon's second hearing was in the morning, 10:00 a.m.; I had an appointment with his lawyer at 8:30. What did he want? I'd wait and see. If the fingerprints on the hands didn't match Ken's there wouldn't be a case. And I wouldn't need to talk to Martinez—unless I wanted to satisfy my curiosity.

Chapter 22

ZOLOSKI'S WARM breath tickled my ear. "Morning, Sweetheart," he whispered in a frisky voice. "Time to get up." From what I could feel he was already up.

"You avoiding work or just want to play?" I rolled on top, then glanced at the clock. "Shit! Seven-ten." I rolled off and slid from the bed. "We're supposed to be downtown by eight!" It'd take me half an hour to find a parking place. Zoloski was supposed to interrogate Martinez and meet Brown, but I figured he didn't need me to remind him.

He followed me into the bathroom. "Shower together?"

I grinned and turned on the water.

LO AND BEHOLD, Lon's lawyer had an office in the Ban Roll-on Building; Victor Amerol's elegant monstrosity of polished granite, marble and glass. Had to be a coincidence, I told myself, I'd given Lon the list of lawyers. He'd called one. Simple. Why didn't it feel simple? I figured Lon's lawyer wanted background information, but now I wondered. The last time I'd been here I got a whack on the head. I counted days. Almost two weeks. Nothing had been simple since.

I walked into the massive lobby, heels clicking on the speckled floor. The bank of silver elevators made me look like a squashed munchkin from Oz.

The elevator doors slid open without a sound. Well-oiled machinery meant taken-care-of. Money. Lots of money. I kept seeing the cash in Ken's deposit box, not enough to live forever, but two million was, and it was out there somewhere. I stepped inside the mirrored cavern where a hundred of me divided into infinity.

Slick as snot, the chamber lifted me to the eighth floor. Ken's office, where I first met Amerol was on the twelfth floor. Did Amerol and Jensen know each other? The unsavory, unsettling thought tasted like gunmetal.

How far did coincidence extend? A fatalist would say I was meant to make this appointment. But what else was I meant to do? Was somebody pulling the strings? Ken Woods? Amerol? The FBI?

I pushed open the door to Jensen's suite. Plush raspberry chairs, deep maroon carpet, massive oil landscapes on three walls. Money, money, money. I crossed the entry terrain, sinking up to my ankles in carpet. A middle-aged receptionist, thick glasses, short grey hair, and squinty eyes, glanced up from the manila folder open on the desk. "Yes?"

"I'm Doctor McCue, I have an appointment with Mr. Jensen." I handed her my card.

Her gaze took in my silk suit, Amali shoes, and the hand-carved beads at my throat. The matching earrings pulled on my lobes and I remembered why I never wore the darned things. She picked up the phone, murmured into it, smiled back at me. "He'll be right out. Why don't you have a seat?"

Though I was fifteen minutes late, "Right out" became another ten minutes. Jensen apologized from behind a walrus mustache, his beefy hand extended, giving me a strong, semi-sweaty shake. His face looked thirty, his thinning hair fifty, his physique sixty. A row of half-carat diamonds flashed from his wedding finger as he ushered me into his private office. It smelled of old cigar and musky aftershave. Eau de Walruses in the Sand.

Jensen's taste in furniture favored "legislative": old and powerful, massive and dark, a smear of light splashing between the half-drawn curtains, a glimmer of blue sky beyond the glass like a lighthouse beacon.

He gestured toward a chair, a huge throne that looked about as comfortable as a pin cushion. I sat, eyeing the chair alongside, a modern, padded high-back, covered in files.

"Thanks for coming," he said as he sat behind the desk and leaned back, his eyes half-closed, but still, trained on me.

I waited. This was his party.

He tapped his fingers together, the gesture thoughtful, the slight tightening around his eyes hinting at impatience. "Lon says you've been trying to find whoever might have killed Ken Woods. Have you found anything?"

I edged forward on the chair. Had Jensen been among the group of suits that always seemed to surround Amerol? "I may have something," I hedged. The right side of my brain said Jensen and I were on the same team, but the left suggested books and covers didn't always go together.

An engaging, you-can-trust-me, smile. I waited.

"Well, throw me a bone," he encouraged

"I'm not sure what I can tell you."

The smile faded. "Look, I've got a tight schedule, the bail hearing is at ten, and whatever you give me could help."

I sidestepped, "What do you think his chances are?"

The walrun mustache twitched. "Depends. The DA claims he's suicidal, a bail risk. Nothing's really changed. It'll probably be denied." His tone implied this was all routine. "The preliminary hearing is scheduled for Wednesday. Someone pulled strings to get it so quickly. Probably the DA—doesn't take much more than suspicion to bind over for trial. But if we could produce some evidence...That's where I was hoping for some help. If I can show that Lon isn't the only one with a motive or that there are more likely candidates, he could be released."

I gave him a regretful smile. If he was a top notch lawyer, he had investigators on his payroll. The chair squeaked as he straightened. "As of now, his chances of walking away aren't good." He leaned forward so that only four feet separated our faces. "Not unless you've got information that will help out."

Something flickered in his eyes. Like one of my clients who'd had a relapse. I didn't like it. I was biased. I didn't want to throw out the baby with the bath water, but I had yet to meet a baby in legal duds. "What have *your* investigators found?"

I could almost see the hair go up on his back. He didn't like being questioned. A casual shrug. "Nothing that helps Lon."

I wondered if Jensen knew about Xavier Juarez.

"Lon could get the death penalty." Pause. Jensen tapped a file folder on his desk with his fingers. "He is your friend, isn't he?" Seeing me nod, he said, "He needs help."

I wasn't falling for that line of bull. The case hadn't been held over for trial yet. Conviction was a long way off—of course, if Lon was denied bail again he'd be spending a lot of time in prison. "When I'm sure of what I've got, you'll be the first to know." I faked a sincere smile and picked up my purse.

A glimmer of frustration slipped into a pleasant lip line. "He said you're his best friend." The words sliced the air.

I resisted the urge to say, "I am."

"He said you had something, but didn't know what." A serious, intense look. "We're on the same side here, Doctor. Let's work together."

Was this a fishing expedition for Amerol, or was I getting paranoid?

He walked around the desk. "Lon thinks very highly of you." *But he won't after I relay this conversation,* his eyes added.

I ignored it, thought of Zoloski's words that the charge of Murder One would probably drop. "Is Lon going to be charged with manslaughter?"

The mustache twitched again. "I expected you would know. The DA's charged him with Murder One—I'm trying to negotiate a plea bargain—but they think they have an airtight case..." *Now will you help*? his gaze asked.

My stomach tightened, my mouth threatening to shoot out ammo to help Lon's case. I shut it with a snap. Until I checked this guy out I wasn't spilling my guts. Besides, the prints from the hands would be done today. If the body was Xavier Juarez, the DA would have no case against Lon. *If*. That word always haunted me like heartburn after a slew of chocolate chip cookies. No, Brown would see that the charges were dropped. She had a vested interest. Walrus breath could just stew in his juice a while longer.

On the way out I shook Jensen's hand, stifling the urge to wipe my palm on my "dry clean only" skirt. With an hour until the hearing, I couldn't resist going up to the twelfth floor—pursue the gut feeling that the receptionist knew something about Ken. Hopefully, Victor Amerol wouldn't be there—he wouldn't be glad to see me. Being caught in Ken's office last time had nearly given me a heart attack.

The receptionist was the only person in the lobby. She'd missed being pretty by a couple of centimeters, eyes too close, nose a touch too long, the type of woman I could see Ken using. She looked young and trusting. She glanced up from her polished desk, her smile turning into a frown. She obviously hadn't forgotten the unceremonious way Cain had escorted me to the lobby. She reached for the phone, her movement jerky and flustered.

I strode across the carpet like an imperious Egyptian queen, not as tall as the huge urn in the entry, but I hoped every bit as intimidating as I leaned over her desk, weight on my palms. Amerol wasn't around and I was determined to follow my instincts.

She fumbled the receiver. "You're not supposed to be here. I'm going to call s-security." Her gaze fluttered anxiously left and right.

I gave her the accusing one-eye. "Ken Woods is alive."

Alarm flickered in her grey eyes, but not surprise.

Bingo!

Her hands knitted together. "No." A whisper of denial.

I leaned closer. "And you're protecting him." I felt like a heel, but every intuition said I was right.

She hesitated, one hand moved back to the receiver, the other clenched in her lap.

"I can help him...Get you both out of trouble..." My voice trailed off. Her eyes widened as the implication she could be in danger sank in. I waited.

Her mouth worked, but no words came.

Footsteps. Luck running out? I didn't turn, but slid my business card across the desk. "Call me," I said softly. "I can help."

She slid the card into her lap. I turned around and practically collided with Cain. He gripped my arm and propelled me for the door.

Outside, it was a mild 70 degrees, but I was sweating. Instead of tossing me on my ear, he was moving down the sidewalk, his fingers like steel. He stopped abruptly, right about where I'd gotten whacked on the head. His dark eyes bored into mine. "Next time you won't wake up." His hand fell away. "Stay away from Pronowske."

I stood there, frozen, watching as he ambled back into the Ban building as though nothing had happened. Well, technically, nothing had. So why were my legs like gelatin?

The strings I was pulling were leading to a scary place, but I couldn't stop myself. Maybe that was why Lon asked me to help—he knew my compulsive need to finish what I started. I didn't like the thought any more than harassing the receptionist and getting threatened by Cain.

Chapter 23

I WAS LATE—the bail hearing over. "Bail denied again," Zoloski said when I called him from the courthouse. "Don't worry about the charge, they'll drop it down." I wasn't reassured—too many surprises these days. I started to tell him about Cain when he apologetically said he had another call.

Turning, I moved to one side of the phone and ducked my head. Lon's lawyer walked by. Talking with Amerol! I tried to call Zoloski back, got nowhere.

The rest of the day passed in the same sense of frustration. I saw two clients, finally talked to Zoloski again, just long enough to learn he had another homicide and he'd be home around ten; he'd be at Lon's preliminary hearing Wednesday morning; and he and Brown would go to the bay area that evening. He didn't give me a chance to speak.

Tuesday evening, I watched a public television nature special, and thumbed through the phone book.

C. Pronowske. No address. Damn. I dialed.

"Hello?" Cautious tone.

"Ms. Pronowske?"

A guarded "Yes."

"I'm with Colton, Baker, and Petard Real Estate. We're helping homeowners such as yourself buy and sell. Are you interested in selling your home?"

"I live in an apartment."

"Oh...I thought the apartments were being converted to condos," I murmured. "I heard many of the tenants were looking to buy." I hoped she wouldn't think too hard about what I said.

"Condos?" Incredulousness replaced the annoyance. "This dump? No way." But she sounded slightly unsure.

"Isn't this the complex on L?" I asked in a puzzled tone.

A disgusted reply, "Try 53rd and F." Click.

Okay. I jotted it down, checked the time and decided to wait until the next evening when Zoloski would be out of town.

WEDNESDAY ARRIVED. The Z-man was out the door before me, but promised he'd meet me outside the courtroom at nine forty-five.

My nerves felt frayed as I hurried into the hallowed court of Lady Justice, inner sanctum of law and ancient English ritual. Of course, these days a trial cost the taxpayers a million bucks and then we got the privilege of supporting the convicted in style. In merry old England, after the verdict, they took the chap outside and whacked off his head.

As my heels tapped down the cavernous hallway, now nearly empty, the vision of decapitation coughed up a mental picture of hands chopped off and teeth yanked out. I glanced around, half-expecting Amerol behind me, circling like a Great White. *Nada.*

Zoloski was outside the courtroom, his ear glued to a cellular, his eyes lighting up as he zeroed in on me. A sight for sore eyes. He waved me over. I was dying to tell him about Amerol and Jensen, also about Cain's warning regarding Cynthia Pronowske—we'd only had the one way conversation the day before, and I was eager to hear about his interrogation of Martinez, which he'd sidestepped.

"No," he said into the phone, "I can't. Not until the lab analysis comes back." Pause. "You want guarantees, talk to God." Pause. "Yeah, right." A good natured laugh escaped his lips. "See ya."

He gave me a light hug. "You're late," he murmured, an appreciative glimmer in his green eyes.

I remembered Tuesday morning's hot shower and felt warm all over. "What's up?"

He pointed to the docket beside the door. "Lon's number three. Second one's almost finished."

As we entered, the clerk read Lon's name. He was already at the defense table, Jensen at his side. No Amerol. I felt a combination of relief and disappointment.

The judge looked down from his high throne, his face a railroad map of ancient history, eyes that said he'd seen it all before, an air of impatience cloaked him like an extra black robe.

The Assistant DA, dressed in a charcoal suit that fit like expensive Saran Wrap, made a brief statement, sighting the evidence collected at Lon's apartment before presenting pictures of the wrecked living room and the cut on Lon's hand. He continued, "The defendant has no alibi. But plenty of motive: jealousy and greed."

Great, they knew about Ken's affair with Dimples. Zoloski's doing? He didn't look at me, but stared studiously ahead. Where was Brown?

Finally, the prosecution stated that Lon had committed first degree murder in a jealous rage...then severed the hands of his victim..."

I was shocked. I had thought Brian Jensen was bluffing yesterday about the charge. Lon was in deep kimchee.

The judge's tired gaze swiveled to the defense lawyer with the unspoken statement, Let's get this over with so I can get done by lunch, hanging in the air.

Jensen rose, straightened his tie, unbuttoned his jacket and shuffled across the tile. To give him credit, he took on a Dustin Hoffman vulnerability that a jury might find appealing. "Your honor, my client is innocent. There is absolutely no reason to believe he committed this heinous crime. Yes, he did have a fight with the victim. But the victim was very much alive when he left." Jensen even got the Hoffman whine right. "Mr. Wilson is a man of honor, a hard-working architect, a valued member of society with no past record of wrong-doing. He's already spent a week in jail. He deserves bail."

The judge's craggy-lined face rearranged itself into pure impatience. He looked at Lon. "Bail was denied, is still denied." His gaze swiveled to Jensen. "You have any hard evidence to present?"

"No, your honor."

"How do you plead?"

Jensen managed a hang-dog expression that brought murmurs of compassion from the few onlookers seated in the courtroom. "My client is innocent. We plead not guilty." God, the scales of justice were soapy. Maybe a prerequisite for law school should be acting.

The judge nodded. "Okay," he growled, "a plea of not guilty to first degree murder will be entered." He glanced at his calendar. "Defendant is bound over for trial." He set the date, only a month away, the gavel sounded and another case was called before I could get my bearings. Lon, now a pale, dazed Robert Redford, was whisked out of the room by the bailiff, Jensen talking in his ear. I grabbed Zoloski's arm, pulled him through the doors, and hurried down the hall, just in time to see the elevator shut behind Lon. He hadn't seen me.

I jabbed the button, then glared at Zoloski. "What the hell is going on? I thought Lon was going to be charged with second degree, or manslaughter, or better yet, the charges would be dropped?"

"Hold it down, Blaize!" Zoloski shot back, guiding me from the courthouse to the shade of a huge plantered tree. "I talked to Brown. She's not willing to talk to the DA until she's got her case against Anytime, Inc. sewed up. Mohammed's murder threw a wrench into it. She needs time."

"I want Lon out! She can do that much. Or maybe he should just sue the shit out of her and the government."

Zoloski didn't react.

"Is she after Amerol? I saw him and Jensen together yesterday. Whatever Jensen knows, you can bet Amerol does too."

Zoloski digested the news with his usual calm, the wheels shifting inside his head, rolling behind the concentrated glimmer in his eyes. "You need to talk to Brown," he said.

"About the tapes? Amerol? Jensen?"

He sighed. "Yes, yes, and yes."

"Where is she?"

"Good question." He hustled me across the street and down another block to his office.

While he talked on the phone, looking for Brown, I sat and thought about the people I needed to question.

1. Lon. I needed to tell him about Xavier Juarez and the possibility Ken was alive, *and* warn him about Jensen.

2. Ken's receptionist.

3. Martinez. He claimed he had more information than Brown. Why wasn't he sharing it with her?

Why tell me? I'd find out tonight.

Zoloski hung up. "We're to meet her at the federal building on Cottage Avenue."

THE JAG, SMOOTH sleek curves again, but dull gray instead of yellow, purred under Zoloski's control. I resisted the urge to tell him what a great job he'd done on the hood. It would only remind him of our narrow escape, and the house. "Did Martinez show up yesterday at eight?"

Zoloski nodded. "Looked like a banker, pinstripe suit and all." His mouth tightened. "Federal asshole." A glimmer of satisfaction. "But he slipped once."

"How's that?" Not quite the time to mention my date.

"He said he was working with Nicole the night Ken was murdered. I checked with the company. He's on their roster, but Jackson said he showed up at noon, stayed until nine, then went home. Said he wasn't feeling well. She agreed to cover for him."

"And she just volunteered this?" I asked, my brain reeling. He could have seen who murdered Ken.

He winked. "No. I impressed on her the penalty for perjury."

An image of Zoloski talking softly into Nicole's ear came to mind, pure sex appeal radiating from him like a guy on one of my romance covers.

Your turn, my brain nagged. Despite the sun beating down on the rag top, heating the car to a broil, I went cold. "I've got some news."

Zoloski hit the gas and jockeyed toward the freeway's left lane. I wished I was in the driver's seat. "I'm listening," he said easily.

"I talked to Martinez..."

A snort.

"He said he knew a lot more than Brown, stuff that would help Lon, but I'd have to meet him to get the information."

"The guy's got a thing for you."

"I know."

He cocked an eyebrow, his expression unreadable. "You want to go? See what you can get?"

Well, he hadn't hit the roof, that was a good sign. "I'm curious," I admitted.

"When's he want to meet?"

"Tonight, nine o'clock, his place."

His gaze narrowed thoughtfully. "Bunnie and I will be in San Francisco checking the safety deposit box, impounding its contents, and grilling O'Malley. I won't be back until late. I don't like the idea of you meeting him alone."

My sentiments exactly, but I was also afraid backup might scare him off.

Zoloski shot me an unreadable look. Trust issues? We saw things differently that was for damned sure. "Do I need to chain you to the bed, or will you promise to stay home, talk to Martinez in a couple of days?"

I sidestepped. "Martinez knew you'd be working late."

His jaw tightened, but his pager beeped. He handed me the cellular. "Dial, will you?"

I did, then handed it back.

"Zoloski here. What do you have?" He listened, shot a look at me I couldn't decipher, murmured, "Yeah?" and listened some more. "Okay, good job. Talk to ya later."

I waited.

We got off the freeway at Fulton Avenue, passed a number of used-car lots, hit a red light. His eyes were watchful. "That was the lab. The hands and teeth definitely belong to Xavier Juarez."

Although I'd expected confirmation, I nevertheless felt momentary relief. Still, I wasn't ready to rejoice. "I assume the charges will be dropped," I said, studying Zoloski's profile as he considered.

He shook his head as we zipped past one car lot after another, before turning down Cottage Way. "Maybe not. Let's talk to Brown."

What the hell was there to talk about? I wanted reassurance. "What about my meeting with Martinez?"

"We'll wait and see. Give me a few days, okay?" *Before you do anything rash*, his expression added.

I nodded.

He parked and I followed him inside the large L-shaped two-story. With its dark, floor length windows and panels of concrete, the block-like structure reminded me of a double row of piano keys. No trees, no greenery, no camouflage.

The moment we entered, I felt the surveillance cameras. After casting a smile at the ceiling sprinkler, I scanned the huge entry for a directory. Zoloski started up the stairs.

Normally I run stairs, but not in heels. My toes felt like crushed Wheaties by the time we hit the second floor.

Zoloski held out his hand. "Down here."

I peered at a brightly lit, three-block-long hallway, and stifled a groan. Sure as hell, Brown's office was at the end.

She ushered us inside and closed the door. Just enough room for a desk, computer, file cabinet, and a couple of padded chairs. Out the window I saw the parking lot and Zoloski's Jag. In the corner, her jacket hung on a plastic hanger from a three-pronged coat rack.

Zoloski leaned against the wall, filling Ms. Centerfold in on Jensen. I sat down and flexed my toes. Sweet agony.

He told her everything including my date with Martinez—everything except my go-round with Ken's receptionist, which I'd forgotten to mention. I opened my mouth to fill in the gap, but the look Brown gave Zoloski closed it. She leaned close, drawing his gaze to her magnificent cleavage, her pink tailored blouse open at the neck. I stifled an urge to give him a kick in the shin.

"So what's the deal here?" I interrupted.

Ms. Brown straightened, sat on the edge of her desk and crossed her Barbie doll legs. Damn, what happened to professional demeanor?

Zoloski studied the wall. Lucky for him.

"The deal is," Brown said, "you forget you ever saw the tapes, or heard them. I'll make sure the charges against *your friend,* Mr. Wilson, are dropped." She said "friend" like we were much more than chummy.

I bristled. Oh, so Lon was supposed to be the hostage. Not much of a deal since Ken Woods wasn't the corpse and Lon would have no reason to kill some guy he never knew. I said as much, pushing back the thought of Lon being an accomplice.

Brown smirked. "Wilson knew Xavier Juarez. We know they met at least once at Crawdad's, and we know Juarez went to Wilson's condo the night he was murdered."

My mouth dropped. I felt like I'd swallowed my tongue. A lover's triangle? With look-alikes? Talk about the Narcissus complex.

Brown crossed her arms, a triumphant gleam in her eyes. "I think Wilson and his lover Ken Woods planned the murder and carried it out. And I think Martinez saw what happened that night and is playing some inside game." She pressed back on the desk with her palms and leaned forward. "For *whatever* reason, I think he wants to tell you. I want you to reschedule your meeting with Martinez for tomorrow night. We'll equip you with a wire, be with you every step."

Zoloski shook his head. "No way."

Had he hoped to talk me out of the meeting? Or did he not want Brown involved? It didn't matter. I knew what I had to do. I stood. "I want to talk to Lon. Alone. No one listening in. If I get the right answers, I'll do it."

Zoloski scowled.

Brown nodded, picked up the phone and handed it to me. "Call Martinez. I'll arrange your meeting with Wilson."

Martinez answered on the third ring, his voice raspy with sleep. Working overtime in bed?

"This is Blaize McCue. I've got an emergency with a client. Attempted suicide. Can't meet tonight."

Brown's eyes gleamed and she nodded. Zoloski paced to the window and looked out.

I hurried on, "I can meet you tomorrow night. Zoloski has a volleyball game. He won't be home til eleven."

Martinez' breath whistled into the phone. I imagined his lips pursed. "All right. Tomorrow. Same time." Pause. "Don't be late." *Click.*

I handed the phone to Brown. "Tomorrow night, nine o'clock."

She set up my meeting with Lon, then hung up. "Twelve-thirty. You get twenty minutes alone."

I glanced at my watch. 11:40. We'd have to hustle back downtown—good old lunch time traffic.

She walked to the door and opened it. "Detective Zoloski and I have some details to discuss. I'll have my assistant drive you to the jail, then bring you back for the wire, go over procedure."

"Procedure?"

An impatient gesture with her hand. "How close you need to be to

pick up voices. What you should say if you get in trouble."
Condescension lay in her tone—like I was a moron.

"Martinez said no weapons, no wires, or no information."

"No problem." The words rolled off her tongue a bit too easy, but
I figured I'd pursue that kettle of fish later. She led the way into the hall
where the assistant she'd mentioned was waiting like an eager puppy.
For some reason, his stuck-out ears made me think of a beagle. She said
to me, "Come in tomorrow for another run through." She glanced at
Zoloski. "We like to be thorough..."   When he didn't respond to her
innuendo, she looked at me again. "Four o'clock okay?"

Thursday. No clients that late. "Fine."

"I'll drive her downtown," Zoloski broke in, "bring her back.
We'll talk then."

Brown masked irritation behind a gracious smile. "Over lunch?"

I stifled the image of her knees pressed against his beneath a table.

Zoloski shrugged. "Fine."

The beagle looked confused as I left on Zoloski's arm. The Z-man
remained ominously quiet all the way to the parking lot. "Dammitall
Blaize, you're driving me crazy!" he said in a low, intense voice. "I
don't want you walking into a potential trap like fish bait!"

I had my own fire. "How long have you known that Juarez and
Lon knew each other?"

Stoney silence.

"You keep holding back, but you want me to tell you everything!
And why the switch upstairs—you didn't seem to mind me meeting
Martinez with you as backup."

"I had my reasons," Zoloski ground out. "I don't trust Brown."

"It's just a conversation. Martinez is a cop."

"*I'm the detective! Remember*?"

Now I knew what the issue was. I was treading on his territory. I
knew this was coming...so why did I feel like I'd been kicked in the
teeth? Well, I couldn't back down now—wouldn't. Looking at his tight
jaw, angry eyes, I almost hated him. Almost—the operative word. I
didn't want to lose him, but he had to accept me, flaws and all. I hoped
push wouldn't come to shove.

Chapter 24

ABOUT HALFWAY TO the jail, Zoloski broke the wall of silence. "When's your first client?"

I felt remote, like I was already distancing myself from him in case the worst happened, my mind focused on Lon.

"You said you had appointments this afternoon," he added when I didn't respond right away.

Oh yeah. I swiveled in the bucket seat, mentally shifting gears. "First appointment's at two."

I thought he would follow with another ice breaker, but he lapsed into more silence. I studied his profile, the angular planes of his jaw, the straight nose, shadow of beard. I felt like I'd known him for halfway to forever. Too long to just walk away like I might have done in my twenties.

I mustered up a soft voice. "What do you think's going on, Stephanos?"

Like a shadow, an equivocal look crossed his face. "Will you stay home tomorrow night if I answer? Stay away from anyone and everyone connected to this case?" His tone said he anticipated a refusal.

Would it be the end if I said no? I hesitated. Cars whined by on the freeway like jackals zooming in on a carcass. Lunchtime. Heading for the trough.

He shot me a look that flickered with pain. He didn't like where we were at right now any better than I. His voice was soft. "I think Lon's involved up to his pretty blue eyeballs."

Not what I wanted to hear.

"But Brown said she'd get the charges dropped."

"She has her own theory. I have mine." He shot me an unreadable look. "I might buy an unwilling accomplice theory." Pause. "However Lon got involved, I think he got a hell of a lot more than he bargained for."

Was he just offering comfort, or did he mean it? I believed Lon was innocent—I'd seen his anguish over Ken's disappearance, his reaction to identifying the body at the morgue—real stuff—not an act. Yet he knew something. All along I'd felt he was holding back and hadn't pushed. Now I had to.

WITH THE Z-MAN waiting outside, a guard escorted me through the sallyport and into a small interrogation room. The walls were bare, the metal table and two chairs like leftovers from the city dump. I sat down, the door opened and Lon was ushered in. The guard nodded at me, backed out and closed the door. The lock clicked and I felt like holding my breath until I got out. I took a deep breath instead, squelching butterflies.

Lon, dressed in drab blue prison garb looked more forlorn than ever.

I hardened my resolve not to fall for the easy smile that had often accompanied shared confidences. All the times I'd spent on the phone with him, or chatting over dinner, enjoying his friendship haunted me as I studied him in silence, determined not to fall for those pretty blues. He hadn't leveled with me about Juarez. Would he lie to me again?

"I didn't see you this morning," he said, his voice raspy. Dark circles shadowed his eyes.

"I was in the back. Came in late."

"So—" His gaze asked what this was about.

I remembered the cigarettes I'd brought and pulled them from my jacket. As I handed them over, I noticed he'd bitten his fingernails to the nub.

He managed a smile after the second drag. "Thanks."

I leaned forward, my arms on the table, and dropped my voice. "We have twenty minutes. No one's listening, or watching."

"Doctor—patient?"

"Yes."

"So, you think I killed Ken?"

It came so unexpectedly, so out of left field, that I couldn't think what to say. I stared. "No," I said. "I think there's a lot you haven't told me. Ken's alive. Xavier Juarez is dead."

He blanched and I wondered which half of the news caused it.

"Jesus," he mumbled, the cigarette bobbing between his lips.

"The FBI thinks you and Ken murdered Juarez."

He shook his head, his gaze pensive as he glanced around the room.

"You knew Juarez. Trent at Crawdad's said he saw the two of you," I passed on Brown's information.

"That's impossible!" Lon snapped. "I met *Ken* there all the time. Trent has them confused."

I leaned forward, our eyes a foot apart. My voice was hard and I hated the anger welling up inside me, but he'd lied to me, and damn it, I wasn't buying this time. "I want the whole story. Now. You've got fifteen minutes. You talk or I walk." He wasn't asking the right questions, like "Who the hell's Juarez?" and he obviously knew Ken and Juarez looked alike. Would he flush our friendship and all I'd done down the sewer?

"Blaize, I'm sorry...I didn't know it would go this far, that Ken would—" He shuddered. "I was just trying to help...nothing else. I swear I didn't do anything."

I stared at his hands, thought about the friendly comfort his arms had offered, the hours he'd listened to my gripes and groans as I worked out problems aloud. Now I wondered just what those hands were capable of. Given the right circumstances people were capable of anything. But what circumstances?

I took a cigarette, lit a match and inhaled. The nicotine made me dizzy, almost sick. I put it out. "Did you know Ken was alive when you ID'd the body?"

A quick "No."

"But you knew before today?"

A slight hesitation, eyes on the floor, then a nod.

"Tell me."

Lon looked at me. "Everything I told you about Ken's secretiveness, his drinking, is true."

I thought about Martinez' information that drug money was involved. "Was Ken using?"

Something flickered in his eyes and my brain made a leap.

"Is that where you got the heroin when you OD'd? From Ken?" More questions lined up in my head.

A nod. "I found it when I was packing his things." A spark of addict's lust shaded his expression as he looked past me at the blank wall, inhaling nicotine down to his toes. "I figured, just once..." A self-belittling snort finished the sentence.

"So Ken was drinking, using, and secretive." I summarized.

A nod. He fingered the matches. "Mid-August he broke down. Cried. Told me he had a client who was crooked. That he'd accepted bribes. God, once he started talking...I couldn't believe it! Ken working both sides, helping the FBI get evidence to nail the guy..." He shrugged.

Drug money.

"They offered him immunity and protection." Lon sucked on his cigarette like a vacuum cleaner. "What Ken didn't tell them was that he'd stolen money from his client."

"How much?"

"I don't know. A lot." He rubbed out his cigarette and lit another.

I bore in with my eyes as I thought of the two million. "Enough to kill for?"

"No!" But his gaze skidded away.

Oh, how I wanted to believe him. "Who was Ken's contact in the FBI?"

Lon shook his head. "He never told me."

I gave him another hard look.

"I don't know," he insisted.

"What happened next?"

Lon's gaze grew cloudy. "Near the end of August, Ken asked me to meet him at Crawdad's after work."

"Why?"

"He said he thought the condo might be under surveillance. He didn't feel safe." His lips curled. "I told him he was crazy. He told me his client might have found out about the missing money. That he might wind up dead."

Lon glanced at me, then away.

"Go on."

"It seemed too fantastic, like a movie or something. I really didn't believe his life was in danger. He loved to overreact."

"Did he tell you who his client was?"

"He mentioned a group of investors, said the man in charge was powerful."

Victor Amerol? "Let's get back to Juarez."

Lon hand trembled as he brought the cigarette to his mouth, took a deep pull, exhaled, sighed. "That Friday, when Ken disappeared, I came home, planned a nice dinner. He staggered in around eleven, half-lit." Lon looked away. "Juarez was with him. Ken introduced us." He closed his eyes. "The way he said his name...I knew..."

I could almost taste Lon's anguish, feel the betrayal. Had Ken told him this was the first time? Was that why Lon had been so shocked in San Francisco by Dimple's admission regarding the Ken/Karla Woods affair? It made sense.

"I wanted to kill him." His gaze shifted uneasily.

Bad choice of words? I held my breath.

"He tried to pass Juarez off as someone he'd met at Crawdad's, but it was too late..."

I swallowed, Lon's words creating a scene in my brain like a bad play:

Ken hitting Lon, Lon swinging back, Juarez getting into it, blood everywhere. A real melee. Lon gets a shiner, and a broken coffee table, Ken gets a split lip and mean mouth. Ken and Juarez leaving together.

"Ah shit." Lon finished his cigarette, his eyes downcast. "He never explained why he brought Xavier."

"Because he knew you'd fly off the handle. Maybe he set you up."

His face twisted in denial, but I could see he believed it. "No."

The fight would explain all the blood, but not Juarez's death. Eight minutes left. "Didn't you notice the resemblance between Ken and Juarez?"

A sharp look. "I was too pissed to notice." His hand shook as he lit another smoke. "Lot's of guys have dark hair, dark eyes and that kind of build."

But he noticed at some point. Anybody would. "Then what?"

A note of regret tinged his voice, "I never saw either of them again."

I believed him, but I had to test the waters. "If you killed Juarez in a fit of passion it's second degree murder. Think about it."

Lon studied the ceiling. "I didn't kill him." The softness in his voice sounded like an admission of guilt.

I brought out the heavy ammo. "You identified Juarez as Ken at the morgue." I couldn't keep the betrayal out of my tone. One minute he claimed he didn't notice the resemblance, and the next he wanted me to understand how he could identify the wrong man as his lover.

Lon crossed his arms, leaned over his knees as though sick. "I thought it was Ken! I didn't find out until—"

I got up, went over and crouched beside him. "Until when?"

"Until Ken called me," he croaked. "At Curly and Moe's. That's why I got plastered." A pause. "I thought it was a joke, but the voice..." He rubbed his eyes. "He said he knew who killed Juarez. That he was next if he didn't get out of town. But he had a deal to finish up. Told me he'd call in a few days." He glanced around. "But I haven't been home...You called to say Zoloski was on the way to arrest me."

"Did Ken tell you who killed Juarez?"

"No."

A damn good story. Too good? My brain backtracked. "Why didn't you tell me? Zoloski and I nearly got ourselves killed in Ken's apartment." I pressed, "After you ID'd Ken, you must have thought Juarez killed Ken. Why didn't you say anything? Because you knew

Ken was alive?" I wanted every detail, some convincing evidence that would assure me he was telling the truth.

"I was ashamed." His voice dropped, low, hoarse, tortured. "I thought Ken was dead. Dragging his name through the mud by mentioning Juarez..."

"No," I interrupted, in no mood for BS. "You didn't want *your* name dragged through the mud." A lover's triangle would have made splashy headlines. But an unidentified body buried as John Doe—who would care?

His head snapped up. "It wasn't like that."

I remembered him begging and pleading for me to search for Ken. "Then why didn't you tell me the truth about the fight?" God, I hated playing the heavy.

He rubbed out the cigarette and lit another. He'd gone through half a pack. "I didn't want to admit Ken wasn't faithful...Didn't want to face it..." He shrunk inside his skin like a penis in a cold shower. His voice rang with sincerity, but it was the anguish in his eyes I believed. God, denial ran deep. How often had I refused to see the signs of Ross' infidelity before confronting it? It wasn't something I wanted to broadcast.

I waited.

Lon inhaled half the cigarette, put it out abruptly, then snorted derisively. "I've always needed someone, Blaize. Man or woman—didn't matter. Anything not to feel abandoned." A pained smile tore at his face.

His words and seeing him like this hurt, but I was finally getting the truth.

"God, with every relationship abandonment hits me all over again." His hands clenched. His lips disappeared into a tight agonized line. "Ken was just like my dad. Couldn't keep his pants zipped. I was such a fucking failure...and I couldn't bear the thought of you knowing..." His head sank lower as he leaned over his knees again.

"You're like a brother to me," I said slowly. "Always have been. I may have jumped to the conclusion that you were gay, but only because I wanted our relationship to be a friendship. I liked you because of your humor—the way you could make me laugh at life's aches and pains." I made myself go on. "I needed to learn how to laugh. You gave me that." I reached out and squeezed his hand, then slowly got to my feet, easing the tightness in my knees.

He didn't look up.

A rap on the door startled me.

Damn. I wanted more time to sort through my feelings.

Lon stood awkwardly, his athlete's grace gone.

A wave of love and sorrow engulfed me. God knows, I wasn't perfect. He'd lied—come clean—that was an amends of sorts...I hugged him, arms closing around a wooden soldier who now seemed hell bent on self-destruction.

The jingle of keys, the sound of the door. Lon softened, returned my hug, and whispered, "I didn't kill him."

The guard led him away.

I believed him. But if he didn't, who did? Nerves jangled like crossed telephone wires, I tried to suppress everything and turn it into a smile as I joined Zoloski. Wordlessly he handed me my purse, slid an arm around my shoulder and walked me to the car. God knows what he saw on my face. Street noise hummed and buzzed in my ears like a drone of bees. I felt as twisted inside as a pair of nylons run through the washing machine. Still trying to get my head on straight, I wondered where I should go next with finding the killer and freeing Lon?

On the way to my car, Zoloski asked, "What'd he say?"

I sighed, would have liked to bounce everything off the Z-man, except damn it he was a fucking cop. No way I was going to violate my doctor—patient oath.

"Whatever he said upset you," Zoloski said.

Concern or curiosity? I studied his profile but it told me nothing. I knew it would irritate him, but I said, "I can't talk about it."

He frowned. "Can't or won't?"

"Can't."

"Did he shoot my theory of Ken coercing him into helping with the body?"

The man never gave up.

"Did he explain why Juarez's blood was found in his living room?" Zoloski goaded as he pulled up beside my Saturn. "The fact Juarez was wearing Ken's clothes?"

No way would I blurt out Lon's story. "Ask Lon." I climbed out of the Jag. "See you in Brown's office."

Zoloski's tight expression said he would get back to me later. He sped off, and I felt forlorn as I climbed in my car.

My thoughts moved to Martinez. He knew something. But whatever he told me, the FBI would be recording. What if his information hurt Lon? Would I be setting Lon up for the gas chamber?

If only I could find Ken. *Cynthia Pronowske.* I remembered Ken's receptionist's worried frown, the spark of knowledge and fear in her eyes. She knew he was alive. And Cain didn't want me near her. I would talk to her, see what I could find out.

My life was full of good intentions.

Chapter 25

BACK AT THE federal building, Centerfold Brown wanted me to wear a cigarette pack-sized recorder that looked like junk and weighed down my jacket. "He sees that and he'll be shoving me out the door."

She handed it to the worshipful beagle-eared assistant. "See what's available."

Beagle Ears left and Zoloski came in. "Had to stop by the office." His expression was not exactly happy and the tension between us as wide as the Grand Canyon. He didn't want me here. I wanted to do this.

The beagle returned with a small clip mike and transmitter the size of a quarter, and a lipstick-sized repeater transmitter. Brown put the wireless in my palm. "You can wear it in your bra. It'll pick up everything within four or five feet. The repeater transmitter will stay in your purse. It'll pick up the low level transmissions from the mike and blast it to any recorder set to this frequency—which we'll have set up in a van. No matter how far away you are, as long as you and the transmitters aren't too far apart, we'll record everything your mike picks up."

Not reassuring if Martinez' information hurt Lon.

Her eyes narrowed. "Make sure you're facing him when he talks to you."

Just so long as he keeps his hands to himself. I went to the ladies restroom, snuggled the mike down between my less than Double-D mounds, put the repeater transmitter in my purse, and gave the mike a test. At her desk, Brown caught every word with my little voice-activated recorder set to the correct frequency. Worked like a charm. Hope I remembered to wash my hands.

Brown actually smiled as she ushered me to the door. "See you tomorrow." But then she was going to be in San Francisco with Zoloski for the night. And he and I were barely speaking to each other. Peachy keen.

Zoloski walked me to my car. "I'll call you from the hotel. If something comes up, you can page me." But the words sounded stiff. Where was Bogie when I needed him?

Would Pronowske lead me to Ken? "Nothing's going to come up. Drive safe." I dropped my voice, did a terrible Bogart imitation, "Okay,

Sweetheart?"

Despite his anger, a smile cut across his face. He shook his head at me as though he didn't know whether to lecture me or hug me.

I slipped my arms around him. "I'll miss you."

"We'll talk when I get back," he conceded, his green eyes softening. He looked pensive as I waved goodbye. I watched his long-legged stride take him back into the building. I missed him already.

I BARELY BEAT my first client into the office. Scooping mail into a pile, I ignored the blinking red eye of Ma Bell.

Eleanor, my first client, walked in. Fifty minutes whizzed by. She'd gone to two more Co-SLAA meetings, gotten phone numbers, made some calls—was starting to get support from others beside her boyfriend. Good. Two more clients passed in a blur of passive-aggressive messages. The third was having a bad hair day. After a good dose of mirroring his words and body language with empathy, he managed some acceptance.

My last client blathered a million reasons why she should quit therapy, quit AA, and join a monastery. "Sounds like an addict looking for a parent and some boundaries," I offered knowing she wouldn't like hearing it. She scowled. Like a dog chasing its tail, she circled a little more, then laughed. "God, am I feeling sorry for myself! Guess I better hit a meeting, get an attitude adjustment and count my blessings."

I smiled back. "See you next week." Damn it's great to win some. Feeling satisfied, I shut the door, jotted a few notes and closed her file. On my desk, the red eye still glared. I hit the button. Listening to messages I rummaged through my bottom drawer for the pair of flats. No matter how great they made my legs look, I would never buy another pair of three-inch heels.

I called Pat to talk to her about some of the shit going on between Zoloski and me. I still felt unsettled by our superficial parting. But she was on vacation for the week. Hubby Arnie was ruining my good friend's availability. I'd have to work this out on my own.

"Ms. McCue." The muffled male voice from the recorder caught my ear. "Stay away from Martinez. Stay home tonight. Stay safe."

Jeez, Louise. I replayed the message. The guy had a faint accent, not Zoloski's deep baritone playing a joke. I'd changed the meeting to tomorrow night. Whoever called thought the meeting was tonight. I listened to it again. A far off bell tolled in my brain, but whatever tidbit I wanted seemed masticated in my memory files. Frustrated, I squelched the desire for a cigarette. Who knew I was meeting

Martinez? Brown, Zoloski, Beagle Ears, and Martinez. None of them had an accent. But Mohammed, Amerol, and possibly Cain, did.

Mohammed was dead. Why would Amerol or his henchman Cain want to warn me away? If Martinez was a threat to their operation, why warn me off? Afraid to mess with the feds?

Did the caller think I'd really listen? Not if they knew me very well.

Another unsettling thought. If Amerol was reluctant to mess with a cop, then his other option would be to murder me—as a warning to Martinez.

I found a piece of gum, stuffed it in my mouth, and listened to the message a third time. "...Stay home. Stay safe."

I round-filed the junk mail and headed for the club. Despite the arsenal in my purse, my nerves jittered all the way down the elevator. At 5:30 it was light out, but would anyone notice if someone smashed my head in, or slid a knife between my ribs. Imagination overload. I hurried to my car, drove straight to the club.

In the back of my brain a refrain kept repeating itself. "Your life ain't worth a plug nickel, Sweetheart." After a couple rounds of weights, the parrot quieted. Thirty minutes on the treadmill and his beak was sealed. Once again in charge, I felt great. Maybe I *was* a control freak...

It was nearly 8:00. What was Zoloski doing? Not Brown, I hoped.

Antsy as hell, glad for the .32 in my purse, I went home, searched the place, and reassured myself there was no bomb waiting, or a slasher in the closet, I ate a quick meal.

Just in case the Z-man finished in the City early and was headed home, I jotted down Pronowske's address along with her phone number, and headed out the door. I could use my conversation with Pronowske as a test run for the hidden mike/transmitter. See how well everything worked.

The phone rang as I opened the door. I ran back into the kitchen, snatched up the receiver and heard the blare of Zoloski's voice before the phone reached my ear.

He was pumped. "Hey, Sweetheart, having a good time?"

"Ze place iz a leetle lonely," I murmured in a mongrel accent with a dash of Marlene Dietrich mixed with Marilyn Monroe. "Vere haf you bean?"

He laughed, the sound warm. "Busy. It's going to be a long night. We've impounded the hundred grand and are checking the computer records for every bank in the City." A tremble of excitement. "Looks like Ken had more than four million stashed."

I whistled.

"Just a sec..." I heard the murmur of Brown's voice, then Zoloski's.

Shit, had she been listening in on our conversation?

He came back. "You going to curl up on the couch and read one of those steamy romances you keep hiding?"

I stared guiltily at my keys and the tape recorder. "It's called substitution. Until you pry yourself away from Brown."

Dead silence. Was he grinning or had I struck fire?

"Actually," I said, "I'm going to the store, pick up some ice cream." Stop by Pronowske's apartment.

A smile crept into his voice. "I'll help you work it off when I get home."

I considered telling him about the receptionist, but it felt too much like asking for approval. And I didn't want Brown in on it yet. "Want me to call when I get back?" I asked, thinking I could tell him then, if I discovered anything.

He hesitated. "I'll call you. Eleven okay?"

"*No problemo.*" I had an image of Agent Centerfold standing by, prodding him to get off the phone. "Want me to say goodnight to Brown?" I offered.

He laughed. The sound warmed me to my toes. "Wouldn't win you any points." His voice softened, "Talk to ya later, Sweetheart."

"Later, Gator." I hung up, realizing I hadn't told him about the warning, "Stay home, stay safe." Kicking myself, I stared at my purse and told myself I could just go for the ice cream. But that felt too much like "Sit down, shut up, and be a good girl" the message of my youth.

Damn it, I was an adult, not a child. I could take care of myself. I was perfectly capable of facing Ms. Pronowske on my own.

Chapter 26

I HEADED TO Pronowske's, arguing with myself part of the way. But hey, Zoloski didn't need my approval for every thing he did, I didn't need his. I took the H Street exit, rolled slowly past McKinley Park. In the summer twilight children's happy voices echoed from the playground, and the steady hum of traffic droned comfortingly from all sides. I eyed the lighted rose gardens, thought it had been eons since Zoloski and I had dropped by and walked through, fed the ducks on the lake...

I zoomed on, the script fixed in my brain. Like a good novel, I had to finish it.

Ten minutes later I parked at 53rd and F. Pronowske's apartment complex was in a short u-shaped block of two-story structures, all in desperate need of a face lift. Vines crept up the brick facade on the front walls. Under the setting sun's red glow, the peeling paint looked like long jagged tears in the stucco, the vegetation like mold.

I turned on the voice-activated recorder, adjusted the mike in my bra, and pulled on a short-sleeved sweater over my tank top.

Pronowske's apartment was situated in the center of the complex. Top floor. I gripped the warm iron railing and followed the stairs to a concrete landing and unlit front door. Heavy metal music blared from inside, the bass thumping like an irritated drum, the kind of music I did unpleasant housework to.

I knocked, waited, knocked again, perspiration running down my back. The waistband of my shorts felt too tight. The shadows lengthened as I shifted from one leg to the other, knocked again. Damn. Who could hear with the stereo jacked up?

I tried the doorknob. It turned unimpeded. I stuck my head inside. "Ms. Pronowske!" My gaze skimming from the red eyes of the stereo on my right to the brightly lit kitchen on my left, I saw the edge of a counter, the wall phone, and the refrigerator. Old yellow linoleum dissolved into dark brown carpet.

My gaze shifted past the vague outline of a dining room table and four chairs to the dark hallway. The door at the end was ajar, light spilling through the opening. "Ms. Pronowske?" I yelled louder. Should I go in? "Anybody home?" If she was in the building's laundry room, would she have left the door open? I wouldn't have.

The stillness made me edgy. My neck hairs prickled. "Anybody home?" I called again, leaning inside a bit more.

A hand closed on my wrist and jerked me inside. The door slammed shut. I twisted free, facing the short, slim figure, silhouetted by the kitchen light, my hand sliding into my purse.

"Cain," I croaked, my voice sounding like I had swallowed a boatload of crackers. He stared at me, the gun in his gloved hand huge as a cannon. Music loud enough to cover a twenty-one gun salute. Shit, what had I stepped into? No one wears gloves in a heat wave. I trembled slightly.

"Ms. Pronowske?" I rasped my worry aloud, the music swallowed it, my brain felt disengaged. The adrenalin hadn't even hit yet.

He moved past me to the living room. Switched off the stereo.

My throat closed. My stomach roiled. Amerol's henchman had beat me to Pronowske. To Ken too? "What are you doing here?"

"Same thing as you, I think. Looking for Woods."

"Where's Pronowske?"

His dark eyes narrowed. He gestured toward the hallway. "In the bedroom. Where's Zoloski?"

How much did the guy know about me? If I said he was on his way, would Cain kill me faster? Or would the lie keep me alive? I shrugged.

He gave me an uninterpretable look. "Jesus." His tone was angry. "You have been a thorn in my side."

One scared thorn. Right now I was trying to figure a way out of being shot. "Could you put the gun down?"

His eyebrows drew together forming a continuous dark disapproving line above his eyes. "Drop the purse on the floor and sit down."

I remained standing, feeling like a fish on land, an easy target. "What do you want?"

"Cooperation. And to keep you alive."

Incredulous, I said, "Right. You're just my guardian angel."

His face hardened, his accent becoming more pronounced, "I'm taking you into protective custody."

I backed up a step. Cain a cop? No way. No way I was going to fall for that line that was for damn sure. For all I knew he was another cousin of Amerol's.

"I can shoot you for resisting arrest," he threatened. "But maybe a look at Pronowske will make you realize you need protection."

No way I wanted to go back there. Until he waved the gun. "Move." He stepped closer, and I didn't know whether he'd shoot me or not. "You talked to her yesterday at the office, didn't you, Ms. McCue," he whispered, as I backed down the hall. "What did she tell you?"

"Nothing."

"I'm a cop. You can trust me. I arrived here two minutes ahead of you. Time could be crucial."

"For who?"

"For all I know we're not alone."

Well, I could have told him that. I figured Ms. Pronowske was here, in body if not in spirit. The door loomed ahead. I tried to take a breath, get my heart back into my chest. But it preferred to choke me.

The bedroom door barred a brightly lit cave. "Nudge it open with your foot. Don't touch anything."

Why whisper? Why the concern about fingerprints when he was wearing gloves? Could he be a cop? I felt like all my brain synapses had fired at once and burned out the main computer.

We entered the room like dirty spoons stuck together. He jerked me to one side, his grip saying I wasn't going anywhere without permission.

My gaze flew from the walnut headboard, bright spring-flowered bedspread and matching drapes on the small open window, to the half-closed closet doors. A half-empty suitcase lay on the bed. The dresser drawers stood open, some empty, some not.

Cain nodded toward the bathroom.

Goosebumps rippled down my arms.

Details flooded through my eyes and pounded my brain like a storm of asteroids obliterating a starship:

A hand towel hanging over the open shower curtain, a field of light blue dipped in muddy brown. Brownish splotches on the faded linoleum. A white tub. Stray tendrils of brown hair hanging over the edge. Oh God! Hair!

I shuddered, my dinner rising but only a croak coming from my throat. His fingers dug into my arm, cutting off my voice and my escape. Hot nauseous acid rose in my stomach at the image forming in my brain.

We moved in tandem toward the tub. I stifled a scream at our reflections in the mirror. Cain's grip tightened as my legs threatened to give out.

"Look!" His command forced me forward. "The bastard who did

this is after Ken. May have found him by now."

Don't throw up. I repeated the mantra, my gaze flickering from the cigarette burns on Pronowske's hands to the dark splotches of blood on her nude body. Stab wounds.

Skin gaped at her neck, a grisly second mouth. My hand jumped to the thin scar that ran beneath my jawbone. Cutting memories. The adrenalin overload was about to push my racing heart over the edge.

I tried to back away and stepped on Cain's foot. Do something! my brain screamed, but the moment was gone before it registered. Pronowske's glassy-eyed stare watched me. I prayed it wasn't happening and any moment she would blink, sit up, and yell, "Surprise!" and I'd faint.

I suddenly remembered the microphone in my bra—my tape recorder in the car. Jesus, what a test run. "If you didn't kill her, who did?"

Cain didn't respond. Like a sack of potatoes, he dragged me back to the living room. I felt like spuds being mashed into a blob. He released the death grip on my arm and let me sit down.

Although his actions said he didn't kill Pronowske, I was scared shitless. He worked for Amerol. One way to find out if he was a cop would be to run. If he didn't blow a hole the size of Montana through my chest, I'd know. The outside door was still unlocked. Could I make it to my car? "If you didn't kill her, who did?" I repeated.

He shook his head, looking worried. "I'm not sure."

"I'd guess you," I said, watching for his reaction.

"Then you'd be wrong, Ms. McCue."

A great act? The truth? "Doctor McCue." Asshole. "Mr. ah—" If I was going to get shot I wanted the guy's name on tape so Zoloski could take posthumous revenge.

His gaze narrowed. "Cain is sufficient."

Was I about to become Abel? I eyed my purse. What good was my .32 or pepper spray when I couldn't get to it?

He sat down across from me on the coffee table, the gun out of reach. "You talked to Ms. Pronowske yesterday. Did you see anyone while you were in the office?"

I shook my head.

He looked pleased at my obedient response and it pissed me off. "What did she tell you?" he asked.

"She liked my suit."

His mouth turned down and his voice grew cold. "I trust you didn't miss the cigarette burns on her hands?" Yours could be next, his dark eyes threatened. Maybe he did kill her.

I shivered, regretting my sarcasm. But since when had that ever stopped me?

"Brown should have locked you up. Kept you out of trouble."

He knew about Brown too? Did Amerol? A part of me said he was sounding and acting more like a cop. But acting was the key word. Neither Brown or Zoloski had mentioned another cop in the works.

He stood and gestured with the muzzle toward the door. "Let's go."

"Where?"

"Someplace safe," he said.

For whom?

He threw my purse at me like a football. "Open the door."

I fumbled the catch.

"Pick it up." No patience left in his voice. Maybe I could hit him with it, and he'd misfire, sing soprano for life.

My pulse raced as I gripped the knob and turned. Perspiration dampened my palms. I tightened my hold on the handle of my purse and swung.

Touchdown!

The gun flew out of his hand. He swore as I lunged toward the landing.

Thwack! Concrete rushed at my face. My forearms screamed as skin peeled off. His body slammed the air from my lungs. I sucked air, rolled left and drove my elbow into Cain's ribs.

He grunted, "Shit!" and caught my right arm, twisting it up behind my back until I froze.

Standing, he straddled me and yanked me up. Sharp needles shot through my wrist, elbow and shoulder. Dragging me back inside the apartment, he murmured a furious string of guttural curses as he retrieved my purse.

"You are making this exceedingly difficult!" he hissed.

Next thing I knew he had my hands in cuffs behind my back.

"Now, shall we try this again?" He bent to retrieve his weapon, his body tightening as though in pain. Good, he deserved all the pain he could get.

I tried to find life in my arm, and remembered the tape. "Where are we going?"

A hiss of exasperation. "If it will make you more cooperative—to the federal building."

"Right." And I'm Houdini.

"Believe what you like. But no sudden moves this time." He slung my purse over his shoulder. "What do you keep in this thing, the bathroom sink?"

"Ha, ha."

Slipping the gun into his jacket pocket, he put the jacket over my shoulders, then slid his arm across my back and his hand into the pocket. The barrel pressed into my side. Would a bullet plow a field through my kidney and lung and come out my shoulder, or maybe just take a chunk out of my spine? "Just walk where I tell you and everything will be okay."

"Zoloski will punch your lights out," I remarked with more spunk than I felt. The only card up my sleeve was the recorder and I didn't see how it might save me.

"You should have stayed home and stayed safe," he said in a low voice.

God, the message on my answering machine! It was Cain's voice! I felt thick-witted.

We moved across the landing side-by-side, his hip glued to mine. I was tempted to bolt down the stairs, but my forearms and palms were raw from concrete, and I figured if I damaged my knees I'd louse up a getaway chance later on—not to mention he had my purse, my car keys, my gun, and me—handcuffed, and a .45 appendage in his jacket pocket.

On the sidewalk, we passed my car. A half a block away, we stopped beside a dark green Ford sedan. Two teenagers were leaning against it. Cain stiffened.

Now was the time to yell. But I kept feeling a bullet, like a rat, chewing its way through organs I needed.

He shoved me in the passenger seat and locked the door. Before I could do more than ease the pain in my shoulders, he was in the driver's seat, the engine humming.

"Nice Ford," I said, hoping my recorder took good notes.

He smiled grimly and pulled into traffic. If he slammed on the breaks I'd fly straight into the windshield. Ugly thought. "Driving without a seatbelt is illegal."

A sideways glance. "If you don't distract me, we'll both arrive safely."

I heard the ring of a cellular. Did I have mine in my purse? I glanced toward the backseat. Cain pulled a phone from his jacket.

"Cain," he said, throwing an unreadable glance at me. "Now? I'm in the middle of something..." His face darkened. "Okay, I'll swing by and pick it up. Tell Vic, no problem."

The phone went back into his pocket. We headed down H street. "You missed the freeway exit," I murmured to my right boob.

"I have a stop to make."

"For Vic?"

"This is damned bad timing," he muttered, rummaging through his pockets and lighting a cigarette. What was he anxious about? I was the one wearing bracelets. My nerves were still hanging in Pronowske's bathroom.

We continued down H. I glanced at the dash clock. "Not much traffic for ten-thirty," Was my tape recorder still picking up the signal or was I wasting my breath? Brown had assured me I could drive to the next state and the repeater unit in my purse would transmit from the smaller, low-powered transmitter/mike in my bra.

We drove over the railroad tracks to nineteenth street and turned left.

My mouth tasted like dry sand. "The Ban building?"

Cain shot me a look that seemed to question if I was talking to him or to myself. As long as he didn't search my bra.

Was Amerol waiting inside? Did Cain want his boss' okay before he axed me? He pulled into the underground garage and parked in an unlit corner. Where were all the late-night workaholics? "This doesn't look like the federal building."

He rubbed out his cigarette in the ashtray, got out, came around to my side, opened the door, and pushed on my back. "Lean over."

Oh God. My head pressed between my knees, I braced for a bullet. I heard a cuff bracelet snap open. Relief flooded my synapses. Until he twisted my right arm behind my back and up to my shoulder blades.

"Ow!"

"Put your left hand on the dash."

I complied, the handcuff dangling from it. Keeping the tension on my right arm, he grabbed my left, pulled it across my body and locked it around the handle grip above the window.

"Now stay quiet and out of sight and you'll stay alive."

He sounded like he meant it—the alive part—but brains hear what they want to hear and I wasn't going to bet my life on it.

When he was gone, I opened the glove box with my right hand. There had to be something I could use. I'd picked door locks before. How hard could a handcuff be? But the pantry was bare. Damn.

Twisting my head, my neck cracking in protest, I spied my purse.

No way in hell to reach across my body and behind the driver's seat.

I found the lever under my seat and pressed the back into a horizontal position. Scrambling onto my knees, I turned 180 degrees and faced the rear of the car.

Leaning as far as I could, right hand outstretched, my fingertips only brushed the soft leather. God, another inch! Just another inch! I pulled with all my might against the cuff, but only gained a half inch, bruising the hell out of my wrist as the metal tightened. Jeez, Louise. What a wimp. Trapped wolves chewed off their feet.

I decided I'd rather die intact. He hadn't killed Pronowske or he would have killed me, I told myself.

Sweat streamed into my eyes, down my back, across my chest. The car was warm, but my nerves made it feel like an oven. I glanced around the parking lot. No sign of Cain. No sign of anyone. Yet.

What would Stephanos do? The thought of his long legs gave me the answer. I unpried my right foot from under my backside and stretched my leg into the back seat foot area. Gingerly, I snagged the strap on my instep and dragged the bag forward. I felt like a wide receiver on his way to the goal line. "Come on, Baby." The thing weighed a ton, but I hadn't done all those leg extensions for nothing.

My hand wrapped around the bag and I lifted it into my lap. Plowing through the contents, I dug out my pepper spray, laid it down just beneath the seat, then dredged the bottom for my lock picking tools. Triple damn. They'd been in the purse that was stolen! I dragged my fingernails across the bottom again: lipstick pencil, a small penknife, and a paper clip. I stuck the lipstick pencil and penknife in my pockets, then eyed the clip. It always worked in the movies. I clenched the end between my molars and slowly uncurled the wire. As I jammed it in the lock, I realized I needed another wire. Shit. Cain would be back soon. It didn't take long to go up fourteen floors on an elevator. Less time to put a bullet in my brain.

I burrowed through my purse again, straining to hear footsteps, sure the car door would jerk open any moment.

My fingers closed round a jumbo clip. It tasted like lead as I jammed it between my teeth and unbent one side.

I blinked away sweat and eyed the metal bracelet.

Footsteps. My throat closed or I would have swallowed the clip. I spit it out, crammed everything into my purse and tossed it in the backseat.

The trunk popped open. The car rocked slightly. A murmur of soft voices. I did a three second contortion act to turn around and straighten in my seat. My left hand felt bruised and battered, half-gnawed off. Still I reached beneath the seat, found the pepper spray and slipped it into the waistband of my shorts.

The trunk slammed shut. I leaned against the seat, the small canister digging reassuringly into my spine.

A face pressed against the window. Heart thudding, my shout came out a croak of joy. "Martinez! Help!"

He unlocked the door, eyebrows raised in surprise. "Blaize." He gave me a once over and his lips curled with lecherous appreciation. "Of all places to run into you."

I pulled on the handcuff. "Unlock it before Cain gets back!"

He fingered the keys.

My excited relief plummeted fifty floors, my stomach with it. How did he get Cain's key's? Unless Cain was a cop and they were working together. No. Martinez must have followed Cain and overpowered him. Relief again.

But the slow smile on Martinez' face curdled the dinner in my stomach. Had I gotten everything backwards? Was Martinez crooked and he and Cain working together? They'd probably just stuck a ton of heroin into the trunk.

"Cain isn't coming back." Martinez wore a smirk of one-upmanship.

My heart lodged in my throat. "Why not?" I fought down terror. God, had I gotten it twisted? Was Cain a good guy? And Martinez working for Amerol? The look on Martinez' face and my gut said yes. *Think,* don't panic. I had to make him believe I believed..." Cain murdered Pronowske, Ken's receptionist. I caught him in her apartment."

An eyebrow twitched. "Looks like he caught you."

"Get me out of here. We can joke later."

Martinez looked unconvinced.

"Cain tried to make me believe some bull about being a cop..." I recalled the tapes in Ken/Karla's apartment. Was Martinez the threatening voice on the tape? Although Martinez was built like a pit bull, Cain like a bantamweight boxer, their voices were similar. Burying the sickening prickles rolling over my skin, I mustered the "I love cops" look I'd used in the gym.

His biceps swelled along with his head. Or I thought they did until he said coldly, "Where's Zoloski?"

"Probably porking Brown—I don't know." Forgive the slur, Z-man. "Will you unlock this sucker?"

Still wearing a grin that gave me goosebumps, he singled out the handcuff key. His gaze narrowed unpleasantly, his hand poised in mid-air. "Didn't you have a suicidal client to take care of tonight?"

Oh Shit. "I checked her into UCD. Seventy-two hour watch. Finished early." Was my voice shaking or just my insides?

"And your curiosity got the best of you?"

"You mean Pronowske?" Where was he leading? Obviously Cain hadn't told him about me. Just as obviously, he was trying to decide what to do. "She called me." I lowered my voice as though offering a juicy secret. "She said Ken's alive. Damn it, undo the iron!"

From the set of his face this was old news. He eyed my chest.

I wished I was wearing a turtleneck instead of my light short-sleeved sweater—unbuttoned—and silk tank top.

"She called you today?" he questioned.

I'd talked to her yesterday, but I nodded, wanting him to think she'd told me about Ken. "Are you going to unlock this?"

"Sure." He reached up and tugged on the bracelet instead.

As pain shot up my arm, fear clogged my arteries. I knew right then that he wasn't about to unlock the cuff, that he was no good guy, that I was in big trouble.

"Tight." Martinez' light brown eyes lit with pleasure, while his gaze did a slow crawl over my body.

My stomach clenched. "Where's Cain?" I rasped.

"You'll know soon enough."

He locked the passenger door and walked around the front. The car leaned momentarily as he slid onto the seat. I remembered his two-fifty bench press and wished our positions were reversed. This test run had turned into the real thing. Only I had no backup. Wherever Cain was, I didn't think he'd be leaping to my defense.

The dash clock said ten past midnight. Would Zoloski panic when he couldn't reach me?

No, he'd think I'd fallen asleep with my steamy romance. Thoughts of escape and rescue collided with circuit overload as Martinez revved the engine.

I moved my knee away from the stick shift and his gloved hand. Leather gloves in summer. Gloves streaked with red. I shivered and concentrated on the canister of pepper spray.

In minutes we were on J Street. We turned right, cut through an alley, and turned left. We were headed toward highway 80. I fumbled with the window, got it down as we slowed for a light, and let the lipstick pencil tumble out. Would anyone notice a breadcrumb trail?

Not likely.

Martinez spun the wheel, throwing me against the seat as he pulled to a stop in a dark alley. I screamed.

His hand smacked across my cheek, snapping my head back. "Goddamnit! Shut up!" My face stung as he leaned across, taking my breath with an elbow jab to my solar plexus before starting to roll up the window.

I sprayed the pepper in his eyes.

He howled and jerked backwards. Swearing, he knocked my hand away with a lucky swipe, groped blindly behind him for the door handle. Wiping at his eyes, tears streaming down his face, hurling curses, he shoved the door open and fell onto the pavement.

I yanked the car keys out of the ignition.

Face twisted in agony, Martinez staggered to his feet and groped his way around the front of the car.

My hand shook as I sifted through the keys. Hurry!

He came around the right headlight.

The window was open, but the door was locked. I jammed a key into the cuff. Eureka. I lurched across the damned stick shift as Martinez popped the lock.

The car rocked as he lunged at me and caught a handful of sweater and tank top.

I twisted, tried to tear free. The side of the car scraped down my back as I slid to the ground, dragging him across the driver seat on his belly.

He blinked furiously, tears still streaming down his cheeks, and hung on like a bulldog.

I scrambled to my knees. Martinez got some foot leverage and tackled me, grappling for a hold on my arms. I toppled and smacked the concrete like a ton of rock. This time I took the impact on my shoulder, and rolled.

Martinez was all over me.

I screamed.

His fist connected to my stomach.

The stars came out. I couldn't move or breathe, then gasped like a runner at the end of a marathon.

Sirens wailed in the distance. Martinez stiffened. I inhaled and jabbed his throat with my thumb. He grunted and jerked back. His fingers closed around my bruised wrist and squeezed. His other hand connected to my jaw. More stars. Pain shot across my eyes. The world spun. I tasted blood. Salty, sweet.

He jerked me to my feet, caught me around the middle and dragged me to the back of the car. "You want to see Cain?" He popped the trunk.

Shit!

Denial. Anger. I stared at Cain's body. The stab wound in his chest, the blood. I smelled noxious diesel and oil.

Martinez jabbed something sharp against my spine. "Get in."

Not me, please. I opened my mouth to try to bargain—every smart ass spark in me dead. His brown eyes flattened, just as dead.

Fear uncoiled like a snake in my belly.

Martinez pressed a long, slim blade to my throat. "You want me to punch holes in you right now? Get in. You got three seconds."

I trembled, tried to hide it. My leg felt like lead as I placed one foot in the trunk. No, this wasn't happening.

Who's on top now? his gaze asked as I drew my other leg in and crouched down. My voice a croak, I whispered, "There's not enough room." What did I have to bargain with?

"There's room. Shove 'im back."

Cringing, I slid my hand under the body and inched it back. My hands came away damp, sticky.

Martinez' bloodshot eyes were puffy slits as he reveled in my horror. He grabbed the lid.

I clutched the edge for a second, then slid down to one elbow, leaving a bloody fingerprint on the outside of the car. Would anyone notice? "Where are we going?" I stalled.

"To get rid of you and all the other evidence that's piled up today. Lay down." A mean smile.

I scooted my hips; Cain and I were almost head to head.

Martinez' smile grew even more menacing. "Should have taken me up on the swim. Would have been more fun for you." *But this will be more fun for me,* his narrowed gaze promised.

Then I knew—he'd killed Pronowske. She'd been beaten, burned, and had her throat slit. I thought of Mohammed, his throat had been slit too. And Juarez's hands chopped off—before he died? I was next. Blood roared in my ears.

He slammed the trunk closed.

Chapter 27

WHILE I FUMBLED in the pitch black dark, the car jostled like a boat on choppy water. I found Cain's carotid, felt a pulse. Frantic, I got my blasted sweater off, bunched it up and pressed it against his chest wound. Was I wasting my time? I groped his waist, found his belt and unfastened the buckle.

"Honey, not here..." he rasped.

My hand jerked. "Jesus!" My racing pulse threatened a heart attack. Reaching for his belt again, I slowly pulled it free of his pants. "I thought you were out." I tried for a funny, "I'm rendering first aid here, you can relax and enjoy it!"

"Mmm..."

Like threading a needle, I managed to get the belt around his back and across his chest. As I tightened the leather over my sweater compress, questions stampeded through my brain. "Cain?"

His breath tickled my ear. "Under the carp...." Then more a sigh than a whisper: "Jack... han..."

Carp? Jack? "What?"

The car bumped and swerved left, then picked up speed. My elbow banged against the metal side, shooting needles of pain up my arm. Why was it called the funny bone? Nothing funny about any of this. My best guess, we were hitting the freeway—Highway 50 toward Placerville, or 80 toward Auburn—lots of good places to dump bodies. "Cain?"

No answer. Dead or did talking hurt too much? I felt his light breath.

Martinez maintained a constant speed for a good forty-five minutes, then slowed as though going uphill and down, taking mountain curves. I watched the luminous dial on my watch click off minutes as my brain worked with "carp, jack, han." Riddles. Fish, jackrabbits, but han? I felt like Bilbo Baggins in Tolkien's *The Hobbit* with good ole Gollum whispering life and death questions in his ear. What iss it, my precious? Only this time, Gollum had turned out to be a good guy.

"Carp, jack, han," I muttered over and over. Jack handle! The lovely image of bending it over Martinez' head tantalized my brain.

I found the edge of the carpet and pulled it back, snaked my hand underneath. Nothing. Panicky, I reached for the other corner and peeled the carpet as far as I could. Rubber. A chunk of metal. I pulled.

"Can't get it," I muttered in frustration.

"Bol..." Cain's soft voice jangled my nerves. I jiggled his arm, put my ear to his mouth until I got a ragged whisper—heard the t. "Bolt."

Shoving my hand deeper, I found the bolt and twisted. The damn thing must have been soldered on; no way that baby was coming off. I wanted to scream, and swore instead, refusing to give up, twisting at the damned thing.

Like a true compulsive personality, I checked my watch every few minutes. We'd been on the road over fifty minutes.

Martinez slowed. Adrenalin pumped through me like a jolt of 100 proof, and I jammed my fingers around the jack, feeling for the rod beneath. Yes! It slipped out like a dream.

We bumped over large ruts. I conked my head. Gravel crunched beneath the tires. We bounced some more, then hit smooth road, slowed, sped up, slowed, twisted and turned. Then, sickeningly, we stopped.

Pulse racing, I shoved the carpet back down, stretched into my original position, head-to-head with Cain—and waited.

And waited.

Even at midnight, trunks are hot. Hard. Uncomfortable.

My forearms burned, my side ached and I had to pee.

I found Cain's wrist, felt for a pulse, wanting reassurance, wanting not to feel alone. Nothing, but hell—half the time I couldn't feel my own pulse. I squeezed his hand. A slight squeeze back.

"If I could get that bolt off, I could use the jack to open the trunk. But I need pliers or a wrench. This is your car. Is there anything back here I can use? Squeeze once for yes, twice for no."

Two short squeezes.

Fucking great! What was he planning to do if he had a flat? Use his teeth? I pulled back the carpet and tried to get the bolt off anyway. Broke every nail on my right hand.

Sweaty as a horse, I tamped the carpet back as best I could and laid back. It was sooo hot, and it smelled like a concoction of BO and blood. "You think I could get us out with just the bar? Use it like a wedge?"

Two squeezes.

Pessimist. "You think he'll leave us in here?"

One short squeeze.

That's what I was beginning to be afraid of.

Then came two slight squeezes. Good news or bad? I lay in the dark, my thoughts tumbling like laundry in a dryer. Out of nowhere I thought of how my brother and I would hold hands in preschool while we waited to be picked up, taken home—wondering but never saying it aloud, if we'd be left there. I tried to think of anything but my hatred of dark, small enclosed spaces, and my bladder.

Good guy/bad guy riddles swirled through my brain—Uncle Sam paid Martinez, but he was also working for himself, or for Amerol. I thought of the heroin, and nudged Cain. "You DEA?"

A slight squeeze.

Jeez, Louise.

"Did Amerol find out?"

He inhaled noisily as though gathering strength.

Don't talk, I wanted to say. Keep breathing. But chances were we'd be dead by the time Martinez opened the trunk. I wanted answers before I died.

More raspy breaths. He said, "Martinez suspic...."

"So Amerol sicced him on you?"

No answer.

I thought of Pronowske's fate. "Does Martinez know where Ken is?"

His fingers twitched, then squeezed once. Yes.

"Do you?"

They squeezed twice, then once.

No and yes? "Maybe?"

"Dead," he croaked.

"No," I muttered, feeling a sense of impatience along with impending doom. "Xavier Juarez is dead."

He coughed, the sound jarring in the enclosed space.

"They're both dead?" I guessed.

He squeezed once.

Jesus. I squeezed his hand just for comfort. It remained slack. "Cain?" I squeezed hard. No response. My heart belly-flopped. "Cain?" I pressed my fingers to his neck. A slight pulse. But for how long?

Martinez must have abandoned the car. I grabbed the jack handle and tried to wedge it between the lid and chassis, near the lock. It slipped, and slipped, and slipped. Maybe I could beat my way out. Trunks were made to keep people out, not in.

I hammered at the lid, then yelled until I was hoarse. An hour passed. My hair clung to my forehead, my top and shorts soaked in sweat. I rested and banged again. Rested. My watch said 3:00 a.m. and I thumped some more.

My grip finally gave out, my right arm heavy as rock, muscles on fire. The bar thunked to the floor. Lungs burning, I flopped back against Cain's inert body. When the sun came up we'd fry.

Dizziness and fatigue washed over me. I needed to rest, save my strength, close my eyes for a moment, come up with a brilliant plan. I blinked. God, I was tired. I ached everywhere. I closed my eyes again. An idea would come. I just needed to give it time...A blackness deeper than a tomb sucked me down into a vortex of smothering nightmares.

The last was a recurring one from my teens. Werewolves owned the night, my neighborhood, my home. Snarling, howling, powerful beasts. If they caught me I'd be ripped to shreds. The only place I felt safe was the car. I threaded my way down pitch black hallways, through a dark garage, trying to reach the safety of the car, to get inside. Just as I hit the door locks, the beasts beat at the windows, clawed at the door handles, trying to get to me. I screamed....

But this time I had the keys, started the car and ran over the bastards. The nightmare faded.

Then I was alone on the highway. Near the ocean. I left the car and walked along the beach. I liked this dream. Fresh air cooled my skin. Hands lifted me. I tried to grip the crusty sand with my toes, but it disintegrated.

This wasn't a dream! An arm tightened around my waist, lifting me from the trunk. Solid ground. Body warmth against my back. Zoloski? No. Wrong smell.

Panic. I heard the rippling of water, smelled wet moss, fish, gulped air. Too clear. Too real. Too late.

The jack! I struggled, light from an unknown source stabbing my eyes. My tongue felt like steel wool.

"She's still kicking."

"Good." Martinez! Off to my left. His voice turned my blood cold. Who had me? Where were we?

"You park above the bridge?" Martinez asked.

"Yeah."

What bridge? I racked my brain. I had the feeling we were in the foothills.

"I'll take her inside. You get rid of Cain."

I could see Cain, unmoving in the rear of the trunk. Where was the jack handle?

Keys jingled. My captor's grip loosened. Swaying, I pulled free and flopped halfway into the trunk. Banged my head convincingly and moaned while frantically searching the space shadowed by my body. I groaned as though out of commission, my heart slamming against my ribs as my fingers found the bar.

The man behind me grabbed my shoulder. "Let's fuck her, then burn 'em together."

Adrenalin shot through my arm. I spun around, and swung. The bar landed just above the man's ear. The metal sank slightly, like hitting a bag of sand, and he crumpled to the ground. He wouldn't be getting up.

A boot heel scraped behind me. I whirled, straight into the barrel of a .45. "Drop it," Martinez snarled, his eyes red, angry, and full of hate.

The jack handle thunked on the ground.

His knuckles whitened as his grip tightened on the gun. His gaze flickered to the thug I'd hit and he gave the lump a disgusted kick in the ribs. The man didn't move.

I shifted my weight from one leg to the other, ready to lunge. As though sensing my intention, he eyes were on me again.

He stared at me like a gorilla who couldn't decide whether to peel the banana or just crush it between his teeth. His skin was blotchy, his eyes red as roses, his smile lethal. I saw a rip in his expensive suit jacket, another at his knee. His eyes burned into mine. "Wiggle and I'll shoot you in the leg." He grabbed my arm and led me across a crumbling asphalt pad toward a derelict shack.

Fun and games before he did away with me? I stifled thoughts about Pronowske, tried to figure out where we were. The American River? The Sacramento? A tangle of undergrowth and three hundred year old oaks, like twisted giants, blocked out the half-moon. A square of white light spilled from the window of the shack, laying on the asphalt like a trap door. To hell? We'd driven over fifty minutes, maybe longer, to get here. I'd been in left in the trunk over two hours— had to be past midnight. If we were off I-80 we had to be above Auburn. Foresthill? Colfax?

A bullfrog croaked. A splash. The river was close, closer than I'd thought. In the distance, higher up, a lone flash of light stabbed the dark, briefly illuminating what could have been a bridge beam. Headlights? A road on the other side of the river? I'd rafted down the American River many times, spent my childhood and teens exploring its nooks and crannies. It had a wild, desolate quality that always attracted me. But now all I felt was sheer terror as he pulled me toward the shack. What good did it do to know where I was? Still, a person likes to know where they're going to die.

Martinez kicked open the door. The unholy stench jerked me out of my skin and slammed me back into it—excrement, urine, vomit. I gagged.

Light from a giant flashlight drew my attention to a rickety table. I followed the beam to a mop of dark hair topping a slack figure in the corner. A sluggish fly buzzed above the head and landed on the cheek, crawled into the ear and disappeared. I covered my mouth and nose, wondering if I'd finally caught up with Ken.

With quick efficiency, Martinez closed the door and pulled a strip of cloth over the window. Were we nearer to civilization than he wanted me to believe? He shoved me down into an old wooden slat chair, tied my hands behind me, the rope tight, but bearable. Looping the rope around the side bars of the chair and down to my feet, he gave it a vicious tug as he finished. Now, the rope cut into my wrists and ankles.

Crouching beside me, he leaned close. "As soon as I take care of Cain and that bozo Vic sent, we'll get to know each other." The nasty glimmer in his eyes sent chills through my gut.

I forced words past the bubble in my throat. "You'll never get away with this."

He traced the scar along my jaw. "Oh yes I will." His hand dropped to my breast and squeezed, like a shopper testing for a good cantaloupe. The pain shocked me into remembering the mike in my bra—other boob. Martinez kept squeezing. An image of him cutting the mike off, my breast with it, careened through my consciousness as pain radiated through my chest.

I sucked down a mouthful of air, gagged on the smell, but couldn't move. A black void hovered at the edge of my consciousness. Damn, I wasn't the fainting type.

A vicious smile played across his face, his breath rotten as his heart. His grip loosened, fell away. "I really enjoyed ripping up your boyfriend's place; enjoyed Pronowske more, but you'll be the best."

I fought to clear my head. "You killed Juarez, didn't you?"

Another smile. "Couldn't turn my back on four million could I?" His leer slithered from my breasts to my crotch. "Amerol wanted Woods dead. I needed a body."

My gaze slid to the corner. I could hear the blood in my veins, thin and whispery.

"So you cut a deal with Ken?"

Louise Crawford 209

"A temporary one." Martinez guffawed as if he'd told a bad joke, his gaze resting momentarily on Ken. "Greedy bastard. Thought he could cheat me out of the money."

I hoped the transmitter in my purse was doing its job and my little tape recorder in my car was getting every word. Or would the mountains screw it up?

"But Pronowske knew where he was." He chuckled. "Oh yes, she did." His predator smile said he'd loved every minute of prying the information from her lips.

I wanted to throw up. "Why put Juarez's hands and teeth in Lon's locker?"

"Brown was nosing around. Figured it would slow her down." A flicker of impatience. He took out his knife, straddled my legs, his weight crushing my thighs into the chair. The blade flickered in the light as he brought it to my throat. I didn't blink, didn't breathe.

He moved it lower. With a quick flick, he cut my tank top across the shoulder. His eyes drilled into mine. The son-of-a-bitch was feeding off my fear!

Do something! my mind screamed. If he cut the other side, he'd find more than my boobs to play with.

Something brushed by the door. A surge of hope shot through me as Martinez leaped to the window, peered out carefully. "Damn raccoons." But the high-pitched roar of a cougar broke the night. Local news stories recommended pet owners keep their dogs and cats inside. Too bad Martinez wasn't out there with a raw steak tied to his balls.

He put the knife in his belt and turned back to me. "When I'm through you'll be happy to join Ken." His lips curled, promising he'd relish every moment. "Think about it." His breath made me think of the burns on Pronowske's hands. I willed myself not to react. He shoved a rag that tasted like blood into my mouth, tied it between my teeth. It bit the corners of my mouth. I tried not to think of where it had been before.

Was he going outside? Relief rushed through me at the thought. But he pinched my nose. I struggled to twist free, siphon air.

He let go abruptly, his mouth a lopsided curve of dark pleasure. "Fucking with a bag over your head's a real thrill." He patted my cheek as though promising a firsthand experience, then moved behind me, his boots clomping on the plank floor. I twisted but couldn't see what he was doing, wished he'd turned the chair the other direction toward the door. Behind me, the door opened and clicked shut. Silence. A shudder of repulsion ripped through my body as I thought of what he intended.

A moth fluttered around the flashlight as though desperate to get inside the glass. I strained against the rope in desperation as a tinge of numbness began to prickle my feet. The side slats of the chair had kept the rope from tightening more around my wrists. I twisted my hands, working the rope—tight, loose, tight, loose—ignoring the pain, gaining millimeters of slack.

I heard the car door open. Was he putting the bozo I'd hit inside? What about Cain? I wished I could see what the SOB was up to, but I didn't have time to worry.

Another fly hummed. With daylight, they'd descend like locusts to feed on our remains. Or maybe he'd burn everything, leaving two charred skeletons behind. The bitter taste of acid filled my mouth.

I started to shake—shock setting in. Not now! I clenched my teeth fighting the nausea. *Fall apart later, my mind hissed. Right now, you've got to get out of here. Focus.*

With little movements I rotated my right hand, peeling away the skin, coaxing the rope to give. Little by little the bond slid. I twisted and pulled, twisted and pulled, all the while straining to hear above the drone of insects.

I heard a metallic clunk. How much time did I have left? I gave another yank and felt the rope scrape along my fingers and drop to the floor. Elated and terrified, I ripped off the gag, spit it out, and fumbled at the knot around my ankles. A knot from hell. The fingernails ripped on my left hand. A matched set. I didn't even feel it.

Another memory jolt...the penknife. I fumbled in my pocket. Would Zoloski find my car, the recorder, Martinez' confession? How much tape was left?

"Martinez murdered...well, you heard...I'm near a river. The American, north fork, I think. Around Foresthill or Colfax. There's an old bridge, and a road. Lots of underbrush and old trees." Would he get the gist? I stifled the anxious urge to laugh. "There's a fishing shack and a pad of asphalt that might have been a private road or something. Dark green Ford. Cain's in the trunk. Martinez stabbed him. He's still alive, I think. Needs blood."

I snapped open the knife. Its tiny blade winked in the light.

"I'm going for the river. Head downstream. If I don't make it, nail the asshole." I sawed the rope at my ankles. After what seemed eons, the cord fell away. I cut the remaining rope from my left wrist and stood awkwardly, needles of pain in every muscle.

I gritted my teeth, tiptoed to the door and cracked it. Martinez was about forty feet away, dousing the car in gas.

Stepping outside, I fought the urge to slink into the shadows. I couldn't. I had to lead Martinez away, lose him in the trees, and circle back for Cain.

After a hesitation in which I told myself I was a damned fool, I slammed the door.

Martinez dropped the gas can, and spun toward me, his hand moving to his jacket.

I ran like hell for the river.

Chapter 28

MARTINEZ HOWLED "Fuck!" and charged after me.

Gravel crunched under my feet for about ten feet, then turned to dirt. I dashed through the moonlit dark, heedless of the brambles and the stab of twigs, sprinting toward the sound of water. Hitting a running target at night, I told myself, was harder than it looked in the movies. If I could lose Martinez and manage to swim across downstream, I might find help.

Abruptly, the ground dropped away. I slid on dry weeds and loose rock, all shades of black and grey under the filtered moonlight and hit hard, scraping on sharp stone. My butt felt like it had been stung by a thousand hornets as I scrambled to my feet. Crouching, hidden by foliage, I listened for Martinez, my breath ragged in my ears. Then suddenly the whir of helicopter blades, downriver and moving further away, broke the quiet.

Highway patrol? My brief flicker of hope died as the sound faded.

I heard Martinez' boots scraping across the rock, maybe twenty yards away. I eased down the bank toward the glimmer of water. It looked like oil, dark, deep, eerie.

My feet suddenly sank into gritty mud. Icy cold seeped through my shoes, making them feel like five pound weights. I grabbed a handful of mud and covered my arms, neck, and face; mother earth camouflage. Like a beckoning shadow, I could see the opposite bank, no more than 100 yards away. Still, I hesitated, with no idea how deep the water was or how swift the current, I could join the ranks of drowning victims.

Pebbles skittered over nearby rocks. In a low angry hiss, Martinez spit out a string of curses. He was closing in. The trees along the bank didn't block the moonlight completely. He could see me. Time to move out. I slipped into the water, holding my breath as it inched quickly up to my thighs.

A twig snapped. "Fucking bitch."

I looked back, could see Martinez moving along the bank, his flashlight sweeping the rocks. Could he see where I'd gone in? The cone of light paused near the spot I'd entered the water. My breath froze in my chest, my pulse racing. I slipped lower in the water, letting the current carry me downstream. One of Martinez' snake skin boots slipped in, eliciting another string of low curses as the flashlight beam swung out over the water. It caught me in the face, and I dove. A muffled blast registered. Something skimmed across my back, a fiery sting like barbed wire scratching skin.

The black cold closed over me and doused the pain. Like an olympiad swimmer I kicked hard, pulling against the current. My shoes felt like fifty pound weights attached to my feet. I kicked, pulled with my arms, kicked again. Forward. Sideways. Forward. Sideways. The need for air screamed through my brain. A little farther. A little farther. My lungs burned.

I came up, inhaled greedily, the sound loud in my ears. Where was Martinez? I was nearly halfway across the river, but could still touch bottom. I could see Martinez' light whisking over the water. He was fifty feet upstream, plowing through the tall grass along the bank. Had anyone heard the shot he'd fired? It must have sounded like a cannon. Maybe they'd think someone was shooting at skunks.

The current rushed around me, sucking at my shorts, pulling at my torn top with icy fingers, my arms and legs numb. I crammed my feet down between the rocks so as not to move. The mud would be washed off my face, I'd be easier to spot.

"There's rapids down there—heard of the Devil's Sink?" He called, his tone cool and reasonable. "Come back, we can still work this out."

Yeah, right, I'd just mosey on over and sit down next to Ken. I waited, wondering if he could see my head turn, my gaze sweep the banks, gauging distances as I listened to the quickening sound of rushing water, realized the dark was fading into grey—visibility would only get better—for both of us.

I was in good shape and a good swimmer, but this had been one hell of a day. I was tired, cold, hungry. *Well, at least I no longer had to pee,* my mind quipped. I snapped my synapses back on track: how the hell to get out of this jam. Except for the glow of Martinez' torch, I couldn't see worth a damn yet. Rapids were nothing to mess with. I didn't move, hoping he'd give up. I should have known better. He stepped into the water, the beam of his flashlight passing a few yards from my head.

Every muscle in my body tensed. I was afraid to move, but couldn't hold my position much longer. My teeth were beginning to chatter.

The water climbed to his knees. The flashlight bobbed and

dipped. He suddenly wobbled, sinking another foot into the water, and fell backwards. The gun flew, splashed and disappeared into the dark swirl. "Goddamn, motherfucking sonofabitch!"

I shoved off toward the far bank as he scrambled to his feet. The light found me a second later.

He lunged, quicker than I imagined, splashing, cutting through the water like a hungry shark. I dived, pulling my arms through the water with every ounce of strength I could muster. It was like swimming in molasses, the current holding me back. When I broke the surface the water level was barely to my thighs, Martinez almost on me. He caught me by the hair and yanked.

Instead of pulling away, I threw myself back at him and dropped down under water, twisting towards him, my fingers scraping across his body, down to his crotch. I found his balls and squeezed with every ounce of power I had left.

He let go with a yell.

Erupting from beneath the surface, my chest heaving like heavy artillery, I shot toward the bank and scrambled up the rocky, muddy embankment. Every breath burned like fire in my lungs.

The squish of his boots came right behind me.

He slammed into me like a linebacker.

Tree limbs, black sky, stars flew by as I crashed into ground. Like a stuck balloon, air shot from my lungs.

No knife. Just hands. Big strong hands. His fingers closed around my throat.

I sucked for breath, for life.

Murder in his eyes, his grip tightened. In the hazy grey dawn, I could see every murderous line of his face, the dark fury in his black eyes.

I scraped my hand along the muck. Nothing. I stretched further, fingers touching something. Darkness fringed my vision. I kicked, gaining an inch. My fingers closed around a fist-sized rock. I slammed it against his nose.

He howled, blood spattered down his face. He let go.

I shoved him off. Coughing, wheezing, I struggled to my feet, stumbled a step away. *Breathe! Breathe!* I coaxed my lungs, staving off the black aura hovering on the edge of my vision. I heard the whir of machinery, a vague familiar sound that hardly registered. *Go, go*, I told my rubbery legs.

Martinez wiped at his face, smearing the blood across his cheek like war paint. He reached inside his jacket, then seemed to remember the river had his weapons.

I whirled and staggered up the hill, my leg muscles burning. Tree limbs caught at my hair, snagged my top. Stickers dug into my calves.

He crashed after me, but not nearly as fast.

I found a narrow trail and followed it. Saw a rickety old bridge up above. Maybe I could waylay a car.

His footsteps grew softer. I was losing him.

I darted on, afraid to look back. A rusty shape caught my eye, small, handy. An old railroad spike. God, I used to collect the damned things as a kid. I snatched it up and kept running.

It grew quiet. Had I lost him? I crouched. Still nothing. My breath rasped in my ears. I sat back.

Out of nowhere, he lunged, diving towards me. Pure reflex made me bring up the spike. It hit him in the stomach, all his weight driving it through his flesh as he fell on top of me. Blood gushed across my chest like warm rain. His eyes widened in shock, fluttered. He tried to get up, one hand convulsively closing on the spike before he fell beside me.

He didn't move.

I thought of a spider pinned to a board. A trembling spasm crawled up my legs, caught hold of the rest of me and shook with all the violence of a hurricane. I stared, expecting him to move, pull the metal from his gut, get up and come after me again.

"Blaize!" Footsteps raced toward me.

My legs gave way as Zoloski caught me. I found myself sobbing in his arms. I couldn't stop shaking, even with the soothing murmur of his voice. I clung to his warmth.

He held me for a long time. "Blaize." He whispered my name tenderly and rubbed my back. "Sweetheart."

I flinched as he touched my shoulder blade and he loosened his hold.

"Holy shit!" He twisted his head toward someone further up. "Get an ambulance!"

"It's just a few scratches," I mumbled. *Just look at the other guy,* I wanted to say, but it never came. I leaned against him and inhaled. No one else had that wonderful smell. No one else could make me feel so safe. I was home.

Chapter 29

THE FAMILIAR VOICE that drew me from a pleasant dream of walking hand-in-hand with Zoloski was Lon's. "Hey Blaize..."

From my hospital bed, I blinked his blurry image into focus. He looked like a new penny, light blue pressed shirt, dark blue tie and slacks. Only the pallor of his skin hinted at where he'd spent the last week. He set a bouquet of red roses on the bedside table. "Where's Zoloski?" I asked.

"Talking to the doctor. He'll be here in a minute."

I sat up, flinching as my stomach twinged where Martinez had punched me, suddenly conscious of my tangled hair and hospital gown. Eyeing the flowers, I said, "Thank you." I felt ridiculously happy to see him and anxious at the same time. Lon was like a brother—had been for a long time.

He didn't sit on the edge of the bed like he might have once done, just stood beside it, looking down at me, gratitude in his eyes.

I patted the mattress. "I won't bite."

A flicker of sorrow. He faked a smile and sank against the edge of the bed, touched my hand as though it were made of glass. His gaze skidded around the room, then returned. "I wanted to say thank you, but now it seems hardly enough."

I pushed thoughts of my mortality down, but an image of Martinez' dying face—eyes filled with surprise—rose up instead. Determined not to let him haunt me, I forced a jaunty tone. "How about lunch at Weatherspoon's and a chess game?" We both loved the rundown coffee hangout.

A genuine smile cracked the handsome veneer. "Friends?"

"Just like gum on my shoe."

He swallowed. "You know, Zoloski, uh, Stephanos, asked me to join him for a workout next week."

My jaw dropped. Stephanos, not Steve, which half the force called him and he didn't like?

Lon grinned. "He's okay."

"Yeah." I sighed, feeling happy. "He is."

A rap sounded on the open door.

I looked past Lon, expectantly, was surprised to see Ms. Olympia,

Nicole Jackson.

"Just thought I'd stick my head in and see how you're doing. Only have a minute."

I waved her to come in and winced. The bullet graze on my shoulder blade was only superficial, but the concrete burn on my forearms and backside snapped, crackled, and popped.

Nicole Jackson wore what I had already decided was her standard uniform. Blue work coveralls zipped up from the crotch to her waist, empty uniform arms hanging behind her legs, a black exercise bra top showing off her muscles and her tan. Her torso gleamed with sweat, emphasizing her buffed upper body. If she hadn't yet won the title of Ms. Olympia she definitely deserved to.

Lon shook her hand. Did I imagine a spark?

She brushed back an errant tendril of black, curly hair and fixed her eyes on me. "Martinez really had me fooled." Concern flickered in her snappy black eyes. "You okay?"

I nodded. "You with Treasury too?"

A wry grin broke across her face. "After this mess, I'll either be put back on tax forms, or busted to Paramedic."

"You do a mean nasal enema," I quipped, hoping I'd never have another one.

"Too bad I can't do one on Al. I'd use a rubber hose." Her face grew somber. "You did us all a favor."

I thought of the railroad spike and shivered. "Yeah. Great public service." Killing someone—no matter how deserved—was horrifying. If I were a gunslinger in the Old West I'd have two notches on my pearl-handled .45's, and a bad-ass reputation. HP, just put me back in my counselor's chair, I thought. But in the back of my mind I wondered how long I'd last without the excitement of a chase, a puzzle...

Would I ever forget Al Martinez' mocking pit bull face?

Lon seemed to sense my mood. He patted my hand again.

Nicole Jackson grinned at him. "How about you? How are you doing?"

His face flamed. Remembering his drug overdose? "I'm fine. Just need a bit of fresh air, some sun..."

He leaned over and gave me a brotherly hug, kissed my cheek. "Brush up on your chess."

"Beat you with my eyes closed," I shot back.

A blond eyebrow rose in challenge. "We'll see." He stood, and walked to the door, his stride almost like the old Lon again.

Nicole joined him, but glanced back at me, pausing at the door.

"Cain's going to be okay. You saved his life."

"What about the thug I hit with the jack handle?"

An apologetic shrug. "Dead."

That made three notches on my .45s. I felt sick. "Amerol?"

"Gone back to the Middle East."

I remembered his flat, dead eyes, and felt relieved.

"Well...I've got a report to write, and a five-year-old to retrieve. If you want to work out together...."

I smiled. Most of the time I worked out alone—Zoloski's schedule seldom permitted a *pas de deux*. Company sounded good. "Give me a week."

She nodded. "You got it."

Lon held the door. They left talking about weights and health regimes.

I thought about showering, fancying up, before Zoloski saw me, but I didn't want to move. I could imagine what I looked like now. The irony made me laugh. The laugh hurt like hell and I closed my eyes and groaned.

"What?" The Z-man's timing was impecable.

I was not about to admit my vanity or my chagrin at having him see me looking like a worn-out, bruised and battered, pin-cushion. I opened one eye. He looked rumped. With both eyes open, he looked damned good. "Water?"

He poured me a cup.

It tasted cold, wet, wonderful. "You missed Lon and Nicole."

"I said hello."

We eyed each other in a long silence that made me uneasy. He cleared his throat. "You collect people as prickly and independent as yourself, have you ever noticed that?"

I snorted. "A few times."

I thought of our relationship, the fact I'd moved into his house. Biggest risk I'd ever taken, scariest step of my life, and the most rewarding.

He brushed the hair back from my face, then sat on the edge of the bed. His gaze grew somber and I could feel a lecture coming on. "You were damned lucky I found your car, and the recorder."

A pause.

"You lied to me, Blaize." His quiet, disappointed tone took my breath away. While he'd been in San Francisco with Brown, I'd run off to interview Pronowske, not get ice cream. I remembered his fury at Piatti's after I'd spewed my guts, spilled my activities into his lap and handed over the tapes. "The best damned dinner I never ate," he'd said. Was this the last straw? I had an image of us as two kids duking it out for power in the relationship. Teamwork was an alien concept we were both striving for. Was it too late? Emotions lodged behind my ribs like a basketball, squeezing my chest. "I don't want to lose you, Stephanos..." I twisted the bedsheet, feeling vulnerable, not liking it, yet telling myself it was for a good cause.

"Dammit, Blaize. You could have ended up like Pronowske."

I heard concern, hurt, and it cut deep. We still had a few trust issues to work out.

He seemed to read my thoughts. His hand found mine and squeezed lightly. "Sometimes you really know how to yank my chain." His voice softened. "If I'd talked to you more, kept you informed, would you have stayed on the sidelines?"

I looked him in the eyes, searching my soul for truth. "I have a hard time trusting that things will get done without me—I've never liked the sidelines."

"Is there a maybe in there somewhere?"

I nodded, smiled. "Lon told me you two are working out together next week."

"Figured you wouldn't be in shape to hit the gym..." His gaze skidded away. He had something else on his mind. "When I left with Brown for San Francisco I was really pissed at you."

The basketball pressed down into my stomach.

"At the hotel, she came on to me. Things got a little hot, before I stopped...but we didn't..."

Screw? No wonder he was Mr. Understanding now. Still, he wasn't hiding it. "No paternity suit in the future?" I cracked.

His lips curved. "She was doing her damndest." He shrugged, Bogie style. "You bring out the best and the worst in me, Sweetheart."

"Goes both ways," I murmured. "What made you come back from the City early?" I wondered aloud. He wouldn't have run from Brown, just put her in her place.

A thoughtful look. His eyebrows rose as though questioning what he was about to say. "A hat trick." What detectives called a sudden mystical inspiration or intuition that solves a case, he'd once explained.

Now he shrugged. "I didn't stop to analyze it or explain to Brown. I just left. Used the siren all the way. Found your note about 53rd and F next to the phone. Found your car. The recorder. Called in a few favors and got a helicopter."

"Just moved heaven and earth," I murmured, impressed. God, I loved the man.

His gaze said I was worth it. He bent down, reaching for something beneath my line of vision. I heard a click, a rustle, a container snapping shut.

He held up a white paper bag, and the steamy romance that looked as mashed, battered, and bruised as I felt. My face heated.

"I skimmed through this. Got some good ideas."

"Oh?"

He reached into the bag. I half-expected him to pull out a pair of edible undies.

But he pulled out a pint of fat-free, chocolate mousse ice cream and two spoons, and set it all on the table. "I figured this would hit the spot about now." His eyes were loving as he handed me a spoon. "Race you to the bottom."

I smiled. "Only if you help me work it off."

A devilish grin of delight appeared and his green, green eyes sparkled. In his best Bogart voice he said, "Anytime, Sweetheart. Anytime."

As he took me ever so gently into his arms, I melted. No doubt the ice cream did, too.

~ The End ~

Louise Crawford

Award winning author Louise Crawford lives in Sacramento with her husband and daughter. She is a member of RWA, MWA, and holds an MA in Psychology.

Louise is published in contemporary romance, short science fiction, fantasy romance, and mystery genres. Louise is happy to hear from readers by email: lcrawford@pobox.com

**Don't miss the first Blaize/Zoloski mystery, *Blaize of Glory*.
Watch for the third mystery *12 Jagged Steps* coming in October 2001!**